M000119761

ALSO BY ANNE RENWICK

The Tin Rose

The Golden Spider

The Silver Skull

The Iron Fin

A Trace of Copper

In Pursuit of Dragons

Kraken and Canals

Rust and Steam

A Reflection of Shadows

An Elemental Web Tale

Anne Renwick

To Sarah,
Watch the shadows!
Anne Renwick

www.annerenwick.com

Publisher's Note: This is a work of fiction. Names, characters, places, and incidents are a product of the author's imagination. Locales and public names are sometimes used for atmospheric purposes. Any resemblance to actual people, living or dead, or to businesses, companies, events, institutions, or locales is completely coincidental.

Book Layout ©2015 BookDesignTemplates.com

A Reflection of Shadows/ Anne Renwick. -- 1st ed.
ISBN 978-1-948359-14-6

Cover design by James T. Egan of Bookfly Design.

Edited by Sandra Sookoo.

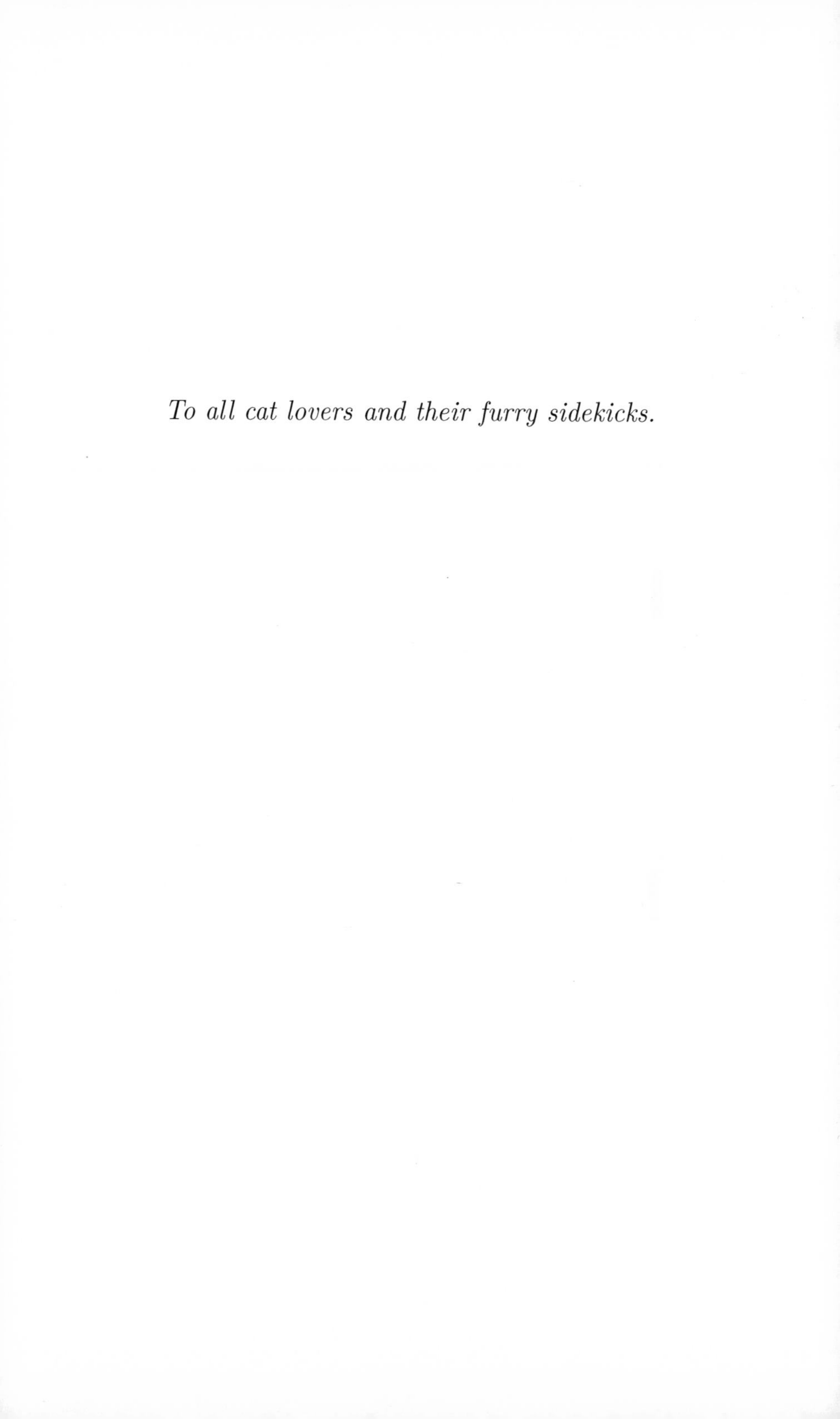

To all cat lovers and their furry sidekicks.

THANK YOU TO…

The Plotmonkeys—Kristan Higgins, Shaunee Cole, Jennifer Iszkiewicz, Stacia Bjarnason and Huntley Fitzpatrick. Though the puns threatened to overwhelm, a story was born.

Sandra Sookoo, my brilliant editor who mercilessly ferrets out weaknesses and sets my work on a better course.

My husband and my two boys.

My mom and dad.

Mr. Fox and his red pen.

Chapter One

February 1885
London

Loops of fine chain coiled as Colleen returned Lady Sophia's golden locket to its velvet pouch. *Done.* She closed the safe, gave the dial a spin and rehung the heavy oil painting to hide the strongbox from view. Odd, that a man of Lord Aldridge's means would choose to stare at blurry haystacks in a field. Years of creeping into the libraries and studies of wealthy gentlemen had taught her that most preferred to gaze upon portraits of themselves. Or of a distinguished ancestor. A favorite dog. Occasionally a beautiful wife.

All, however, kept at least one bottle of single malt scotch whisky on hand. Liquid sunshine in a bottle. Drifting across the dark room to the lord's liquor cabinet, she considered the array of choices before her, tracing the zigs and zags of the pattern cut into a crystal decanter with a leather-clad fingertip.

The household was quiet. All servants had retired. Lord Aldridge himself would be careful to be elsewhere this evening. Still, she shouldn't. Not once in four years had she helped herself to the smallest of nips. But tonight's task had gone smoothly, without the slightest hitch. And she was officially off the job.

Retired.

With a blemish free record.

A smile stole across her face. Already her bags were packed. Soon her cat, Sorcha, would return from her city prowl, and London would be nothing but a sooty memory.

She ought to celebrate. Lord Aldridge wouldn't begrudge her a drink for saving his daughter—and her dowry—from a marriage to a good-for-nothing scoundrel with significant gambling debts, would he? She pulled the stopper from the decanter and poured herself a splash.

Generous dowries made for wonderful bait, but sometimes they hooked a bottom feeder.

Livid, the earl had turned to *Witherspoon and Associates: Private matters handled with discretion.* His daughter had been compromised—a polite way of saying she'd allowed herself to be seduced by a treasure hunter without regard for the consequences. Pressing for an engagement announcement, the reprobate had threatened to display her engraved locket while sharing detailed stories of his conquest. Shameful behavior. And all mere days before the naïve girl was to be presented to society. The very kind of situation which Witherspoon and Associates was often employed to handle. Colleen had retrieved the locket while Mr. Witherspoon himself arranged for the offending gentleman's debt to be called in, casting any nasty rumors that oozed from his mouth into doubt.

Glass in hand, Colleen sank into the large chair behind Lord Aldridge's desk, tipping backward to rest her booted feet on its surface. Swirling the whisky, she took a sip. Dignified, with a seamless blend of rich fruit, spice and just a hint of peat. Aether, she missed Scotland. Missed the quiet countryside surrounding Craigieburn and the nearby village, where none of its populace ever glanced at her askance for, though golden eyes might be rare, there wasn't a single family who couldn't name a relative whose eyes glimmered in the dark.

Everything had changed the night the bridge carrying her parents' train across the River Tay collapsed, killing all aboard. Her chest still ached at the memory of burying empty coffins, of standing in the graveyard surrounded by well-meaning villagers but without a single family member beside her. She'd felt so very alone.

With her father's death, she'd become a laird in her own right, but tied up as her inheritance was in legal verbiage, her title was nominal until she reached her twenty-fifth birthday. Life in London under the thumb of her uncle—her mother's disapproving brother—had become her new reality.

Only three more days to go.

Once she ripped control of the property from her uncle's hands, she could finally tackle the ever-lengthening list of repairs on her family's home and surrounding properties. Five long years had passed since she'd last crossed its borders.

The door creaked.

Abandoning her drink, she dropped her feet to the ground and slipped into the shadows mere moments before another individual slipped into the room. She'd not expected Lord Aldridge's study to be such a popular destination this evening. Was his daughter's dowry so grand that men would have her by whatever means necessary?

Her hand slid to her boot, hovering above the dirk sheathed there. She was a sneak thief, working silently and alone. Unaccustomed to any interference. The blade was for self-defense, not for drawing blood over a silly girl's locket. Not once had she ever needed to resort to violence. Neither, however, did she wish to fail at her last task.

Please, not here. Not tonight.

The man shifted. Heredity, unnatural or otherwise, had provided her with the advantage of keen nighttime vision. The faint light cast by the thin sliver of a waning moon was enough to fully illuminate Mr. Torrington's familiar form. Dark hair. A straight nose. The honed planes and angles of a handsome face. A set to his jaw that spoke of single-minded purpose and a razor-sharp mind.

Friend not foe. Her heart started beating again. With new purpose.

She'd always enjoyed watching the Queen's agent work. Reveled in stepping out of the shadows to materialize beside him. Colleen grinned. The first time she'd tapped his shoulder in the dark, he'd jumped so far and so high that she'd expected his own eyes to reflect the light of his lamp. But not only was Mr. Nicholas Torrington's lineage noble, his family tree contained no inexplicable branches.

Still, they both lived dual lives. One kept hidden from the *ton*, the other highly visible. For years, they'd flirted as their paths crossed. On rooftops, inside locked rooms, down dark alleyways. In ballrooms, at garden parties, in the hallways of the theater. Neither betraying the other's secrets with so much as a stray comment or shared glance at an inopportune moment.

Time passed and small conversations grew longer. An inexplicable bond formed. One that had snapped some months past.

With the coming of fall, gentry retreated to their country estates, and London society thinned. Still, small gatherings were held. On All Hallows' Eve, Mr. Torrington—eyes glittering—had lured her out onto a balcony where torches affixed to the balustrade burned. In the flickering light, he'd pressed a soft kiss to her mouth, and the ground beneath her feet shifted all while dragonflies took wing in her stomach. Would he propose they merge their assorted lives? If so, how would she answer? Forming an attachment to a London gentleman was not at all compatible with her plans.

But a giggling couple had wandered out behind them, and whatever he'd been about to say had died on his lips. The evening ended in disappointment, and no flowers had arrived for her the next day, no note. Not a single indication that he wished to discuss the possibility of joining their two lives. She'd not seen or heard from him since.

Irritation had faded into a dull, empty ache, and she'd thrown herself into work and another flirtation. One that had been decidedly misguided on her part. Her fault for allowing emotion to direct her behavior. Had her dowry not been perceived as worthless, her life might have taken a turn not unlike that of her client's daughter for Mr. Glover was becoming an unavoidable and increasing irritation.

There was a faint click, and a dull, red light flickered to life. A shade with a long wavelength, one barely visible to most human eyes. Curious. Decilamps usually glowed a greenish-blue. A recent advance placed in the hands of the Queen's agents? Mr. Torrington's eye caught upon the unfinished drink as he crossed to the desk, popped open its locked drawers with ease and rifled through its contents.

Was it coincidence that led him to this very study on this particular night?

Possibly. Lord Aldridge sat on the board of the Lister Institute, a group with close ties to the Queen's agents. Still, she needed to be certain.

Frowning, Mr. Torrington prowled about the edges of the room, peering behind paintings. Colleen's heart stopped and she forgot to breathe as he lifted the blurry haystacks, setting the painting aside to contemplate the numbers etched into the dial upon the safe. She couldn't allow anything to leave the lockbox tonight lest she stand accused. Frozen, she watched as he pressed his ear to the door and spun the dial with deft and capable fingers. Left four spins, right for three, left for two, then a twist to the right. *Pop.* The door fell open. She cursed silently as he inspected each box. Gold and silver. Emeralds, rubies and diamonds. But he took nothing. With a soft huff, he closed the door and rehung the painting.

Once again, she breathed.

She ought to stay silent, wait for him to leave, then slide down the drainpipe and disappear. After all, curiosity always killed the cat. But something about him still tugged at her heart, and soon she would quit London, never to see him again. With the necklace—and all of the contents of the safe—secure, she could afford to indulge a whim. "Can't find what you're looking for?" Mr. Torrington whipped about, lifting his decilamp as he reached for his weapon. The light seared her eyes, and she averted her gaze. "Do you mind?"

"Lady Stewart?" Incredulity laced his voice. "What are you doing here?" The beam of light lowered, and he dropped his hand from his hip, away from the TTX pistol hidden beneath his coat.

Adrenaline buzzed through her veins as the inevitable attraction flared. Impossible to leave now without playing their old game of cat and mouse. This time, however, if he let himself be caught, she had no intention of allowing him to slip away with a mere kiss.

Curving her lips into a smile, she sauntered back to the desk to lift her glass. "Enjoying a glass of whisky, neat. I'd offer you one, but you appear frustrated." Smoothing a gloved hand over the curve of her hip, over her close-fitting trousers, she invited his interest. "As if satisfaction is just beyond your reach..." She let the suggestion hang between them.

"Are you offering to help bring my evening to an exciting finish?" His broad shoulders relaxed, and his eyes—a narrow rim of brilliant blue surrounding dark pupils—flashed. To his credit, only then did his gaze drop. "Or merely offering a professional consultation?"

~~~

Her answering laugh was low and throaty. Despite the gravity of his mission, Nick found it impossible not to respond to her teasing. Like him, Lady Stewart was garbed entirely in black. A hooded cape about her shoulders. A shirt beneath a buckled corset. Pouches hung from a low-slung belt. Leather gloves stretched to her elbows. Trousers hugged her hips and thighs. But the boots... As always, those held his gaze with the tenacity of a pteryform trap. Leather and laced, they rose from her trim ankles, sheathing her long and shapely legs before releasing their grasp a few inches above her knees.
~~~

Those brain cells that had not entirely abandoned work noted the stitching at her calf. Since they'd last crossed paths, she'd added a long—and likely sharp—blade to her attire.

His heart gave a great thud, then took off racing while the room grew warmer by several degrees.

Aether, he'd missed her. Missed the bustled and skirted woman who wore tinted spectacles and hugged the walls at society events. Missed the leather-clad seductress whose amber eyes flashed as they glinted back at him across the dark room, daring him to—

What, exactly?

His eyes lifted to her full lips, and he found himself stepping closer, not at all certain that she wouldn't bite. After disappearing from her life—from London—these past three months, she'd likely draw blood. But, like cream rising to the top, finding out the answer had become an immediate priority.

So much for a formal call that landed them both upon a settee in a parlor while her aunt supervised awkward courtship conversation. Better, perhaps, that they'd met here, where he could speak freely about the possibility of merging their realities.

As soon as he'd claimed a kiss.

He chanced another step closer.

"That would depend, Mr. Torrington, upon your goal." She set down her glass and propped a hip against the desk. "I certainly can't assist you if we're working at cross purposes."

Ah, she did indeed hold a grudge. He couldn't blame her. But the lead he'd chased into Scotland this winter—one involving a snowy owl—had required he depart immediately and under an assumed name. When Nick had finally located the cryptid hunter, the slitty-eyed purveyor of rare and unusual creatures had denied selling any animals, let alone owls, to men involved in medical experimentation. Was he trustworthy? No. But the man swore up and down that he wanted nothing to do with any of "that shape-shifting nonsense." Nick had stopped by the Department of Cryptozoology in Edinburgh, but found it a tangled, bureaucratic mess. Abandoning hope of their assistance, he'd left the north and returned to London to find himself once again an uncle, but his sister's health worsening.

He pushed aside all grim thoughts. There would be plenty of time for them later.

At the moment, the woman he wished to make his bride required his full attention. New leads concerning the shadow committee operating in London had emerged in his absence and, should *those* prove valid, Nick would at last have means to infiltrate the group—which would once again mean abandoning Lady Stewart. This time, however, he vowed he would not leave her wondering at his intentions.

His mouth twitched, fighting a smile. "You want *me* to divulge secrets to an employee of a private agency?" He kept his voice light and teasing.

Nick could, however, do exactly that. Tonight, he wasn't acting as a Queen's agent. Instead he was chasing a rumor, one that promised hope for his ailing sister. For years, he'd worked to develop a treatment, but none of the cardiac medications he'd worked upon improved her condition. If anything, they worsened it. Then, recently, he'd heard a whisper about a medical device used to stimulate a paralyzed heart to beat once more. Quietly, he'd begun asking questions.

A board member involved in the oversight of Lister Laboratories, Lord Aldridge had denied the technology's existence. "I've yet to lay eyes on a convincing blueprint," he'd scoffed. "The theory is in place, but for now it remains nothing but a future possibility." Yet a nagging feeling in Nick's gut insisted that the earl knew something more. If there was a treatment under development that might help his sister, he would find it, and searching the earl's private residence was a first and obvious step. Alas, it fell outside the bounds of the task assigned to him by the duke and, therefore, he could not request direct assistance from the agency.

Tipping his head, he considered the woman before him. Lady Stewart would make a most excellent silent, stealthy partner.

She narrowed her eyes as she pushed off the desk. "If your task this evening does not involve the contents of that safe, we might be able to find common ground." Lean, lithe, and light on her feet, Lady Stewart circled about him, inching closer. But Nick didn't reach for her. He had the distinct feeling that should he make the slightest move in her direction, she might leap out the window.

The open window.

He'd watched her do exactly that too many times to count.

"Was that why you watched from the corners?" he asked, turning to keep her in his sights. "Was there something in the safe *you* wanted?"

"What I want is for all its contents to remain securely locked within."

Nick had found nothing of interest in the safe, nor the entirety of the study. Save a certain lady who had interrupted his search.

"Done." Perhaps Lady Stewart *could* help. He'd never before considered partnering with her—heat swelled in his chest—leastways not in terms of working a job together. His eyes slid once again over her form-fitting trousers. Yet they'd passed each other in the dark for years, prowling about London in the small hours of the night. So many untapped skills paced before him. "Any chance you—and your cat—would consider working with a new partner?" He glanced behind her, searching the shadows. "Where *is* your familiar?" Lady Stewart rarely prowled London at night without the overlarge, black cat who shadowed her every step.

"Sorcha often wanders off on her own. Cat business." She shrugged. "She's always returned. No need to worry."

But she did. Nick could see it in her eyes.

Lady Stewart lifted her eyebrows. "Why would a Queen's agent consider hiring a common sneak thief?"

"Please, you're anything but common," he scoffed. Society might look askance at her unusual eyes, but they conferred upon her amazing nighttime vision. Her other senses were heightened as well, not to mention her physical prowess. "Four years living this dual life and not once caught."

"Five," she corrected, stopping in front of him. Close enough so that he could see the fine locks of hair that had wrestled free from a twisted knot at her nape. "A lady without plans to marry needs to look after herself." The faint, familiar scent of wildflowers drifted past—now mixed with a hint of whisky—and his breath caught, trapping the scent within his lungs.

"Without plans, or without offers?" Yes, he was fishing. And hoping for a glimmer of encouragement. He knew a few agents who mixed business with pleasure. A few ended up married, the exact state to which he aspired. Would a brief alliance with a competent—his gaze skimmed over the curve of her neck—and beautiful thief help or hurt his cause?

Her eyes narrowed. "Does it matter?"

"Only if you're about to inform me I've competition for your attention." Her face froze, and a crack shot through his hopes, threatening to shatter his plans. He prayed she wouldn't mention another man's name. "Work called me away before I had a chance to speak."

"Is that an apology?"

"It is." He stared into her amber eyes. "I've missed you."

"Marriage," she huffed. "I've no interest in agreeing to terms that would force me to curtail any of my activities."

"Nor should you." The crack retreated, and he found himself able to breathe deeply once more.

A single step brought her body mere inches away from his. "Most of the *ton*—most men—would disagree."

"Not this man." He struggled to hold on to the thread of their conversation. "A woman should not be forced to waste her talents."

Her eyes flashed. "Yet, more often than not, we must hide them."

As she had hers. "But not from me."

"Trust that I place in your word as a gentleman and a Queen's agent… and our mutual ability to reveal the other's predilection for nighttime prowling…"

"From which you've announced your retirement. I do hope you'll reconsider, but in the meantime, do you propose to resume your celebration?"

"Possibly." She tipped her head. "Provided you've no conditions, no assumptions that what we share here, tonight, will lead any further?"

"None. Hopes, yes. But I'll not force them upon you." His gaze fixed upon her soft, wide mouth. "Does that qualify me to join the festivities?"

Her fingers wrapped about the black, silk cravat at his throat, and she tugged him closer. "It does."

Dropping his hands lightly upon the warm leather encasing her narrow waist, he lowered his mouth to hers, intending to gently explore the shape of her lips, to tease forth her arousal. But as her lips parted, her fingers slid about his neck urging him closer and shattering the last of his preconceptions about her experience. There was no hesitation, no awkwardness to her response that might encourage him to slow down. Instead, her soft moan was pure carnality.

Desire surged, and his tongue slipped inside her mouth to tangle with her own, to drink in her taste. Whisky, rich and seductive with a hint of spice. Warm and intoxicating, like the scent of her skin.

With a throaty growl, he slid his hands down her back, past her bottom to catch at her thighs. Lifting her firmly against his hard length, he spun about to drop her onto the edge of the desk.

Without breaking their kiss, he circled his fingers about her ankles, then dragged his palms upward over leather and lacing until they reached her knees. With a mewl of approval, she spread her legs, inviting him yet closer. A roar rushed through his veins.

Aether, she was a perfect fit.

He nudged against her, and her body shuddered. Kissing her, holding her, touching her was all consuming. His heart raced as fantasies of taking her on the desk swirled through his mind. No, not fantasies, for even now her fingers tugged at the clasps that held his trousers closed. Not in ages had such wild anticipation driven him senseless. He flexed his hips, and she groaned her encouragement.

But one moment his fingers were dipping beneath the rise of her corset, and the next she'd shoved him away. "Did you hear that?" she hissed. "Someone is coming."

Nick heard nothing but the pounding of blood in his ears.

"Go!" She pushed at his shoulder as she dropped onto her feet. "The window!"

He heard the footsteps now—growing closer—and turned to follow. She was already halfway out and reaching for a drainpipe.

"Hurry!" Her eyes flashed green-gold.

He followed quickly, but by the time his feet hit the ground, she was gone.

Chapter Two

"I can't believe Lady Sophia would do such a thing." Isabella shuddered. "She's so quiet and demure... and with her debut tomorrow night!"

Eyebrows arched, Colleen looked over her shoulder to where her aunt—in name only, for Isabella was but two years older—leaned against the bedpost. Her hand smoothed across her lower abdomen where a gentle roundness had begun to announce the eventual arrival of her uncle's heir. For after five years of barrenness, Isabella insisted the child would not dare be anything but male, refusing to discuss any other possibility.

Including the near certainty that the growing babe was *not* her husband's.

Colleen wasn't the only one sneaking in and out of the townhouse windows during the night. Isabella had taken a lover. A nimble one, given the paucity of vegetation surrounding her aunt's window. Though they'd been careful to be quiet, Colleen's ears had heard far more than she wished.

Worried, she'd forced the topic a few nights past. "You're certain my uncle doesn't suspect?" She'd spoken gently. "He has a vindictive streak."

"It was his idea," Isabella had stammered. "I didn't wish to be unfaithful, but he insisted there must be a child. What I didn't expect was to..."

"Fall in love?" Colleen had finished. There was, after all, no longer a need for her paramour's continued attention. Though she wished her aunt every happiness, her uncle's conceit would not tolerate any societal doubt. "Be careful. Of late Mr. Vanderburn has begun conducting nighttime patrols of the grounds. Now that the deed is done, your husband won't chance any rumors clouding the infant's birth." So ended their conversation. Soon after, such visits had ceased, and Isabella had folded into herself, growing quiet and pensive.

Not that it terminated Mr. Vanderburn's steely-eyed vigil. For years, her uncle's thick-necked henchman carried out his errands via the service entrance, rarely lingering longer than it took to steal a treat from the kitchens. Of late, however, he'd begun turning up in the most unlikely places at the most inconvenient of times, hampering her ease of movement. Something she considered suspicious, given it was the dead of winter.

It was a most excellent time to retire.

The steam maid huffed, waiting impatiently for her charge to face forward once more. Steam Adelle—a fancy, new model imported from France—had little patience for her Scottish charge. They were always in conflict, for Colleen refused to bend to the steambot's notions of fashion.

"It's *always* the quiet ones." She ignored the puffs of steam escaping the steambot's collar. "Have you learned nothing from my stories?"

Isabella—her uncle's bride of six months when Colleen arrived—had quickly grown wise to her plea of a headache to absent herself from various social events. Isabella had taken to arriving at her door—curative cup of tea in hand—at inconvenient moments asking questions Colleen did not care to answer. She'd dodged them all… until she'd been caught with one leg out her window.

Ever since, Isabella had become her partner-in-crime. In exchange for scandalous—yet professionally filtered—gossip, her aunt helped conceal Colleen's odd comings and goings, prattling on about her niece's delicate health.

"Enough to deftly navigate the tangles of society. The occasional well-placed comment has kept the sharp-tongued matrons at bay." Isabella threw her a satisfied smile. "No worries, I've not once even hinted at my source."

"Nor have I intentionally applied my skills to interfere with your… diversion." For they kept each other's secrets close. "I've no idea who he is, but if there's ever trouble, you need only ask for my assistance."

Isabella gave a nod, but her gaze fell away. "He's said much the same." She crossed to the window—always cracked open, even in the dead of winter—and peered down at the saucer of milk that balanced on a ledge outside. Legend insisted that such offerings would dispose the cat sìth to offer good blessings in return. "Sorcha's been away for nearly two weeks now. Longer than usual."

An undisguised appeal for another topic of conversation.

Aside from Colleen, Isabella was the only other human whose touch the cat permitted. The cat sìth was more wildcat than house cat and belonged in northern Scotland where several of her kind freely roamed the woods upon Stewart lands and beyond. Such cats were considered by many to be fairy creatures and featured prominently in the myths and legends of Scotland, including farfetched stories explaining her family's origins. Rarely did any condescend to live inside four walls.

Sorcha was an exception. Colleen's steadfast companion since before her parents' death, the cat sìth had refused to stay behind when her favorite human was forced from her home, leaping onto the steam carriage as it carried Colleen away to London.

Though her uncle took a narrow-eyed view of his niece's pet, he'd allowed the cat to stay, provided the creature remained above stairs or outside. The household at large took a dim view of her pet for most found Sorcha's steady, golden stare unnerving and had a tendency to mutter with suspicion—and the atavistic fear that encompassed centuries of superstition—about the similarity of the cat's eyes to Colleen's.

Here in the city, her cat was less revered and more feared. She'd heard the word "familiar" muttered more than once. Only Mr. Torrington used the term in lighthearted jest.

"She'll be back," Colleen insisted, though her assurance sounded false even to her own ears. Three weeks was the longest the cat had ever vanished. Of late, she had begun to visit Sorcha's London haunts, hoping to catch a glimpse of the feline.

"Are you certain you truly wish to retire, to leave town? I'll miss you." Isabella's lips curved upward and a hint of cunning lit her eyes. "And the gossip. Perhaps when things grow dull or difficult, I'll follow you north and fling myself upon your hospitality."

"I will, of course, return for the child's birth." Colleen wouldn't miss it. Assuming her uncle did not object. Steam Adelle let out a prolonged spout of steam, and Colleen turned back toward the dressing table to let the steam maid continue the work she found so necessary. "Though you—and your baby—will always be welcome at my home in Scotland. The air is fresh, and the landscape is stunning," she sighed at the memory, "but you might grow weary of the quiet and the cold."

Would she, rattling around the tower house all alone?

Years spent slinking about the gritty streets of London in the wee hours had honed her skills in a way that rural life could not. Houses here in the city were close enough that one might leap from roof to roof, feet never touching the ground. Gargoyled drainpipes and corniced ledges provided quick and convenient vertical ascents, with the ever-present crank hacks and steam carriages useful obstacles to dart between when one needed to evade a pursuer.

And a certain Queen's agent might turn up at any moment. She'd miss their flirtations most of all.

The steam maid stabbed a final hairpin into Colleen's hair, then rolled back, crossed her arms and huffed. A puff of acrid smoke escaped before she clamped her metal mouth shut. It was always the same silent argument with Steam Adelle. On the dressing table before Colleen was spread an assortment of punch cards, all programs for elaborate and popular upsweeps. All of which she'd rejected in favor of her usual, a simple chignon.

"As I've explained too many times to count, Steam Adelle," Colleen grumbled, "plain is a necessity for afternoon tea."

It was especially hard to hide in the small, brightly-lit parlor. But with no cosmetics and her spectacles—tinted a smoky gray with cerium to hide her amber eyes and block the glare of over-bright lights—no gentleman caller dared compliment her beauty lest he risk sounding like a fool. She smiled at her reflection in the mirror. Her walking dress—a muted blue and green tartan set with red—was but one more layer of camouflage. It over-emphasized her heritage and gave would-be suitors pause. The precise reason Colleen loved it. Fading into the background was an underappreciated talent.

"Are you certain you've told me *everything* about last night?" Isabella squinted at Colleen with suspicion. "Mr.

Glover has returned from his journey and is certain to call, yet the usual irritation isn't etched into your face." She tapped her chin. "In fact, you look rather... high-spirited, considering your eyes have a touch of exhaustion about them."

She cringed. With no plans to marry, Colleen had discreetly taken an occasional lover over the past few years, ones who assured her they had no designs upon matrimony. Women, after all, had the same urges as men, whether they wished to admit to it or not. Alas, her most recent affair had gone... badly.

Curiosity—and perhaps a touch of bored irritation—had convinced her to permit one Mr. Travis Glover—tall, blond, and handsome—to coax her down a hallway and into a locked room while others still whirled upon the dance floor. A regrettable decision. Without preamble, he'd tossed her onto a divan and lifted her skirts. The experience had been a stunning disappointment. One she had no desire to repeat with him. Ever. Which had made his impassioned proposal the following day mystifying. She'd declined, of course. Yet ever since, he'd made a pest of himself.

He called at tea time and peppered her with endless questions about her Scottish estate, insisted upon a dance at every ball, and established an ill-defined partnership with her uncle. Of late, every time she turned about, he was present, staring at her with possessive eyes before making yet another attempt to worm his way into her life. It was exasperating.

This morning, flowers had arrived—an enormous bouquet of roses—and she'd allowed herself to hope. Were they from a certain man whose recent absence had stolen away the joy from her work, from her life? Whose unexpected return had flooded her heart with warmth?

Alas, they weren't from Mr. Torrington. And they ought to be. For after years of turning her nose up at what the marriage mart had to offer, there was at last one particular eligible London gentleman whose suit she would consider. *Consider.* For though his words had hinted at a full partnership, both as his wife and as a business partner, she needed to be certain.

He knew about her lands in the north—and her unusual eyes bothered him not one bit. If he proposed, ought she accept? Scotland called to her, and she needed to go. Still, she clung to the possibility that could have the best of both worlds, spending time at Craigieburn in the north as well as in London.

Unless Mr. Torrington had reconsidered in the bright light of day? For there was no indication that he intended to make his romantic interest in her common knowledge. No note. No flowers. No meeting arranged to speak with her uncle, formality though it would be.

A forlorn ache settled beneath her ribs. The uncertainty would drive her mad.

"What *is* wrong with Mr. Glover?" her uncle had snarled at her across the breakfast table, fingers crumpling the edges of his neatly pressed newspaper. "He's asked for your hand, and I've given my consent."

Where to begin? But her uncle wanted her agreement, not her objections. Nothing good ever came from crossing him, so Colleen had kept her thoughts close and her gaze demurely lowered. "I don't believe we suit," she'd answered vaguely. As always, she had fixed her eyes upon a faint char mark, where a spark from a steambot had vaulted from its firebox onto the polished wood of the table.

"How many gentlemen have declared themselves willing to overlook your paltry dowry and low-bred background?"

"None." Circumstances she'd actively encouraged. But her tone was respectful, as expected.

"Precisely." He'd muttered about his sister abandoning her heritage to elope with an aberrant Scotsman. "Mr. Glover is a second son and holds a satisfactory position in society. Your stubborn refusal to consider his bid for your hand is unacceptable. There will be no more playing the invalid under my roof. You will attend any and all social events to which you have been invited—including the Aldridge girl's debutant ball—wherein I expect you to entertain Mr. Glover's attentions while you reconsider your stance." His nostrils flared. "Am I clear?

"Yes, sir." It was the expected reply, but gone were the days when a guardian could force a marriage. Had her father not seen fit to leave his estate in her uncle's care until she was twenty-five, Colleen would have left this household the moment she reached her majority some four years past. Why her uncle had taken a sudden interest in seeing her married after so many years of virtual neglect, she could not begin to imagine, but she could certainly endure another three days of Mr. Glover's stiff—if overly saccharine—courtship.

Particularly if Mr. Torrington also saw fit to reappear at *ton* gatherings. He could provide her with a public excuse to turn her back on Mr. Glover. Her heart gave a great thud.

Lying awake last night, Colleen's mind had replayed their encounter over and over. A single kiss had tilted her world upon its axis, and a second had sent it spinning. Had they not been interrupted, where might the moment have led?

She'd barely slept at all.

"So? Is there a new gentleman in your life?" Isabella was still awaiting an answer. But Colleen wouldn't be detailing how very exciting it had been to be dropped upon a solid desk and kissed by a man as if only she could quench the fire that burned within him.

"It's nothing. Merely a close encounter with the competition." Mr. Torrington's intentions were not yet clear. Until he made them so, she would keep his words to herself. She pressed her fingertips against her flushed cheeks. This wouldn't do. Much as she would welcome Mr. Torrington's presence were he to call, she had difficulty imagining him perched on the overstuffed divan in the parlor. Mr. Glover, however, would certainly be in attendance, and she did not wish to give him the slightest encouragement.

"Nothing?" Isabella tugged a folded letter from her bodice. Pinched between thumb and forefinger, she dangled it just out of Colleen's reach. "Then you weren't expecting a missive from…"

With a single swipe, she snagged the missive. Her pulse leapt. A renewed offer from Mr. Torrington? As Isabella laughed, she tore open the envelope and unfolded the paper within.

Lady Stewart,

It is with great regret that I write to inform you that there has been a most unfortunate accident. A contingent of boys from the Gordon Academy were en route to Inverness when they experienced a small fire aboard the school dirigible. Though ignition of hydrogen was averted when all hands rushed to extinguish the flames, the helm was abandoned and the airship crashed into the south-west corner. The boys were rescued and sustained only a few minor injuries, but the roof has suffered considerable damage.

Your servant,
Watts

Her estate manager had attached a quote for the roof's repair. Stonework, wooden beams, slate shingles… the supplies required were lengthy. And that was before they accounted for wages to pay the workmen. Her stomach slid to her toes, and her heart dropped to the floor beside it. All the extra funds she'd saved for an emergency? Gone.

Isabella, who had been reading over her shoulder, sighed, "Oh, Colleen. I'm so sorry."

She nodded absently, her mind already leaping ahead to the only logical solution: she needed speak with Mr. Witherspoon. The safer, smaller—and ethically principled—jobs she usually insisted upon would keep her in London for months—and under her uncle's thumb. Taking a room at a hotel would increase costs and extend her stay in the city indefinitely. But if she asked her employer for riskier tasks, ones with generous compensation, she need only complete a handful of jobs.

Her uncle would be furious if—when—he learned she'd failed to present herself at tea. But there was no time to waste. She lifted her gaze and met Isabella's knowing grin. "Will you cover for me one more time?"

Chapter Three

Told to watch for a blonde woman with a distracted air who favored pink, Nick strolled past the entrance to the Rankine Institute for what felt like the hundredth time. Though the Queen's agents had ties to the engineering school, he preferred to keep his unofficial inquiries carefully away from any eavesdropping bureaucratic ears. Hence his reluctance to enter the building.

He had, however, attracted unwanted attention. A particularly burly guard—who had taken up his post an hour ago—now tracked his every step. Eyes narrowed and arms crossed, his scowl suggested he would like to grab Nick by the scruff of his neck and drag him into a dark alley. Only his gentlemanly attire—the cut of his coat's lapels and the fall of his trousers—kept him safe.

Though he'd failed to find any incriminating evidence, Nick could not dismiss his suspicions of Lord Aldridge. While the man's desk had revealed nothing—save the woman he wished to marry was more adventurous than he'd dared hope—there might yet be more information hidden in less obvious locations within the house. Or at the Lister Institute but, much as Nick longed to search the gentleman's office, security was extremely high. That would be his last resort.

A polished steam carriage pulled to the side of the street and stopped, waiting. More and more crank hacks rattled and clicked past on the street as the well-to-do working middle class hired transport home. Foot traffic also increased, forcing him to step to the side of the pavement. The sun hung low in the sky as he tugged his pocket watch from his waistcoat to confirm the time. Mr. Jackson had suggested that the engineer he sought—a newlywed keen to bask in the afterglow of a honeymoon—made a habit of leaving promptly at five. Except when she didn't. A Queen's agent in training, unexpected assignments were guaranteed.

It was now five past.

He'd contemplated paying a call at Lady Stewart's residence, but wanted to present her with a lead, not merely a ring. *Gah*, his mother had been far too excited when he'd asked her for the heirloom, flapping her hands and darting from her chair to hug him tight. The anticipation of more grandchildren always set her face alight.

"I've yet to propose," he'd cautioned her. "She might decline."

"I've seen how she looks at you." His mother had pinched his cheek. "She won't."

Nick wasn't nearly as confident. Lady Stewart had an independent streak a mile long. Not that he wished to cage or leash her. No, he wanted a wife that was his equal. What better way to show her exactly that, than by taking her out on the town while most of the city slept? Which is why he paced the street in the growing dark hoping to latch on to another lead. Not solely motivated by saving his sister, but also by a growing emotion that he struggled to name. It was more than desire, but was it love?

The attraction had been instantaneous that first night they'd met eye to eye on a dark rooftop. A shock of awareness had rippled through him and set his pulse racing like a runaway steam train careening down a mountainside. He'd teased. She'd laughed... and responded with a flirtatious comment of her own. Encounter had followed encounter—both while running free across the cityscape or whirling across the confines of a dance floor—and their conversations deepened. The death of her parents, her unusual eyes, and her desire to leave London. His frustration with laboratory work, the irritations of being a second spare, his sister's heart condition.

The birth of his precious niece had exacerbated his sister's heart condition. Blue fingernails and fainting spells—otherwise known as Adams-Stokes syncope and seizures—were now commonplace rather than occasional events, and Anna's pulse rarely exceeded forty beats per minute, a severe bradycardia that even atropine injections could not accelerate.

At any moment, her heart could simply... stop.

Her husband—a Naval officer on assignment in the South China Sea—had been sent for, though at the rate his sister continued to deteriorate, he wasn't at all certain an airship could carry the lieutenant home fast enough.

Nick unclenched his jaw and rolled his shoulders. Strolling, he reminded himself, not stalking.

"There's nothing you—or anyone—can do, Nicholas," Anna had murmured, cradling her infant daughter and smiling down upon the sleeping child with wonder. Marriage and the wished for pregnancy had been a risk she'd taken despite all medical advice. "I've accepted my fate and regret nothing. My daughter is a miracle, nothing less."

It was a miracle that Anna had survived the delivery. But he'd bit his tongue. Anna might be resigned to an invalid's life and an early death, but he wanted nothing but health and happiness for his sister. He wanted his niece to know her mother, but without a method to restart Anna's heart when it ceased beating...

He'd glanced at the collection of contraptions gathering dust in the corner of her room. All generated low levels of harmless electricity, designed to stimulate the nervous system and prod her heart to greater effort.

"None of the... less invasive medical devices worked?"

"None."

Which explained the newest contraption—P.C. Hutchinson's Magneto-Shock Machine—and the full-time nurse. Covered in knobs and dials, it hummed at a low level, ready to generate a burst of electricity. All well and good until one took note that it sported a metal probe designed to be inserted through the chest wall and directly into the ventricles of the heart. *That* was just as likely to be deadly as curative.

He'd quizzed the nurse directly and reached the horrified conclusion that there was merit in such a device, if also a high risk of infection. The machine would only be used if Anna's heart refused to beat after three minutes, before which a less invasive approach—percussive pacing and chest compressions—would be attempted. It hadn't made him feel any better, but at the four-minute time point, brain death would threaten. Such an action would be a last-ditch effort.

"But know that I've not given up hope." He never had. Never would. "I'm still looking for a solution."

Anna had squeezed his hand. "I know."

For three years he'd served as co-investigator of a cardiophysiology laboratory in the basement of Lister Laboratories. They'd isolated and studied a number of cardiac glycosides, chemicals with structures similar to that of digitalis—a drug extracted from the foxglove plant that strengthened the force of a heartbeat—but though many had proven to be alternative treatments for those suffering from congestive heart failure, for Anna, each had proved toxic. Only atropine—a derivative of deadly nightshade—had increased her heart rate. Until, with the worsening of her condition, it didn't.

This past year, work as a Queen's agent had placed increasing demands on Nick's time, and he'd spent less and less time in the laboratory. Instead, he'd found himself chasing reports about a small group in London who believed in such nonsense as selkies, werewolves and witches, in creatures who could alter their physical form. Believing was one thing, but attempting to force it was another. Rumors midst the cryptid hunter community were rife, but when confronted directly none—like his lead in Scotland—could provide any proof or name names. Locating—forget infiltrating—this shadow committee suspected of such unethical behavior was proving difficult.

When he wasn't chasing down men suspected of animal cruelty, Nick had turned his attention to chasing another whisper he'd heard uttered in the hallowed halls of Lister Laboratories. He'd taken that rumor directly to one particular board member. Lord Aldridge. The man had hesitated—for the briefest of moments—before denying that he knew of any such researcher.

"I've caught word of an independent scientist working upon a novel method to restart the heart once it has stopped beating. Not," he waved his hand at the monstrous, invasive machine beside them, "this. But a small, miniaturized, cardio-pacing device that can be implanted into the chest wall, one that will monitor the heartbeat and deliver a tiny, well-timed electrical burst to the cardiac tissue when it detects no beats."

"I'd rather," Anna hadn't met his gaze, "that you spend your time courting Lady Stewart, for I'd very much like to see you married before I..." The baby had begun to cry in her cradle, and his sister had scooped up Clara, jiggling and cooing as she rocked the infant back to sleep.

He'd taken that as his cue to depart.

Marriage. Device hunting. Stop a ring of gentlemen from turning their interests in shape-shifting creatures upon humans. While he waited for new information on the last, he thought he might combine the pursuit of the first two activities and take Lady Stewart prowling about London in an attempt to win her heart.

The sun hung low in the sky by the time a young woman wearing a rose walking dress stepped forth from the building and paused beneath the portico, pinning a straw hat to tousled and crimped blonde hair.

"Mrs. Leighton?" Nick inquired.

Her hand slipped into the folds of her skirts and into a conveniently located pocket. No doubt her fingers wrapped about the hilt of a knife or the handle of a small firearm. Her eyebrows lifted. "Have we met?"

"Allow me to introduce myself." Careful to maintain a respectful distance between them, Nick doffed his top hat and bowed. "Mr. Torrington, begging a few moments of your time. I'm sorry if my approach caused you concern." He straightened and drew back the edge of his coat, providing her with a glimpse of his TTX pistol. The burly man stepped into the doorframe, his fingers curling into a fist, but the weapon gave him pause. Nick shot him a smug glance. "We have a mutual colleague. Mr. Jackson suggested you might be able to provide insight into a particular conundrum I've encountered."

Mrs. Leighton held up a hand. "It's fine, Cyrus." She led Nick a few steps away to stand beside a lamppost. Foot traffic flowed about them, and the street noise of passing clockwork horses, crank hacks and steam carriages provided a certain measure of privacy. But her hand didn't leave her pocket; not all the suspicion had left her eyes. "What information is it you seek?"

Nick ducked to avoid losing an eye to the prong of a parasol. "Mr. Jackson informed me your work encompasses the miniaturization of portable energy sources, a Markoid battery was mentioned."

Her eyes slid sideways and she frowned. "Mr. Jackson should not have spoken so freely, but go on."

"There is rumor of a new medical device, one that proposes to stimulate the heart should it cease to beat by delivering an electrical impulse."

Concern—and maybe a touch of horror—furrowed her brow. "I make it a point never to associate with galvanists."

That drew him up short. "I wasn't..." Or was he? If his search for information had exhausted reputable sources, ought he look elsewhere? Most galvanists were charlatans, preying upon a family's desperation to bring a relative back to life, but... "I'm not looking for a confidence man who has constructed a grand device, one that fills a room with wires and spinning gears to produce impressive arcs of electricity that would cause a corpse to twitch and jerk, but rather someone with a more furtive bent. A scientist who works toward his own ends quietly, out of the public eye, focusing primarily upon the heart. One disinclined to publish his or her findings and who may have escaped the notice of the larger scientific community."

"And you came to me because...?" She shifted on her feet. Uncomfortable with the concept or did she know something?

"Because the device I'm searching for would be intended for the living. To keep their heart beating, jolting it back into motion mere seconds after it ceased to beat." His effort was aimed at keeping Anna's heart beating steadily and fast enough to sustain life. "The power source would need to be small, compact and safe. Mr. Jackson insinuated that your research into alternate power sources for automatons occasionally brings you into contact with some of the more unsavory characters who occupy the fringes of your field of study."

"He would," she quipped, "after a particularly unfortunate incident on the train." But her shoulders relaxed. "This past summer an unscrupulous foreign investor attempted to steal my prototype. He was caught and interrogated. A list of people interested in purchasing my battery was compiled, but most sought to power automatons. But as to biological uses…" She tapped two gloved fingers upon her lips. "One woman, a spiritualist, was convinced that regular stimuli to the occipital lobe of the brain might allow an individual to detect—to see—the presence of spirits."

"No." Nick shook his head.

"Another," Mrs. Leighton's voice dropped, "hoped to revive flagging male virility."

Heat crept into his cheeks. "Certainly not."

A tiny smile crept onto her face. "The heart is a muscle, is it not?"

"It is."

"Then you might want to speak with the third scientist. Classically trained at the University of Edinburgh, Dr. Gregory Farquhar's thesis presented a study of how the electrical stimulation of nerves causes muscle fibers to contract." A certain gleam entered her eyes and Nick realized she'd been toying with him, tweaking his nose with the nonsensical possibilities of her battery before finally handing over the information he sought. "He's quite mad, however. His intended use of my battery? To power a portable device to jolt the bodies of dead animals in the hopes that they might reanimate in an altered form."

In short, transmutation. The transformation of one species into another. Not over the course of generations, but via a process best described as sorcery. And by a mere battery. Was such a thing even possible?

Nick fought to keep his jaw off the pavement. Had his hunt for a remedy for Anna's heart condition uncovered new information pointing directly to a key member of the shadow committee he sought?

"Thank you, Mrs. Leighton." He bowed. "You've provided me with much to consider."

"You're quite welcome, Mr. Torrington." She lifted a hand and the driver of the steam carriage hopped down to hold open a door. "Please keep all information about my research under tight wraps."

"Of course." He handed her into the waiting steam carriage.

With a solid lead in his pocket, he'd intended to hasten to Lady Stewart's side to present her with the promise of an adventure. He was certain she would prefer such a gift to hothouse flowers. But if this information fell under the umbrella of Queen's agents' business, could he justify the risk of sharing such a promising detail?

Chapter Four

Reflexively, Colleen glanced over her uncle's shoulder to assess the light levels in Lord Aldridge's ballroom. In a nod to tradition, the crystal drops of the central chandelier glittered in the flickering light of wax candles. Along the walls, gas jets burned within milky-white globes to cast a steadier light. Not a single Lucifer lamp was in evidence as its harsher blue-white light was considered unflattering to a lady's complexion.

Bright enough that any odd reflections from Colleen's eyes would likely go unnoticed were she to tuck her tinted lenses away. Yet given the antics she planned this evening, it was best if she left her spectacles perched upon her nose. It would not be her eccentricities she wished commented upon when tongues wagged about tonight's events.

In the receiving line, Lady Aldridge stood beside her daughter, Lady Sophia, whose gown—what with its profusion of pale blue ruffles and lace—threatened to swallow her whole. Though her deportment was demure and polite, there were faint shadows beneath her eyes and a certain tightness to her shoulders. She had the look of a cat subjected to a leash. Or a cage. Lady Sophia glanced up, their eyes locked, and Colleen could swear she saw a flash of fire deep inside those pale, silver eyes.

Had the young woman *deliberately* left her distinctive necklace in a forbidden man's bed? She fought the upward curve of her lips. Colleen counted it as a distinct possibility. If Lady Sophia also possessed claws, there would be more trouble before her parents managed to shove her down the aisle. *If* they succeeded in forcing her to wed at all.

"Come along." Isabella hooked her arm about Colleen's, leaning close as they stepped into the ballroom. "This had best work. My husband made an unanticipated appearance in my dressing room in which I was *instructed* to begin planning your wedding to Mr. Glover."

Colleen sucked a breath of air past her teeth. "Do not overexert yourself."

Out of the coal scuttle and into the grate. Anger and annoyance clasped hands and began to whirl deep inside her chest. Of all the nights! The moment Mr. Glover had her in his sights, he would stick to her like taffy on teeth.

Isabella snorted. "If there's another gentleman in your life, now would be a good time for him to present himself as an alternative."

Anger ran down her spine like molten steel, then cooled, stiffening her resolve. "I'll rescue *myself* from Mr. Glover." Though Mr. Torrington might offer for her hand, she was still contemplating the merits of such a union. First, she needed to complete her new assignment. The task was simple, but she *needed* the money.

She scanned the ballroom. In one corner, a steam orchestra hidden behind a wall of potted rhododendrons played a waltz as guests whirled and swirled about the floor. Mr. Glover was not among them, but a refreshment room opened off the ballroom and bustled with activity. What with his sweet tooth, they were almost certain to find him within.

"Do you remember the plan?" Colleen steered them in the direction of the refreshment room.

"I do."

It was a touch risky. She'd never caused a public scene before, but Mr. Glover's persistent advances must be terminated *and* the package must be placed. Guests were still arriving, making their way up the grand staircase to the ballroom which meant *now* was the best time to put her plan into action. To the right of the entryway was Lord Aldridge's library. If all went well, both tasks would be accomplished in quick succession. Her heart began to pound. Her uncle might well turn her out on the doorstep tomorrow morning, but if she accomplished her aim, there would be more than enough in her bank account to pay for a room at Claridge's.

He was already irritated at his wife and niece's impromptu "shopping trip," one that had left the steam butler turning guests—and one Mr. Glover—away from the townhome during regularly scheduled calling hours. Though they'd later purchased silk stockings, their first stop had been at her employer's door.

"Back so soon?" Mr. Witherspoon had looked up from his desk, amused, as she stepped into his office. Dark and wood-paneled, its walls were lined with hefty legal tomes. One might hire him to draft a will, but more often than not, gentlemen arrived with difficulties that required a more unofficial and delicate solution. "Only yesterday you informed me of your retirement."

"An unanticipated situation arose." Embarrassment heated her cheeks. She'd made much of returning to Scotland. "Fixing it requires—"

"Funds." He set aside his fountain pen. "How much?"

The sum she named widened his eyes, and Mr. Witherspoon leaned back in his chair and steepled his fingers. "How quickly, Lady Stewart, do you wish to amass your rewards?"

"Within five days." She swallowed, hoping it wasn't an impossibility. Fixing the roof of Craigieburn Castle before heavy rains could do yet more damage was a pressing matter. "I know I ask the impossible, but—"

"There is an assignment I intended for another associate, but given your exemplary performance over the past few years, I'm happy to place it in your hands. It involves an obfuscation chain that will require you to return to Lord Aldridge's home this very evening. Might you be attending Lady Sophia's debut ball?"

Excitement and relief filled her lungs, restoring her ability to breathe deeply. Was it possible she would not need to alter her plans? "I am."

"There is only one small obstacle you need to overcome." He'd pursed his lips. "Three years ago you declined to work on the more... gray cases."

"Needs must."

"Very well. Listen closely."

The task involved an obfuscation chain. She would be but one link of many and wouldn't know what she was passing along—or why. There was little to no risk involved, beyond being caught with the item in hand. In which case, no one would step forward to protect her. That the compensation for this single job was enough to cover the cost of roof repairs was telling. Someone was skirting the law, and she would need to bend her morals.

She ignored the queasy flutter in her stomach. "I'll take it."

Though she'd not asked, it was unlikely Lord Aldridge knew his home was the platform for yet another operation carried out by Witherspoon and Associates. Not that he'd be surprised. Ballrooms were always filled with undercurrents of activity.

"Ready?" Her aunt snapped her attention back to the task at hand.

She nodded. "Ready." Better to finish this soon, before there was any chance of Mr. Torrington's arrival. She did not wish for him to intervene.

"Mrs. Wilson!" Isabella hailed an acquaintance, abandoning Colleen's side as she began to make her way across the polished floor.

"Miss Stewart," a gentleman whose name she could not recall greeted her. Always "miss" never "lady". How the English hated to acknowledge that an unmarried woman might hold a title, even one that was little more than a courtesy. "Fine, dry weather we've had these past few days."

"Quite lovely," she answered, not meeting his eyes. Indeed, it made the rooftops far less treacherous.

Isabella disappeared into the refreshment room.

A few more acquaintances nodded, some making a weak effort to engage her in polite conversation. Long minutes passed, but her dull answers failed to inspire further comment, and awareness of her existence begin to fade until her silent presence was no more than decorative, much like the wallpaper.

Her pale, yellow ballgown was unremarkable. Its neckline did not plunge. Its sleeves did not bare her shoulders. And the swags that fell from her hips to gather in a generous bustle upon her backside did nothing to accentuate her figure. The only adornment was an overabundance of fabric flowers clustered at one shoulder and upon her opposite hip. When the moment arrived, her sudden change in behavior would draw sharp attention.

It was time. Isabella hadn't reappeared, which meant Mr. Glover was within.

Touching her fingers to the red, tartan rosette she'd tucked in among the other blooms, Colleen stepped into the crush of guests, wending her way toward the refreshment room.

The box suspended beneath her bustle and within its wire cage resumed its soft bumping against the backside of her knees. It was a simple rosewood box inlaid with Mother of Pearl, hinged, and fitted with an ornate lock to which she had not been given a key. Despite its small size, the carriage ride here had been most uncomfortable, and she longed to be rid of her package. Not to mention Mr. Glover's unflagging courtship.

The refreshment table groaned beneath all manner of delicacies. A tall centerpiece lifted a much-embellished pineapple aloft. Towering artistic cakes that rose at intervals were surrounded by lower arrangements of ices, biscuits and iced cakes. Champagne and lemonade were among the many offerings.

Isabella stood beside Mr. Glover, who was collecting an assortment of treats upon a plate. Powdered sugar dusted his mustache. A gentle touch to his sleeve and a murmured word from her aunt shifted his attention toward the door. His gaze caught hers. An ingratiating smile stretched across his face, and he quickly abandoned his plate to snatch up two glasses of champagne.

As she'd suspected. Unable to wring assent from her in private, he would now attempt a more public venue.

The chase was on.

Pivoting on her heel, she exited the room and threaded her way through guests—jostling elbows and knocking dance cards from the hands of more than one gentleman. Irritated young ladies hissed their displeasure as she passed.

"Miss Stewart!" Irritation twisted through Mr. Glover's voice as she exited the ballroom. Gleeful at his consternation, Colleen bit down on her lip, fighting an entirely unprofessional urge to laugh as she grabbed at the doorframe and rounded the corner into the upper hall. Clutching at her skirts, she rushed down the stairs past the new arrivals—whose eyes widened to stare—and into the empty library.

Thrusting a hand beneath her bustle, her fingers found the clasps that held the package within. *Click. Click.* The rosewood box fell free. Drawing it from beneath the silk swags, Colleen placed it on the table beside the globe—as instructed—then hurried across the room to stand before a window overlooking the street. Across the street stretched Hyde Park, cultivated and clipped for the pleasures of London's populace. Nature, tamed and domesticated. But at least outside a cool breeze could ruffle the leaves upon branches and moonlight reached the ground unfiltered by thick panes of wavy glass.

"Colleen!" Mr. Glover boomed as he strode into the library, his hands—now empty of celebratory champagne—spread wide. Annoyance and confusion twisted his face. Had he even noticed that he had addressed her in a most improper and informal manner?

Arms crossed, she drew herself up straight as she turned to face him, peering down her nose through her gray lenses. "Lady Stewart."

A few guests appeared at the doorway with unabashed curiosity written across their faces. She fought back any hint of satisfaction from her face. The perfect audience.

Mr. Glover came to a halt before her and swept a bow. "My apologies, The Much Honored Lady Stewart of Craigieburn." Though his movements and words gave every impression of a courtly greeting, his voice was tight. "I spoke with your uncle and explained that we *must* marry. He's given us his blessing and has begun the paperwork."

How dare they? The impudence! "I don't wish to—" A thought struck her like a blow to the stomach. "You..." She couldn't force the words past her lips. If he'd detailed their—incredibly brief and disappointing—affair, that would explain her uncle's sudden insistence that she marry. Fire ignited inside her chest. If Mr. Glover had indeed besmirched her honor, she would see him suffer.

He took a step forward. "I've been to Scotland."

"To Craigieburn Castle?" Was that where he had disappeared to these last few weeks? A cold trickle of fear ran through her body at such an excessive act of devotion. She took a small step sideways, shifting away.

He nodded, his eyes feverish. "Your dowry is beautiful. It's a tall and stately tower house, a castle in its own right. We'll make it our home."

"No, Mr. Glover, we will not." Keeping her voice civil was a struggle. In three days Craigieburn and its lands would be under *her* control, and she wouldn't be signing it over to anyone. Ever. "I've declined your offer and asked you to cease pressing your attentions upon me."

"This ridiculousness must end." His eyes narrowed, and he blew out an exasperated huff. "We've been intimate. We must marry."

"I disagree." Why was he so insistent? Why her? She wasn't an heiress. She brought him no social connections. And this certainly wasn't a love match. Save a brief fumble in the dark, they shared nothing. *Nothing.* "There were no consequences," she informed him in a soft voice. Her precautions had been effective, thank goodness.

"Miss Stewart?" Her voice trembling with the effort to oppose ingrained instincts that private conversations were not to be interrupted, a young woman stepped into the library. "Do you require assistance?"

Mr. Glover called over his shoulder, "Miss Stewart has made me the happiest of men by agreeing to become my fiancée."

"I've done no such thing!" Colleen cried, raising her voice for the benefit of their audience. Her anger was tempered by the thought that no one would link her presence in the library with anything save this argument. The obfuscation chain—her part in it—had been executed perfectly. "I've given you my answer, and it's my consent, not my uncle's, that you require. Do stop. You're making a scene."

"Stop being so difficult," he hissed. From his pocket, he withdrew a ring. "Now slip this on, and let us return to the ball. We'll share the next waltz." He reached for her, and she jumped back.

"How dare you take such liberties!" She raised a hand to slap his face, but he caught her wrist midair.

The audience gasped. A gentleman broke free from the gaping crowd at the doorway. One Mr. Nicholas Torrington. "Sir, this is unseemly."

Colleen's stomach sank. Not only had she wished to rescue herself, she didn't want him to see her playing the role of a woman teetering on the edge of hysteria. But, alas, he was present. And if they were to work as partners, she might as well test his mettle. Would he see through her charade? Step onstage and carve himself a role in this dramatic production?

Mr. Glover ignored him and spoke through clenched teeth. "Come now, be reasonable. You permitted my attentions. I did not drag you into that room. It was you who misled *me*. Such behavior comes with an implicit agreement."

"I agreed to a brief liaison," she said. "Not a lifetime!"

"I believe Lady Stewart has made her position clear." Mr. Torrington's hand landed on Mr. Glover's shoulder, wheeling him about so that *he* stood face to face with Mr. Glover, his broad back and wide shoulders blocking her humiliation from onlookers.

Aether! He'd been close enough to overhear their last exchange. Blood rushed to her face, and she closed her eyes for a moment, reminding herself that she'd *wanted* a public scene. If not this particular one. Not one in which

Mr. Glover refused to concede defeat. Her last days in London would be a misery. And if he followed her to Scotland, what then?

Colleen forced her eyes open, bracing herself for more ugliness. Mr. Torrington's right hand had moved to the small of his back. Pinched between his thumb and forefinger was a silver filigree ring set with an amber stone.

"Your behavior is presumptuous, sir," Mr. Torrington chided. "I too have been courting Lady Stewart." He waggled the ring.

He'd planned to propose tonight? Her stomach twisted. She still wasn't certain marriage was something she wanted. Did he truly expect her to place his ring on her finger?

While accepting an offer of marriage was not at all the end to the public commotion she had planned, it would serve nicely. And, with her latest task complete, she was free to take on new employment. She drew in a deep breath. A betrothal *would* allow them to spend time together without inviting too much censure. Perhaps if she viewed it as a trial engagement while she assisted him with his endeavors? Might they also find time to trial their... physical compatibility?

"Moreover," he continued, waggling the ring again, insistently. She plucked the silver band from his fingers and slid it over her glove and onto her finger. It wasn't as if she'd be required to follow through with an actual wedding. A young lady was entitled to change her mind, though the gratification that swelled his next words hinted that his actions might not at all be a performance. "She has accepted me and wears *my* ring."

Chapter Five

Clasping his fiancée's hand, Nick drew her forward, displaying the ring upon her finger to the audience before them. Hushed whispers erupted as speculation spread through the crowd. For years, he'd managed to steer clear of the marriage mart. It helped that two brothers stood between him and the eventual inheritance of a viscount's title. Still, irritation would curdle the features of a number of mothers and daughters once the news reached the guests upstairs.

Though he forced a pleasant smile onto his face, inwardly he cringed. What should have been a shared private moment following an impassioned proposal involving actual words had been turned into a spectacle played out before a roomful of gossip-inclined *ton.* Not ideal. He never would have dared attempt such a stunt had he not known how adverse she was to societal attention.

"I'm sorry, Mr. Glover." Lady Stewart lifted her voice, and he had the decided impression she carefully chose the words that would appear on tomorrow's scandal sheets. A niggling suspicion that she'd staged this altercation warned him that there was more at play here than a lover's spat. "My heart belongs to another."

"Impossible," Glover barked. Fury set his mustache quivering like a hairy caterpillar having heart palpitations. "I would have been informed. Your uncle—"

"Perhaps you'd best take that up with him." Nick's tone would have warned off a normal man, but Lady Stewart's admirer had a fervent look about his eyes that suggested—no, promised—he would be trouble.

"You may count on it."

Glaring, Glover turned on his heel and stormed from the room, off to lodge a loud and vociferous complaint to her uncle. Trouble would come next from that direction. Her guardian, Lord Maynard, was known for his uncharitable business ventures. Whatever arrangements he and Glover had arrived at, Nick's sudden intervention wouldn't be welcome. Not that he cared.

Would that he could toss Lady Stewart in a waiting steam carriage and take to the streets to settle things between them privately. Alas, that would only inflame the situation. As their time together here could now be measured in mere minutes, he cupped her elbow and drew her toward a service door fitted into the room's paneling. "Come," he said, "let's find you a quiet corner to regain your composure."

She sniffed, but held her tongue and allowed him to lead her down the hall, past a servant's staircase—sidestepping a clockwork hoist that carried stacks of empty plates and fingerprint smudged crystal along a downward track toward the kitchens—and into the conservatory.

He drew her into an alcove behind a potted plant where they could face each other and speak in relative privacy.

"Regain my composure?" His fiancée lifted an eyebrow. "How very patronizing." Indignant amber eyes flashed behind her grey lenses, and Nick was struck by a desire to pluck them from her face that he might bask in the full heat of their brilliance, in the golden glow that was almost an exact match to the color of the amber ring that now adorned her finger.

Nick cleared his throat. "Apologies, but what kind of agent would I be, shattering the carefully crafted illusion you present to the *ton*? Though Mr. Glover's bleating tonight has drawn unprecedented attention in your direction, you might still aspire to slip quietly from the role of wallflower into that of stately matron."

"A wallflower potted and rooted and content to remain upon the shelf." Her chin lifted.

"Is that so?" he countered. "Then you should not have encouraged the attentions of Mr. Glover, a man with a tendency to boast within the confines of his club."

"He did not!" Her eyes grew tight as she muttered a curse. "Of course he did. What did you hear?"

"You won't like it."

"Nonetheless, I prefer to know, lest I be taken by surprise. What nasty rumors has he spread? Leave nothing out."

With the name Dr. Gregory Farquhar in hand, Nick had headed to a club favored by second and third sons who eschewed the tradition of military or church service to pursue alternative paths. Among them were a number of physicians who might know something of this cardiologist's past, of his present.

And so one had. "Stay far, far away from him," he was cautioned. "Whatever promise he once showed, he's descended into madness and no longer even pretends to see patients. His wife grows ever more bitter as her husband toils away in that basement laboratory of his doing aether knows what." With some reluctance and repeated warnings, he'd been given Dr. Farquhar's direction.

Though the hour grew late, Nick had decided a brief visit was in order. Perhaps if he approached Dr. Farquhar as one scientist to another, offering flattery and a willing ear, the man might invite him into his laboratory. Unlikely, but worth a try.

Fortifying himself, Nick had tossed back his drink and rose. En route to the door, he'd passed a rowdy bunch of gentlemen, tormenting one of their own about his supposed "conquest".

"Are you insane? She has no dowry. Leastways, not one worth mentioning."

"You don't have to marry the first woman you bed, Glover. Not even if you leave a bun in the oven."

"She's hardly the first," he'd snapped. "And it's not her that I value, but what she will bring to our marriage."

Sniggers erupted. "She's a freak," a second man said. "Hiding those strange eyes of hers behind smoky glass, slipping in and out of rooms when no one's looking."

Nick had slowed his steps, wondering.

"Save yourself," a third advised. "She turned down your offer. Consider yourself fortunate. We'll take you to Mrs. Fowler's house..."

A brothel. He'd heard enough.

Dr. Farquhar lived in a relatively new townhome—terraced—on a respectable street not far from The British Museum. The man's steam butler had taken Nick's card, but declared the good doctor not at home and unable to say when he would return. The usual lies, for Nick had not missed the twitch of a curtain that covered an upper window. For a brief moment, he'd stared into the wild eyes of a white-haired man. The physician himself?

With a normal, civilized conversation ruled out, Nick had returned home to dress for the ball and arrived at Lord Aldridge's front door to find chaos and turmoil surrounding the very woman that drew him to tonight's societal event.

"Mr. Torrington, tell me." Lady Stewart scowled, correctly anticipating what he had to share.

"Much what you'd expect." He cleared his throat. She deserved to know. "Bets were being taken. Odds were rather in favor of you declining his offer, despite... well... his boasts of sexual conquest that would force you to accept his suit."

"I will claw his eyes out." Her face flushed, but she did not turn away from Nick's gaze. "But I won't pretend I've been chaste all these years in London. Are you certain you don't wish to retract your unspoken offer?" She lifted her hand and began to slide the ring from her finger.

He caught her hand with his. "No." Were there certain primitive instincts fixed in his brainstem that objected? Yes. But the higher centers of his brain admired her refusal to conceal the truth. "I'll admit to a selfish urge to guard your reputation and an inclination to defend your honor by resurrecting the tradition of pistols at dawn, but it's not your maidenly virtue that draws me." The corner of his mouth kicked up. The words he'd practiced in his mind fell away. Instead he spoke the raw truth. "Not only do I like you, Lady Colleen Stewart, I admire you. Your quick mind, your skills as a sneak thief, your refusal to conform to society's will. And," he trailed a finger down the side of her face, "your kisses send fire racing through my veins. You're the only woman I wish to make my bride. But if *I* don't suit *you*, then by all means, return my ring."

The pulse at her throat fluttered. The attraction between them was palpable. No, combustible. Yet her hesitation spoke volumes and her words, when they finally came, were soft. "Might we... consider this a trial engagement?"

"A trial engagement." He lifted an eyebrow.

"We've known each other for years now, but only in fleeting snatches." She took a deep breath. "I'd not thought to marry anyone. Not before you. But—"

"You wish to know me better first."

She nodded. "And you ought to know me better as well. There are freedoms I do not wish to relinquish."

"You wish to discuss terms." Fair enough, especially given her uncle certainly wouldn't be inclined to negotiate a favorable marriage contract on her behalf. "Contracts and finances."

"Of course. Much as I loved my father, he tied me—legally—to an awful man he himself did not respect—and all due to a misplaced view of a woman's abilities. I'll not willingly or blindly speak vows without securing my future rights."

"The last thing I want is a reluctant or apprehensive bride."

"Additionally, you might not appreciate the attention an engagement to me brings. Your own reputation will suffer."

"Not nearly as much as yours." Gentlemen were permitted their wild oats, but the slightest hint of indiscretion forever stained an unmarried woman's reputation.

"And," her voice dropped as her lips curved upward, "we ought to see if we... suit."

Heat crept up beneath his collar and cravat. Nick stepped closer. "Are you suggesting—"

She flicked her fingers against his waistcoat, directly over his concealed TTX pistol. "I wish to see how you conduct yourself in the field."

"You want me to lead you into excitement and danger upon the dark streets of nighttime London?" Never had he thought to woo a woman in such a manner, but he found himself warming to the many possibilities that long hours of prolonged surveillance might provide.

"I do." She laughed, then became all business. "Now, tell me what you have in mind for our first outing together, and what is it you seek."

A tiny, irritating voice counseled him that he ought not include her on tonight's undertaking, reminding him that the scientist might well be employed by the Committee for the Exploration of Anthropomorphic Peculiarities, or CEAP as it was sometimes referred to among the Queen's agents. Nick could do this alone. He could sneak into Dr. Farquhar's laboratory without assistance. A partner to watch one's back was valuable, but not imperative. So asserted his mind. Other parts of his anatomy continued to insist that the presence of this particular woman was, in fact, very necessary. But those parts—ones that were upright and alert—had no business running a mission.

Still, when put to a vote, his gray matter lost.

"A medical device. One merely rumored to exist, so finding it is not a certainty. To begin, I've a basement laboratory I wish to search. Quietly and discreetly." For her, he tried to separate the task at hand from any future they might or might not share. "Regardless of the outcome of our trial engagement, you will be paid." He named a sum. "For each evening you assist my endeavors. A bonus of twice that if—when—we find the device."

A titter of laughter met their ears and though the other couple that wandered past was lost in each other's eyes, he stepped yet closer to Lady Stewart, dropping a hand lightly upon her waist to discourage any interruption of their conversation.

"A generous offer." She leaned forward, breathing her next question into his ear. "And what of our trial engagement?" Her fingertips smoothed the lapel upon his jacket.

"Formal and chaste." He swallowed, fixing his gaze upon the unremarkable cluster of fabric flowers pinned to her shoulder.

"Is that so." She bit her lower lip, toying with the top button of his waistcoat. "How... disappointing."

He laughed, then pulled her into his arms so that she might feel his stiffness against the soft swell of her stomach. "Unless you wish otherwise. Though it is by no means a condition of either our engagement or your employment."

"Well, then, let's see what opportunities present themselves." She dropped her hand, then slid her arms beneath his coat and about his waist. "Shall we begin tonight?"

"Yes." His cock twitched, but he ignored its enthusiasm. This was not the place for anything but a kiss. People—some of them irate—would soon come looking for her. For them. Not only would her uncle take offense, but their scene in the library might well have overshadowed Lady Sophia's debut. "When will your household be asleep?"

She rolled her eyes. "After Mr. Glover's uncalled for furor? My uncle will rant, but my aunt will silently applaud my actions. By three in the morning, I will have been sent to my room. Any further outrage will be set aside for breakfast pleasantries."

He snorted. "Taken to task over tea and toast?"

"It does tend to put off one's appetite."

"Colleen?" a voice called in the distance. Their time was up.

"My aunt," she said, but didn't pull away. "Now that we're engaged, you may call me by my given name."

"As a fiancé ought. Might he also be permitted a liberty?"

"If I may call you by yours?"

"Of course."

"Well, then. But only a small one for the moment." Her fingers slipped beneath the edge of his waistcoat and ran over the linen of his shirt, tracing the muscle that ran down his back. "Appearances must be maintained, Nicholas."

He brushed his lips along the edge of her jaw and whispered, "Not Nicholas. Nick." Then he captured her mouth with his own, tasting honey and soft sighs as he explored its sweet shape. A perfect fit. He was about to deepen their embrace when the leaves beside him rustled.

"Colleen!" her aunt exclaimed, staring openly through the foliage. "What is this I hear of an engagement?"

He took a step back, releasing his fiancée. "Soon," he whispered. If there was time to seek out a private corner of London after they searched the laboratory...

Behind her spectacles, Colleen's eyes flashed as if her mind charted a similar course. "The mews," she whispered, then dropped her hands from his waist and—at an impatient huff—turned toward the interruption. "Mr. Torrington, you've met Lady Maynard."

"Many times." He turned and bowed. "Always a pleasure." Colleen's aunt was a classic beauty—and older than her niece by a scant few years. He'd heard speculation about the manner of Lord Maynard's first wife's death. None of them pleasant, all of them centered around her inability to provide an heir.

"So *this* is the gentleman that kept you up at night and has set the ball abuzz." Lady Maynard threw him a saucy glance.

Nick slid his questioning gaze back to Colleen.

"She knows only about *my* occupation."

In other words, Nick's employment with the Queen's agents had not been discussed.

"And the cat's," Lady Maynard added. "Your timing leaves much to be desired, but better late than never. Not that my irate husband agrees. I'll do what I can to smooth your path, but you had best pay a visit tomorrow. My advice? Bring a competent solicitor."

"A solicitor?" Nick asked.

Lady Maynard's eyes widened as she glanced from him to Colleen. "Does it not strike you as odd that your uncle is—after years of ignoring your presence—suddenly so very interested in finding you a husband? One of *his* choosing? It's rare his temper flares. He's up to something."

"So noted," Nick replied.

A commotion broke out in the hallway.

Lady Maynard caught up Colleen's hand, grinned at the amber ring, then tugged. "Come. Mr. Glover is grousing about breach of promise, and I've sent for the steam carriage. We have minutes to fabricate a story involving a lengthy courtship and a secret engagement." She winked. "Clearly, the truth won't do."

Chapter Six

By half-past two, the house was perfectly silent, and Colleen slid from her bed. No cat stretched upon the covers or performed brief ablutions before leaping to the ground to twine about her ankles. Instead, the tin of tuna sat untouched upon the windowsill. Each day Colleen's concern grew.

Despite the white patch upon Sorcha's chest, her otherwise black fur always set superstitious individuals on edge, leaving Colleen forever worried that the cat might become a target. But how did one hunt—especially in London—for a wildcat that did not wish to be found? Not that it would stop her. If she wasn't back by morning, Colleen would try.

Stretching, she turned her mind to tonight's activities. The only specifics she'd been given were device, basement and laboratory. Never had she taken on a job so woefully under informed, with little to no control as to its execution. Still, with the funds to repair her roof secured, she could afford this slight indulgence. For once, pay was not a pivotal factor. Adventure—and a handsome, exciting man—called. For the first time, she would roam London's streets for the thrill, rather than the necessity.

A current of excitement shot through her as she lifted the lid of her trunk and contemplated her wardrobe with a smile. What *did* one wear to both explore the laboratory of a—presumably—mad scientist *and* seduce one's partner?

French silk. Blood-red silk bloomers and a matching silk camisole. But that was all the indulgence she could spare. Priorities, as always, involved avoiding discovery and the ability to affect a quick escape. To that end she chose a lightly boned corset, a high-necked blouse and linen breeches that tucked into boots that laced to the knees. All black.

She wound her dark hair into a tight knot, fastening it in place with pins sharp enough to draw blood. A belt followed, one adorned with loops from which she suspended a number of useful items such as lock picks, a coiled Rapunzel rope, and a purse filled with smoke bombs—a useful distraction when one needed to make a hasty exit. She slid a long, thin blade into the sheathe within her boot and swung a hooded cape about her shoulders. While warm, its fabric provided the added advantage of hiding her features and her eyes from anyone who might later recall a flash of unusual brilliance.

And to that end, the amber ring upon her finger must remain behind. A perfect fit and the exact color of her eyes, it was evidence that Nick's proposal, albeit unconventional, was far more than a passing whim. Though she remained wary at the thought of a lifetime commitment, a certain warmth spread through her at the idea of calling him her husband. Placing the ring upon her dressing table, Colleen stepped to her window and searched the misty shadows. Confident her uncle's minion was not about, she climbed out and leapt free, sliding down the drainpipe and into the murky gloom as she made her way to the mews.

At exactly five minutes to three, her ride appeared.

Beneath a lamppost that struggled to cast a dim pool of light through the fog, Nick sat upon a tarnished brass clockwork horse that had seen better days. Soot darkened its leather mane, muck crusted its hooves, and its eyes stared in two different directions, suggesting its winding springs might be wild and unmanageable. Much like its rider's appearance.

He wore brown-striped trousers tucked into tall boots and a long leather coat, one that bore a number of disturbing stains—all unidentifiable in origin—and was fastened closed by a row of brass buckles that marched down his chest. A highwayman of old. Rough and tumble to her sleek and sophisticated. A thrill coursed through her.

With two steps and a leap, she landed behind him on the saddle and wrapped her arms about his waist. He threw an amused glance over his shoulder, then flipped a lever, setting them off at a sedate, non-attention-gathering pace. She pressed her face against his shoulder, inhaling the pleasant scent of gear oil and saddle soap. A far cry from the earlier over-perfumed and sweaty ballroom crowd. "Whom do we hope to rob?"

He huffed a laugh. "Dr. Gregory Farquhar of 28 Bloomsbury Street. He's avoiding me. Our visit will be more exploratory in nature than acquisitive. I've no idea if the device even exists."

They had a bit of a ride ahead of them. Time, then, to admire the taut stomach beneath her arms, the broad back crushed against her chest, and the way her hips slid forward on the poorly sprung saddle with each awkward step the clockwork creature took until they were pressed against his firm rear, their thighs tightly aligned. She had the sneaking suspicion that Nick had chosen this beast for more reasons than its off-putting appearance.

"Why the device?" It was easy to forget that her arms encircled more than a Queen's agent. Mr. Nicholas Torrington was also a scientist. His entire career was spurred by a hunt for a cure—or a treatment—for his sister, Anna, whose heart struggled to beat. On the rare occasions his sister ventured into society, she always appeared vaguely blue. "Have the drugs failed?"

"For Anna, yes." The clockwork horse clopped forward a few steps before he continued. "For years, I've attempted to strengthen her heart, hunting for novel drugs, but finding few. Atropine. Digitalis. Hawthorn.

None have the desired effects. Her only hope now is locating a rumored device that will restart a stalled heart."

Her breath caught as images of cadavers jolted with bolts of electricity sprang to mind. "Is this Dr. Farquhar a galvanist?" Such quacks were little better than the spiritualists a few decades past who had hinted at the possibility of life after death. Under the guise of medicine, some slightly less insane men sold elaborate devices while expounding upon the benefits of electricity to restore health and vigor. She'd seen men with paste-pots and handbills gluing advertisements for electrotherapy clinics to walls.

"He once trained as a cardiac electrophysiologist," Nick said, focusing her mental ramblings. "Today? The exact direction of his work is unclear, but he might well be a galvanist focusing upon cardiac tissue. I should warn you that there's a strong likelihood he's experimenting upon animals."

Animals. Most likely stray ones. But not necessarily. A hired man with a catch pole would snag any convenient animal that had the misfortune to wander past. One such as a roaming cat sìth. Worry twisted her stomach even though her mind insisted Sorcha was far too wild and resourceful to ever find herself trapped. Besides, Dr. Farquhar's house was near The British Museum, far outside her established territory. Still...

"What do you know of heart anatomy and physiology?" Nick asked. His voice broke the grip of her concerns.

"Next to nothing." Save he always made hers beat faster. "What—exactly—is wrong?"

"Are you aware that the heart is composed of a unique kind of muscle tissue that will spontaneously contract?"

"I am now."

"A heartbeat initiates at the top of the heart. First two chambers known as the atria contract, then a signal spreads downward via a net of connecting fibers. When the stimulus reaches the lower two chambers, the ventricles, they contract, pumping blood into the lungs and throughout the body."

She slid her palm upward, until she could feel the beat of his heart. "Thump-thump, thump-thump." At her words, it leapt beneath her hand. Warmed by gratification, she smiled against his back.

"Exactly. Normally, such an electrical impulse travels through the heart at a rate of sixty to seventy times per minute."

Nick tugged on the reins, turning the clockwork horse onto Oxford Street. The street lamps did their best, but the night was moonless and thick with fog. Those out and about moved as if anonymity was assured, as if they were no more than flitting shadows. For them it might be dark, but for Colleen's eyes the gaslight was enough to cast everything in a faint gray light. On their left, a passing figure in leather and wool flicked a cigar stump into the street. A ruffian wearing ragged trousers slept in a doorway beside a mangy dog. A crank hack passed on their right carrying home a man wearing a top hat.

She tugged her hood forward. Better safe than sorry. "And Anna?"

"As low as forty beats per minute." Nick paid no mind to the skulking shapes in the streets. "When we were children, it wasn't as bad. Her heart's rhythm was slow—only fifty beats per minute—and occasionally skipped a beat. From time to time, she might grow lightheaded or a touch dizzy but, for the most part, she was fine. After much fussing, the doctors concluded that her heart was damaged, that something blocked the rhythm from propagating to the lower chambers. But there was nothing to be done." He took a deep breath. "Of late, it has grown much worse."

Sympathy tugged at her chest. "How so?"

"Shortness of breath. Heart palpitations. Her hands are always cold, her fingernails blue. From time to time, she collapses without warning, twitching. To the touch, her slow pulse is seemingly absent. There's nothing to be done save limit her exertions."

"That's awful! What changed?"

For a long moment, Nick fell silent, seeming to struggle with her question. "Anna was advised never to marry."

"But she did." Colleen remembered the announcement. And what often followed some nine months later? Love might pain the heart, though it would do no direct damage. But... "There's a child." One did not require a medical degree to know that childbearing—childbirth—could place a strain on the heart.

"Yes. Though the infant is fine, Anna's condition grew worse following delivery, and she began having fainting attacks." He blew out a sudden breath. "There's a fifty percent chance of mortality within a year of such a seizure."

Meaning each time she collapsed, her family could do nothing but watch and hope that *this* time her heart would restart. And, when it did, brace themselves for the next episode. She tightened her arms about Nick's waist. "If we locate this device, you propose to...?" She trailed off, praying there was hope.

"Evaluate its potential," he finished. "It's time I set aside medications to pay more attention to the work of the electrophysiologists. Anna lives on the sharp edge of fear, preparing daily for the eventuality that the next seizure might well take her life. Imagine if there's a way to guard against that possibility?"

Colleen attempted to digest the enormity of the situation facing his sister. She opened her mouth to ask another question, but a glow of light clouded by dense smoke caught her eye. In the distance, a rattle grew nearer and nearer. And louder and louder.

The dreadful cry of "Fire!" reached her ears at the same moment a great steam pumper fire engine roared onto the street, taking the corner on two wheels and followed closely by a fire wagon carrying coils of hose. People poured from buildings, half-dressed—some in their nightclothes—all shouting and clamoring as they thronged through the streets following the engine like a pack of hounds.

"Hold tight!" Nick shoved the lever forward, sending their clockwork horse into a gallop, weaving expertly through the swelling mob—then reining back to a sudden stop at Bloomsbury Street. In the face of the dull roar of the fire, the fire brigade worked quickly, sending arcs of water onto a blazing townhome while pickpockets threaded through the crowd taking full advantage of the commotion.

Though quiet shadows were preferable, a burning house would be a convenient distraction while they searched the laboratory. She slid from the clockwork horse, but Nick made no move to dismount. Instead, a curse fell from his lips.

No. Could it be— "Is that... 28 Bloomsbury Street?"

"It is." Nick's jaw tightened.

The timing *was* curiously suspicious. Yet they hunted a life-saving medical device, not some secret government technology pursued by biotechnological spies. *Or so she'd been led to believe.* Her gaze slid sideways. "Then *you* should interview its mistress." She pointed to a woman who stood beside the fire wagon—conspicuously alone—with a blanket wrapped about her nightdress. No neighbors rushed to her side to offer comfort. No tears streaked down her soot-blackened face. Odd.

Lips pressed into a grim line, Nick dismounted and paid a boy to watch the clockwork horse, promising far more if they were both still present when he returned. He elbowed his way to the woman's side. "Mrs. Farquhar?"

"Yes?" Suspicion tinged her voice, and she clutched the blanket tighter.

Columns of smoke and steam rose from the burning heap as the firemen doused the fire. Colleen stood to the side, keeping her face well-hidden in the shadows—a challenge beside this blaze—yet with her ear finely tuned to the nuances of their every word.

"I need to speak with your husband," Nick said. "Now. Is he nearby?"

"No," Mrs. Farquhar's eyes sidled away. "So if you're here to collect his findings…"

Nick stiffened. Colleen's ears pricked.

"Don't deny it," the woman grumbled. "That outlandish dress of yours doesn't fool me. You work for *him*. I warned the likes of you that Gregory was a bad gamble. The bastard did a runner."

"And took his invention with him?"

The fire was nearly out, and the crowds began to disperse. The firemen, exhausted, worked quietly to stow their equipment. She squinted. Broken glass. Charred wood. Dripping, soot-blackened water. The house was now uninhabitable, but the gaps in the structure made by flames and collapsing wood made the lowest floor, sunken beneath street level, accessible. Easy enough to pass through the kitchen and reach those rooms behind it where the laboratory would be located.

"Oh, is that what we're calling it?" Mrs. Farquhar groused. "Nasty business, all of this. Why else would he run? Either way, that rosewood box you're after? It's not here."

Ice crystalized in her blood, and a shiver ran across her skin. A rosewood box. She'd bet her entire bank account that she'd had her hands on that very box just a few hours past. Dammit. A sick twist of nausea swirled in her stomach. She had lowered her standards to accept a gray assignment and look where it had led. Anna's life dangled in peril all because—

No. This was not her fault. Colleen took a deep breath and concentrated upon the conversation.

Nick was pressing Mrs. Farquhar for more information. "Did he give you any details about the men he worked for?"

"No." She backed away, shaking her head, all but snarling at Nick. "I'll not fall for any tricks. This is a test, and I'll not fail. You'll not get anything more from me. Go away."

It didn't matter. She knew that the buyer—whomever he was—had arranged for one of Mr. Witherspoon's other associates to meet with Dr. Farquhar, initiating the process by which his invention had been passed along an obfuscation chain. Which meant, quite simply, that it was—or would be—in the hands of another unscrupulous soul. Why, then, this burning of his house? Something felt wrong. Either it was part of the cover up, or someone had secrets to hide. The obvious choice, to question Mr. Witherspoon, was pointless. He would tell her nothing.

That meant they had a laboratory to investigate. Then a scientist to locate.

Chapter Seven

The firemen's backs were turned, presenting Colleen with opportunity. A few long strides and a quick vault over an iron railing dropped her into the front service well of the house. Though it was dark, her eyes needed no more than the tiniest pinpoint of light to see clearly.

As she passed down the charred, acrid remains of the hallway, glancing into various workrooms, numerous damp, brownish-green frogs hopped about her feet, and a dozen rats with soot-streaked and matted fur scurried along the baseboard frantically seeking a way out. More than once, she'd been grateful for her knee-high boots, but never so thankful as she was now.

A heavy, half-closed iron door barred entry to a side room. There was only one reason for such security here in the basement. *This* must be the laboratory. She shoved at the door, forcing it to flex upon its hinges, and a panicked, lightly-singed weasel loped past her ankles seeking a path to freedom.

In the laboratory, the vile smell of chemicals and charred flesh assaulted her nose and sent her stomach roiling. Broken glass crunched beneath her feet, and something squishy shifted and slid. A mistake, looking down at the toes of her boots, for she found herself in the middle of a shallow puddle where thin, white threads twisted and curled as they died a slow death. Worms?

She grimaced and forced herself to survey the room.

Not every experimental subject had escaped. Not even close. Wire cages held blackened lumps of flesh, and glass tanks were occupied by frogs floating belly up. Bile rose to her throat, and she averted her eyes from the lifeless captives, only to find herself face to face with charred shelving and the rows of skulls it held. Small mammals, all of them, none of which she could identify, save those that were feline. Larger than that of house cats, smaller than that of a wildcat.

A frisson of dread ran down her spine. There were multiple skulls of cat sìth. Was it possible that cryptid hunters had found a landholder willing to turn a blind eye to poaching? Alarm morphed into anger.

In the center of the room stood a steel work table. Lining the walls were countertops and cabinets and yet more shelves. Or, rather, there had been. Most were charred, their contents destroyed, shattered or otherwise altered beyond recognition—save a partially collapsed, wood-framed box fitted with cracked and smudged glass panes with metal tubing that led to a low-set window. An experiment of some kind had been set up inside a fume hood and interrupted when the fire broke out.

"Colleen?" Nick called as if from a distance, searching for her, but she didn't answer.

A faint mewl emerged from within the fume hood. One that sounded decidedly like an injured cat. *Exactly* as Sorcha had the night she'd returned home injured, limping with a gash across her leg. Feral animals were always a threat in the dark alleys she roamed.

She dashed across the room, swiping at the glass with her forearm, but only managing to smear the sticky residue. She pushed and rattled at the frame, forcing it to roll upward along two metal tracks. Inside were fluid-filled bottles, wires, a bucket of water, a scalpel and forceps. And a wire cage containing an exceptionally large black cat with a torn ear and a pinch of white upon its chest. Two slitted, golden eyes peered up at her.

"Sorcha!" Her voice was both a wail of grief and one of relief. Only then did she take note of the bandages wound about the cat's legs, the shaved patches of bare skin upon her chest and shoulder. "What did that horrid man do to you?"

Crouching, the cat sìth hissed and bared her sharp teeth.

"It's me, sweetie. Come to take you home." First to her uncle's, but then, yes, all the way back to northern Scotland. "You poor thing." She tugged off a glove and reached out, giving the frightened cat sìth a moment to identify her as friend, not enemy. When they located Dr. Farquhar she'd make him answer for his mistreatments. "The moment we're home, I'll find you a saucer of cream." And spoil her rotten, as a fairy cat ought to be.

The cat sniffed her fingers, then twitched, directing her gaze over Colleen's shoulder. A low growl emanated from the cat sìth's throat seconds before Nick pointed his decilamp at the cat's cage.

"He's a friend," she crooned to the cat, comforting her by letting a little Doric slip into her words. "Nae worrie."

"Colleen?" He stood beside her. "Is that—?"

"My familiar?"

"Sorcha."

"Yes. And she's badly hurt." Her worse fears realized.

Nick pulled a second decilamp from a pocket and handed it to her. "I know your vision is excellent, but…"

She took the offered light. "It does improve things." And it did. They'd never spoken directly about her unusual eyes or any of her other catlike skills, something they would need to address were this engagement to progress beyond its trial status. Something she'd worry about later. "I'll need to keep her in the cage for now, until her panic subsides."

Colleen snapped upright, remembering why they were here. She glanced about the laboratory and said, "Perhaps you can make more sense of what remains. I passed a number of fleeing frogs and rats and even a weasel." She flicked the light across the skull-laden shelves, past the caged corpses. "Dr. Farquhar's other victims weren't so lucky."

For now, dawn approached. They needed to comb through the wreckage for clues. What exactly was Dr. Farquhar about and where might he have run? Reluctantly, she turned away from Sorcha and began to poke through the wreckage.

Nick, however, moved to stand before the fume hood, examining its contents. Sorcha, quiet now, stared at him through narrowed eyes. "A bottle of chloroform, for use as an anesthetic." He traced a length of wire from beneath the cracked window to the remnants of a large mechanical contraption, one that was minimally charred yet still unidentifiable to her eyes. "This machine bears a striking resemblance to the one in my own home, used to send a jolt of electricity to the heart."

Colleen cringed. Both for Anna and for the poor animals—dead and alive—that might have endured its use.

"Disappointing. I was hoping to find evidence of something much smaller." Nick tipped the bucket full of water. "And this was likely filled with ice."

"Ice?" She looked up from the pile of soggy papers she'd tried to separate. Alas, not only were they glued together, but the ink had run to the point of illegibility.

"Extreme cold stops the heart."

"He was—" Her mouth fell open in horror.

"Stopping hearts so that he might practice restarting them?" His voice grew distant. "Yes."

Anger marched up her spine, setting her skin alight. Frogs and rats she could perhaps understand. One had to begin somewhere. But cats?

Wait.

Something about Nick's voice sounded off. She narrowed her eyes. "What is it you're not telling me?"

He hesitated. "Queen's agent's business."

"That's Sorcha in there. That makes it my business too." The words emerged as a growl. "We can work together on this, or at cross purposes. Your choice."

Nick blew out a long breath. "Fine. Dr. Farquhar's sanity is questionable."

Obviously. But she kept her mouth shut, waiting.

"It has been suggested that Dr. Farquhar has an interest in animal transmutation. In short, sorcery."

Or witchcraft.

Which might explain his interest in Sorcha. In the cat sìth. Was it possible he believed the stories?

"Tell me," Nick urged. "Even to my weak eyes, it's as clear as day that you know something more. We are both partners and a betrothed couple. Isn't it time to peel away all pretenses?"

She knew quite a bit more, and he was right. They couldn't work effectively as a team if they kept details—however small—from each other. "Sorcha is no house cat." She hesitated, uncertain how to explain the feline to an Englishman.

"Not new information, Colleen." His voice was flat. "I've watched the two of you skulking about London for years now. What, exactly, is she?"

"Cat sìth, a kind of hybrid cat—part wild, part domesticated. A number of them live in the woods of my family's estate. Some say they're fairy. Others believe that the cat sìth is the animal form of a witch, one who can transform into a cat nine times. Legend, myth, folk tale. Take your pick. Regardless, Dr. Farquhar—by name—is Scottish. He ought to have respected tradition and not subjected a rare and precious animal to such treatment." She crossed her arms. "I can see from your face that this information holds significance."

"It does," Nick admitted. "But it's a long, complicated story that needs to wait." He waved at the fume hood. "This doesn't fit with Mrs. Farquhar's account of the situation."

"What do you mean?" She dropped the ruined papers and crossed to his side.

"If he planned to set fire to his laboratory and bolt with his device, why would he have set up an experiment involving a rare and precious animal?"

Why indeed?

"After you abandoned me," he glanced sideways at her, eyebrow raised, "his wife admitted she'd pressed her husband to demand more money for his work. Denied, she claims he accepted a more lucrative offer." Nick waved his free hand, and Sorcha snarled. "Yet if he was here, working in his laboratory when the fire was set—"

"Then his wife told you a passel of lies."

"Exactly."

"I see no evidence of his body. You?"

"None. Rather, a door open to the rear garden."

So Farquhar had left, run for his life and left the cat sìth to her fate. Were fairies real, the man would have tripped and died on the doorstep while making his exit. Pursing her lips, she threw a final glance about the laboratory. "There's no indication of where he might have gone, and there's nothing else here that's salvageable. Shall we go question her further?"

His expression hardened, turning his face to granite. "Yes."

She hefted Sorcha's cage into her arms.

Ever the gentleman, Nick reached for it, but the cat sìth hissed, and he stepped back. "Something tells me she'll shred my hands and arms through the bars. Should we not simply set her free?" he asked, though from the look on his face, he already knew the answer to that.

"Were she not injured and afraid." Even in Colleen's care, the large cat crouched with narrowed eyes, decidedly displeased and only just managing to tolerate her rescue efforts. "I don't want her to bolt." She wouldn't risk losing Sorcha to the city or men like Dr. Farquhar again.

They tromped back onto the street. Only a few gawkers lingered, staring at the burned-out building, marveling that the firemen had been able to save anything about it. The scent of the fire hung in the air, so thick and pungent Colleen could smell nothing else.

About the still-dark edges of the streets, figures skulked, scampering away like rats when she turned her eyes directly upon them. Though all appeared guilty of something, most were servants, late to their morning posts. Some looked as if they bided their time, hoping for a chance to loot the shell of a building for any valuables that had survived the blaze. One man, in particular, glared at her from across the street, but by the time she turned Nick's attention in his direction, he'd disappeared.

They persisted, but no matter how many people they questioned or the number of dark alleys they stalked, there was no sign of Mrs. Farquhar. Neighbors curled their lips when questioned and denied knowing where she might have sought refuge for the remainder of the night.

As Nick's frustration grew, so too did Colleen's sense of unease. Nick's hunt for a medical device, her participation in an obfuscation chain, and this fire were all tightly linked. And both of them knew more than they were sharing.

As a glimmer of light filled the morning sky, Nick turned to Colleen. "Time to admit defeat. For the moment. You need to return home before your absence is discovered."

Impossible to argue with that statement. Besides, he needed to know about her latest task for Witherspoon and Associates. Sooner rather than later. Once they'd retrieved the clockwork horse, lashed the cage—covered by Nick's coat—to the saddle and were well on their way back to Mayfair, Colleen could no longer suppress her stomach-churning knowledge. She very much doubted her employer would be willing to name names. Not, at least, without first charging Nick an exorbitant fee. "There's something you need to know."

Chapter Eight

Restored by a few hours' sleep and dressed once more like a respectable gentleman, Nick pulled his phaeton to the edge of the street and tossed the clockwork horse's reins to a boy before flipping him a coin. His was not the only vehicle present. Was The Much Honored Colleen Stewart of Craigieburn beset with unwelcome guests? He expected so. Glover and his ugliness were certain to be among them, attempting to claim what was not his.

Despite the mounting frustration that had followed Colleen's horseback revelation, Nick smiled. When he'd seen that man backing Colleen into a corner, his blood pressure had spiked and set his blood on fire. Only later—when reason returned—did he realize that she'd had Glover exactly where she'd wanted him: in a position of public humiliation. As she was normally one to avoid the limelight, it was an excellent move. No one would ever guess what she'd been about. With such drama before them, who would notice the addition of an unassuming rosewood box upon a table beside a globe? He certainly hadn't.

Nick's "rescue" had been entirely unnecessary. Yet she'd accepted his ring. Allowed him to publicly claim her. But convincing her that they belonged together long-term? That would take time and trust, the first tentative bonds of which had been established last night.

As dawn threatened, he'd dropped Colleen in the dark shadow of her choice before returning to the scene of the ball where the house was quiet with exhaustion and oblivious to his reentry.

No surprise. The rosewood box—contents unknown—was gone.

It burned that he'd stood so close.

An obfuscation chain, a rosewood box, a fire, a fairy cat. Not only was it not a coincidence, but Colleen was the common thread running throughout. All those times he'd teased about Sorcha being her "familiar" and not once had she said a word. Upon reflection, he ought to have asked sooner. The creature wasn't a proper house cat. Its legs were a bit too long, its tail a touch too thick. Much like a Scottish wildcat, save it was black, had a white patch of fur upon its chest and was overlarge. And apparently believed by some capable of transforming into a human female. To that end, he needed to bring her into his confidence and inform her of the existence of CEAP and a shadow committee within London itself.

Step one: rid her of Mr. Glover's attentions so that they might progress to step two: a morning drive in the park wherein he might learn her employer's price. Convincing her employer to reveal the name of the ultimate buyer, she'd explained, would cost him dearly—should he agree at all. His family, he'd assured her, could well afford the price. Everything hinged upon learning the buyer's name.

No, not everything. But he expected the task of locating Dr. Farquhar might prove difficult or impossible.

Nick mounted the stairs, took a deep breath and knocked, bracing for objections to his presence.

The door flew open. Lady Maynard herself stood before him, her eyes red-rimmed and her nose pink and swollen. "Thank aether!" she cried, reaching out to catch him by the sleeve, dragging him inside and slamming the door behind him. "You're late. Please tell me your solicitor is not far behind."

"I'm afraid I didn't—"

"Believe me?" she huffed. "Most gentlemen know of my husband's love for legal entanglements and unorthodox dealings."

Stacks of trunks and boxes lined the entryway. Perched atop, a wicker basket. A pair of golden eyes peered forth, watching his every move. Sorcha. Were Colleen and her cat being sent away? If so, he'd offer them sanctuary.

"This is highly irregular, my lady." A flustered steam butler rolled back and forth, clutching a silver salver while attempting to navigate past his mistress to reach Nick.

"Hurry, Mr. Torrington," Lady Maynard urged, ignoring the steambot and pushing him toward a tightly closed door. From within came muffled cries of outrage. Lady Maynard's voice dropped. "This morning Mr. Glover arrived with a special license and a minister. You must do something!"

That explained the luggage. Lord Maynard intended to ship his niece off with her husband. Immediately.

With a curse, he burst into the parlor to find Colleen and a group of squabbling gentlemen gathered about a large desk. In a far corner, a silent, thick-necked man stood. Nick would save the question as to why a man such as Maynard felt it necessary to employ a bodyguard for later.

For now, he had eyes only for his fiancée who stood, arms crossed and jaw clenched, bristling with indignation. Once again, she was dressed every inch the respectable lady. Neatly knotted hair and tinted round spectacles. A somber blue gown and sensible shoes. All fashioned to hide her true spirit.

How many had ever seen her in her element, free and unencumbered by society's restrictions? The flash of amber eyes, the lithe bend and twist of her form, the grin of a woman who dared to sneak kisses from a man. He could swear he'd seen a flash of red silk beneath her black shirt last night and hoped she'd entertained thoughts of seduction. He'd all but cursed the first rays of sunlight that forced him to abandon the chance to learn the answer.

Never had a woman captured his interest so completely.

He was glad to see his ring upon her finger, proof of the claim he was about to make.

"What is the meaning of this?" His voice thundered.

Lord Maynard turned a pinched face in Nick's direction. Like his starched, stiff collar the man never unbent. "You."

Colleen glanced at Nick, and her shoulders dropped ever so slightly. "As I explained, Uncle. Mr. Nicholas Torrington proposed, and I have accepted. This," she waved a hand at the minister, "is an unseemly spectacle."

Mr. Glover flushed an angry red, pointing the fountain pen at Nick as if he might run his competition through. "I saw you at the club. You've heard the rumors. They're all true. Had she wished to take a different husband, Miss Stewart should not have lifted her petticoats. You can't possibly want a compromised woman."

Sharp indrawn breaths sucked all the oxygen from the room at once.

"Mr. Glover!" her uncle warned.

"Bite your tongue!" Nick couldn't say he was happy that she had a past, but so too did he—and Nick would never utter such words about any woman with the intent to shame her into compliance.

"How dare you!" Colleen's eyes flashed with fire behind her tinted lenses. Her fingers clawed into the folds of the blue gown she wore. Had Glover any idea how close he was to having his eyes gouged out? "Not for an entire dragon's hoard would I marry an unsophisticated boor such as yourself."

"He has a valid claim," her uncle insisted in a calm and controlled voice, though irritation narrowed his eyes. "The settlement is quite fair, and Mr. Glover comes from a good family."

Outrage rolled off Nick's back in waves. *This* was how her family protected her? He couldn't begin to imagine treating his sister in such a manner. He opened his mouth to protest, but Colleen spoke first.

"This is the nineteenth century!" Anger shook her body. Behind gray lenses, her eyes flashed. "You can't bind me to a man of your choosing to force his fealty. Find a way to solidify your business dealings that doesn't require some misguided feudal maneuver." She drew breath. "Enough of this. My twenty-fifth birthday is in two days, and I intend to return to Craigieburn to run the estate *myself*."

She'd mis-stepped. Her uncle's gaze slipped to the amber ring upon her finger, and his lips twisted with suspicion.

Nick crossed the room to stand before Lord Maynard. He dropped his voice to a low growl. "When we wed, *Lady* Stewart will retain all rights to funds and properties in her name. And, yes, I promised she herself will oversee the Craigieburn estate." He held out a hand, beckoning Colleen to his side. As she came, tension fell away from his shoulders. His protection wasn't strictly necessary, but it felt good to offer it, to have her accept it without question. "I care not about her romantic past, only her future with me. If family connections matter, may I remind you that my father is a viscount. But more importantly, Lady Stewart has *accepted* my suit."

Her uncle's eyes narrowed. Clearly, the man wished to refuse him.

The clergyman cleared his throat. "I'm afraid the names are already inked. This turn of events will require a new license."

"No!" Mr. Glover cried out. "She is promised to me!"

"It will require no such thing," Nick stated. "We plan to marry in Lady Stewart's own kirk."

Another gasp. But this time it was Lady Maynard, who looked to be suppressing a smile. But it recalled to mind her presence, and her husband's frown etched itself deeper into the granite of his face.

"Unacceptable. Your outrageous behavior caused quite the upset last night, and I want no further disgrace touching my family. You must marry here. As soon as possible." He turned to the clergyman. "How long to obtain a new license?"

Mr. Glover yelled a protest, while the clergyman answered, "A few hours?"

Nick's mind frantically sought a way to delay the actual event. He'd have her as his bride willingly. Or not at all. A special license was too fast, but a wedding in Scotland required twenty-one days of residency. That would provide them with at least three weeks to alter course. He must hold fast to his insistence of a Scottish wedding.

Beside him, Colleen stiffened. "Scandal," she spoke slowly and clearly, "will not touch you," she glanced at her aunt, "or yours. Unless you persist with your protests."

Her uncle's face paled.

Touché. Though he could only guess at the particulars, Nick recognized blackmail when he saw it. He fought to keep the amusement from his face.

"I will marry whomever I choose, whenever and wherever I choose," she continued. "You've never cared about my reputation or marital status before, and I've no idea why you should involve yourself now. I will, however, bow to your sensibilities and vacate the premises. I intend to take a room at Claridge's."

"Nonsense." Nick turned to Colleen. "My family will welcome you with open arms. We've rooms aplenty and both my mother and my sister can serve as chaperones. If you'll gather a few of your most important possessions—"

Lord Maynard slapped his hand down upon his desk, his lips pressed into a white line as he glared at his niece. "Think beyond yourself, beyond the next year. Neither you nor Mr. Torrington have family in Scotland. Speculation will run rampant should you, like your unreasonable mother, persist with this plan. Is that how you wish to begin the next stage of your life?"

At the mention of her mother, Colleen's back snapped ramrod straight yet, much to his annoyance, Nick rather agreed with her uncle on this point. Scandal aside, the Duke of Avesbury wanted him here in London working, not haring off to Scotland at a moment's notice to marry. Not when a ceremony in the city would serve much the same purpose. But he kept his opinion to himself.

Colleen turned her face toward Nick, her eyes full of questions she could not voice aloud in present company. She'd brightened at the mention of marrying in Scotland, but recent developments in London demanded their immediate attention. And they'd yet to discuss any aspect of a future together. He played for time.

"The choice is yours." One did not capture the heart of a wild creature by backing her into a corner. "And not one that must be made this very moment. Better to make a reasoned decision." He watched her internal struggle, noting the moment when logic gained the upper hand.

"Very well," she said. "We will remain in the city for the present while we consider my uncle's perspective. But," eyes filled with apology, Colleen's gaze slid toward her aunt even as her shoulders stiffened, "I refuse to remain here under household arrest with *that man*," she lifted her chin at the thick-necked brute who stood silently in the corner of the room, "dogging my every footstep."

"Fine," her uncle bit out, appearing to capitulate, but there was a stubborn set to his jaw. "Your fiancé's house or a hotel, I care not." He turned his attention to Nick. "Rather than feed the flames of last night's upset, I would prefer we meet later." A pointed glance was thrown at Colleen. "Alone. A meeting wherein two gentlemen discuss possibilities for the future of a favorable relationship between our respective families."

Something oily roiled beneath the surface of the lord's words. An unpleasant conversation lay in Nick's immediate future. "Very well. Tomorrow?"

"Tomorrow. Two o'clock in the afternoon."

"Agreed." That left Nick plenty of time to consult with his solicitor.

Glover's mouth fell open as he stared at Lord Maynard. "Tell me you are not actually considering Torrington!"

"And why not?" The lord snarled at the man he'd thought to welcome into the family not a quarter hour past. "I cannot force her hand, and you failed to secure her interest."

"You will regret this! All of you." Eyes blazing, Glover stormed from the room.

Colleen's uncle reached out and pulled a cord behind his desk. "If you'll see yourselves out, there is much to which I must attend." He crooked his finger at the thick-necked man in the corner. "Mr. Vanderburn..."

The steam butler appeared at the door, ushering them outward and away from the lord's presence.

Chapter Nine

Minutes later, tears ran down Lady Maynard's face as she and Colleen held each other's hands promising the other that this was not a permanent separation. At their feet, Sorcha crouched inside her wicker cage, ears flat and tail switching while a steam footman loaded a single trunk onto his phaeton, lashing it in place. The process drew the attention of the finely dressed. Curious faces turned in their direction then, eyes wide, their steps hastened as they hurried to be the first to spread the news of Lady Stewart's departure with one Mr. Torrington. Fresh scandal, the life and blood of the *ton*. Even if they married, speculation surrounding the circumstances of their engagement would take some time to die down.

Resigned, Nick sighed and turned to pay the boy looking after his clockwork horse.

"No!" Colleen cried, and he spun back to find a man with a shock of wild, unkempt hair attempting to wrest the wicker basket that held Sorcha from her arms. Inside, the cat sìth hissed and spit. A large paw—claws unsheathed—swiped from between two bars and drew blood moments before Nick delivered a sharp left hook to the man's jaw. Hard enough to discourage him, to send him staggering, but not enough to render him unconscious.

Colleen backed away, clutching the basket to her chest.

Hand pressed to his jaw, the attacker's feral gaze jumped from Colleen to Nick and back again. "I was promised the cat sìth would be mine!" Blood welled from the deep gouges scratched into his arm.

"Who made you such promises?" Nick demanded, wondering why the man's face seemed familiar.

"The committee, of course," he spat.

"What is the meaning of this?" The lord's bodyguard, Mr. Vanderburn, scowled from the top of the stairs.

The attacker glanced at the lord's minion, then scuttled off at a dead sprint. Only then did Nick notice his sooty, singed trousers. *The missing scientist, Dr. Farquhar!*

Dammit. Queen's agents were expected to maintain a low public profile. But after six months of failed leads, he wasn't letting this one go. "Stay here," he ordered Colleen, then gave chase.

He wanted answers. "Stop!" he yelled. "Thief!" A lie, perhaps, but one that would draw the attention of the many policemen who patrolled Mayfair. With luck, he might gain assistance and be mistaken for a private citizen trying to regain his stolen purse.

Though the older, spindly-legged scientist was no match for Nick in a foot race, what he lacked in speed, he made up for in lunacy, dashing into the busy street. An ill-advised attempt to weave between clockwork horses and steam carriages sent him bouncing off iron wheels and into a tumble before nearly meeting his end beneath steel hoofs.

Nick cursed. Not a chance he would risk such a death. He waited for an opening, only to see Dr. Farquhar stagger back onto his feet. No. There could be no escape. He needed to end this now. He yanked his TTX pistol free from its holster and took aim.

Zwing. Nick's dart found its mark.

A constable skidded to a halt beside him. "You can't—" His eyes widened as they took in the make and model of Nick's weapon, a sidearm issued only to Queen's agents. In a heartbeat, the policeman became his ally, yanking out his whistle and waving at traffic.

Farquhar was getting away. Again, Nick took aim. *Zwing.* A second dart landed neatly between the man's shoulder blades. He slowed. Wavered. And finally fell.

"Well, that's something to see," the policeman commented, his voice ringing with awe and a bit of dark hope. "I hear a third dart kills?"

"I need him alive," Nick said, irritated that he'd been forced to act in such a public location. "And restrained." Answers would have to wait.

On the far side of the street, a small knot of uncertain people gathered about the paralyzed man. One ventured close to pluck the dart from Farquhar's back and hold it up, peering at it while others, too well-bred to draw close, forced their slack jaws closed, pretending nothing was amiss.

"Yes, sir!" The constable blew hard on his whistle. Wading out into traffic arms spread wide, he brought the entire street to a standstill before waving Nick across.

He snatched back the dart. "If it's potent enough to drop a fleeing suspect, should you be handling it?"

"Well I—" Offended, the man stalked off.

The other onlookers drew back, moving away from the presumed thief as Nick searched Farquhar's pockets, turning up nothing but a smooth snail shell and a handful of loose coins. Added to a missing cravat and the lightly singed, rumpled clothing he wore suggested the man had not intended to leave his home last night. And he looked to have spent a rough night on the street, trailing them here, rather than turning to friends or neighbors.

Where was his wife? Was she an accomplice or an adversary? Why had he not run to his employer, pleading his innocence and begging assistance? And what, exactly, did he plan to do with the cat sìth when his laboratory was a lost cause?

Nick wanted answers to each and every question, but it would be hours before the man woke up, and even then Farquhar would be groggy and disoriented. What to do with him in the meantime? Even now, he could see his phaeton approaching with Colleen at the reins, her expression daring anyone to challenge her as she wove her way through the stopped traffic. He couldn't very well toss off her trunk and replace it with Farquhar's limp body.

Or could he?

No. He shook off the thought. Not only would the Duke of Avesbury have his head for such a public display as it already was, Nick did not wish to invite any aspect of his work into his personal living space or that of his family.

Another constable joined them. "You can't just—" But the first elbowed the second in the ribs, lifting his chin to point at Nick's TTX pistol. "Sorry, sir. My apologies, sir."

"Is there a station house nearby, one with a cell?"

"Of course, sir!" the constable rocked onto his toes. "Not more than two blocks away. Shall we assist him to a cell?"

"Yes, please." A compromise. Treated like a common thief, Farquhar would draw less attention and perhaps lessen the paperwork that was certain to land on Nick's desk. "This man's name is Dr. Gregory Farquhar. He stole something extremely rare and valuable. Moreover, he is wanted for questioning with regards to an intentionally set fire that occurred early this morning. Lock him up, but treat him with kid gloves. He'll wake in a few hours. Send word to me here." He handed the policeman a punch card and a few coins. "By *private* skeet pigeon."

The card would provide the clockwork bird direction and the coins the funds to do so—the municipal flock was notoriously rusty and unreliable—with an extra bonus added to ensure they were motivated to see the task done.

"Will do, sir!" the constable barked.

"Mr. Torrington?" Colleen inquired, stiff and formal from her perch. "Is that—"

Nick vaulted into his vehicle, landing beside her and the voluminous froth of her skirts. "Dr. Farquhar? Yes." The two police officers slung their arms beneath those of the mad scientist and heaved him upward, dragging him down the pavement. "They'll take him into custody. When he wakes, we'll question him."

"We." A note of doubt hung in her voice. She tugged on the reins, pulling the control lever to a sedate, proper level three, then took the corner, directing them toward his family's townhome. A light rain began to fall, dampening the feather that sprouted from a bonnet carefully pinned in place upon her head.

"Yes, we. Partners, remember?" He let his gaze fall upon the black buttons that marched up the front of her coat. "Easiest for us to enter the station dressed as a lord and his lady, but wear sensible shoes. And a skirt that won't brush the floor. Detainees are often ill, and there's no predicting if a mop has touched the floor in recent years."

Colleen threw him a small smile. "A point in your favor, fiancé, that you escort me to such delightful locations."

The burden on his shoulders lifted ever so slightly. "And in yours, if you can resist the temptation to strangle the man who caged your familiar." Behind them, the cat sìth cried a pitiable displeasure at being stuffed in a cage and hauled about London streets. "How is Sorcha?"

"Physically, the wounds are superficial. Dr. Farquhar appears only to have punctured a vein. The patches of shaved skin must have been preparation for further experimentation. The fire stopped him before he could do any significant damage."

"What is supposed to happen," he began, "when you mistreat a fairy cat?"

"Nothing good," she said. "Show a King Cat kindness—a saucer of milk or a fresh-caught fish—and good fortune follows. Mistreat him, and misfortune descends. All the dairy cows go dry. Or, should you be so unlucky to have a death in the family, the cat sìth might steal the soul of the dead before burial."

"Or a wife, for example, might decide to burn your townhome to the ground and lay the blame at your feet."

She laughed. "Exactly." Snapping the reins, Colleen slowed the horse, expertly weaving through a knot of traffic at the intersection.

"And if your cat sìth happens to be a witch?"

"Ah, the darker myth. She can take the form of a cat nine times."

"And after the ninth?"

"Stuck."

"And left wandering the Scottish countryside, perhaps to be trapped by cryptid hunters and sold on the black market as a curiosity." He glanced at the wicker carrier. "Or they accompany young women with beautiful, flashing eyes to London."

Colleen stared straight ahead. "I'm not a witch."

"I didn't think you were." He reached out and squeezed her arm. "I meant only to note the similarities. It can't be coincidence that Sorcha, in particular, ended up in his laboratory."

"Dr. Farquhar values Sorcha—enough to follow us in an attempt to reclaim her—but not over himself, or he wouldn't have abandoned her to the fire." Colleen fell silent, as carts and carriages rattled past them. She slid a glance in his direction. "You mentioned a long, complicated story. Queen's agent's business. Could this mad scientist really believe Sorcha is a witch in cat form?"

He would tell her all about CEAP, all about the shadow committees that the Queen's agents hunted. Not here on the streets, but soon. Before they interviewed Farquhar.

"Aether, I hope not," Nick sighed. "I need answers. A solution to Anna's condition. Not the mentally disordered ramblings of a thwarted researcher who has abandoned key steps of the scientific process in his quest to prove an obscure folk tale from his childhood." He recalled Mrs. Leighton's words. "Unfortunately, it seems he might. There have been whispers of men exploring the possibilities of animal transmutation, a kind of sorcery where an animal shifts into a human form, then back again."

She sucked in a breath. "Like the witches associated with the cat sìth."

"Exactly like that." And though Colleen possessed a number of catlike skills—excellent night vision, good hearing and astounding agility—she was all woman. One who could help him untangle fact from fiction. "He'll wake in a few hours. We'll question him then."

His family's townhome drew into view.

"About your family—"

"They will be thrilled to have you as their guest." He grinned. "Or, rather, in their clutches. My mother wants nothing more than to see all of her children married. But—" He held up his hand as she drew breath to protest. "If you prefer, I will inform her—and my father—that this is a work arrangement. That our engagement is a façade constructed for the benefit of society while we investigate a situation at the Duke of Avesbury's command."

"Perhaps that's best," she said. He tried not to let his disappointment surface. "I want to accept your offer, but what we know about each other has been gained in such snatches. Spending an extended amount of time in each other's company is the only appealing aspect of the situation in which we find ourselves. Well, that and departing my uncle's household." A long, silent moment passed before she slanted him a glance from beneath long, dark lashes and, when she spoke, her voice held a note of invitation. "And when opportunity permits, perhaps we might explore our..." A patch of bright color bloomed high upon her cheeks. "Physical compatibility?"

Nick's heart leapt to life inside his ribcage and began to pound. Other interested portions of his anatomy also took note. "I'd hoped as much, but a gentleman should never presume. Kisses, no matter how hot they burn, need not progress. If you wish, we can discuss terms."

"I'm no innocent," she said. "As you well know. Without any expectations that I would ever marry, I have taken the occasional lover. Quietly and discreetly." Her lips pressed into a flat line. "At least in the past. None have been so crass as to publicly announce such a fact until now."

Once made public, such a perceived transgression was rarely, if one was female and unmarried, forgiven. "What is it you want from an affair?"

"What do I want?" Her odd glance suggested not a single lover had ever asked. "I want…more. I'm no delicate flower." Her very ears were now pink.

Ah, she wanted excitement. Passion. Tightly controlled in the presence of all other *ton*, she thought he might be willing to unleash the woman who prowled through London beneath the moon, slipping in and out of rooms in the dark of night. Aether, he wanted that too.

He leaned close to her ear and growled, "Large, solid desks can be accommodating. It's a shame we were interrupted. Chairs. Walls. Floors." He paused. "Soft mattresses too have their charms."

"And yet are so very prosaic," she breathed. "I was hoping you might have other ideas." Her hands tightened on the reins. "In two days, I celebrate my twenty-fifth birthday. Shall we mark that as the day we decide if a future as husband and wife suits?"

"Two days. Will that be long enough?" he asked, stiff with arousal. Her chest rose and fell quickly beneath her buttoned cape. He blinked, forcing himself to stop speculating about layers that clung more closely to her skin. "Two days of close companionship while we uncover whatever Farquhar is about, and investigate if he's made any discoveries that might prove useful."

"I expect it will be all society is willing to afford us. If that. Now, speaking of Dr. Farquhar..." Without taking her eyes from the road, she reached into a small purse that hung from a chain about her waist and drew forth a long, narrow slip of paper. "I launched a skeet pigeon at dawn and have a response. Mr. Witherspoon is not pleased, but in light of Mrs. Farquhar's arsonist tendencies and Anna's pressing need, he will provide a name for three thousand pounds."

Nick nearly choked. "Three thousand pounds?" He snatched it from her fingers, his eyes focusing on the ink-scrawled figure, upon the bank instructions as to where the money was to be deposited. "For a name?"

"Clients would swiftly abandon him," her lips twisted, "if it became known he was willing to sell their information. Therefore, even as a special favor to me, a breach in client confidentiality does not come cheap."

Chapter Ten

Beside her, Nick fell silent. Overhead, gathering clouds darkened the skies as a faint mist strengthened into a steady rain. Her gray lenses filtered the remaining light such that when she stole a long glance at his tight face, his features stood out in high relief. All of them tense. Three thousand pounds was a small fortune. Far more than most would be willing to spend on an ill relative—particularly a female—for the *chance* at a cure. No, not even a cure, a treatment. One his sister would be reliant upon her entire life. Should it work. And all that dependent upon finding the current whereabouts of one particular rosewood box and the precious object contained within.

"Ready?" They'd arrived at his family's townhome. Tall, terraced and proud, it stood at attention beside its clones, all of them neatly lined up alongside this side of the square.

He took a deep breath. "My family knows I work for the Queen. Nothing specific, but they hold no illusions that I spend all my time locked within four walls of a laboratory. I'll inform my mother that you have a similar profession, that our engagement is temporary, a societal necessity while we work together. But..." He caught up her hand, stroking his thumb over the amber stone. "Not only is this my grandmother's ring, it's an exact match to the color of your eyes. My mother and sister will doubt our story."

"As well they should." The longer she was with Nick, the less she wanted to part ways. "We're playing for time. Time alone. Time to interview a mad scientist."

"Time," he repeated. "That my sister might not have."

"And will therefore use as efficiently as possible." She gave him a weak smile. "What with your swift capture of Dr. Farquhar, the price Mr. Witherspoon demands for a mere name might not be worth paying. Not if you can persuade the scientist to share his secrets. Why, we may have answers before nightfall."

"That may be, but I like to know all the players in a game, to roll over every log to see what crawls out. Whoever purchased the device from Mrs. Farquhar went through much effort to conceal his identity, and I want that name. Regardless, we'll find time for a courtship. Even if we must squeeze it in between interrogations." The corner of his mouth curved upward. "Poetry and roses? Sweet nothings whispered in your ear?"

He hadn't released her fingers, had made no move to climb down from the phaeton, but instead stared into her eyes as if answers could be found deep within their depths. Eyes were often said to be "windows to the soul". What, then, did he imagine he might see?

She cared for him very much. Admired him. Enjoyed his company. Ached for his touch. But she wasn't—not yet—in love with him. Though it wouldn't take much for her to tumble hat over boots. Time to lighten the mood, if only briefly.

"Only if they're suggestive." Colleen leaned close and teased the shell of his ear with her lips, quite satisfied when his hand tightened about hers. "And only if you're prepared to act upon them. Tell me, how seriously will your mother and sister take their assigned role of chaperone?"

"We shouldn't need one on a public street, Lady Stewart," he chided, though lights danced once more in his eyes. Good. She didn't want to dwell on what their future may or may not hold. Not when the present demanded their full attention. "Now hand over the reins to the groom. Sorcha may be Scottish, but you'll never convince me *any* cat enjoys the rain."

She gave him a cheeky grin and reached for the wicker carrier. "If you insist, Mr. Torrington."

If her feet hesitated before crossing the threshold, she blamed the sight before her. She'd left the past five years behind her the moment she exited her uncle's house. Even if she wished it, there would be no reversing course.

Inside, a steam butler waited. Her uncle's was old and creaky with neglect. Forever belching clouds of smoke, the hallways were dark and gloomy, a challenge to keep clean. Here, the black and white marble-tiled floor gleamed. A tall hallway mirror sparkled, and the furniture was glossy. Even the steam butler himself bore the most lustrous metallic accessories she'd ever seen. All polished daily, she expected.

"Lady Stewart, this is Hopsworth." Colleen nodded. "Hopsworth, this is my fiancée." At Nick's announcement, the steambot's wire eyebrows slid to the top of his forehead. "Circumstances dictate that she reside here for the next several days. Have a steam footman retrieve her trunk, then send him to collect the remainder of her luggage from Lord Maynard." He gave the address.

"Yes, sir."

"Is my mother home?"

"Not at present. She is out paying calls. Your sister and niece, however, are in the nursery," Hopsworth tipped his head toward a tightly closed door, "your father in the study."

"Excellent. I'll speak with him while Lady Stewart settles in. Please show her to my old room."

Hinges—forced to bend further than their design permitted—protested with a loud creak as the steambot drew himself ramrod straight. The slightest puff of disapproving steam escaped his neatly crimped collar. "Yours, sir?"

"Don't pop a bolt, Hopsworth. It's not as if I currently occupy it." He flipped back the blanket covering Sorcha's carrier, and the cat hissed, swiping her clawed arm at the steam butler who reeled back, hands raised. Was he afraid his metal casing might scratch? "That wildcat in her arms is accustomed to roaming free," Nick continued, "and requires outside access. My room provides a convenient trellis. As the cat has suffered a recent trauma, she must be given time to familiarize herself with new surroundings. Once Lady Stewart's things are placed in my room, no one save myself is to enter. For any reason. Not even the steam staff. They're to leave a saucer of cream and a tin of tuna on the floor outside the door twice daily."

Such thoughtfulness. Far, far better than any bouquet of roses.

"Yes, sir." Hopsworth's jaw snapped shut with an echoing clang. "Lady Stewart, if you'll follow me?" With a final glance at Sorcha, the steam butler hooked himself to a rail lift, punched a button, and a great clattering and turning of gears yanked the steambot up the stairway.

"One of the latest models," Nick said, "but in his chest beats the mechanical heart of an eighty-year-old." He waved toward the stairs. "Go explore. I've a rather sturdy—if prosaic—bed."

"Don't think I won't assess its possibilities." She winked. "But despite your orders, I'm not at all convinced we won't be interrupted. The entire household will be wondering what we're about."

He laughed and dropped a quick kiss upon her lips. "So they will."

She widened her eyes in mock fear. "Don't leave me to face them alone."

"No worries. I won't be long. I'll speak to my father about transferring the funds to Mr. Witherspoon, then I'll take you to my sister."

A few minutes later, Colleen stepped into Nick's room. Though faint, she caught his scent on the air as it swirled with her entry. Spicy, soapy with a hint of musk. The usual shapes of furniture lined the walls, all failing to catch her attention save one. A large, canopied bed dominated the room. Despite her brazen words, her skin heated, threatening to burst into flame. Would she sleep alone tonight? Or would he climb the aforementioned trellis to join her?

She tore her eyes away, scratching Sorcha's chin through the bars as she crossed to the window, cracking it open. Indeed, the structure was convenient—and not just for prowling felines. "Perfect," she told the cat. "Access to both the ground and the roof. Though I'm certain you miss the moors, the forests and the abundance of lively rabbits, it'll do. We'll be home soon enough." For, despite Isabella's presence, her uncle's townhome had only ever been a temporary residence. A necessary stop before returning to her true life.

Last night—or rather, early this morning—she had scrambled through her window, dragging the monstrous metal cage with her. She'd released Sorcha, then snuck to the kitchens alone, returning with a tray. Ravenous, the cat sìth had consumed an entire leg of mutton before lapping up the promised bowl of cream and executing a lengthy bath before the small fire that burned in the grate. Colleen had crawled into bed and, when she awoke the next morning, found the feline curled into a ball beside her, seemingly no worse for her misadventure.

But there'd been little time to rejoice, for a pounding upon her bedroom door had woken her, and last night's drama surrounding her engagement resumed. "I've been sent to help you pack," Isabella had announced, brushing away tears. "You uncle insists that you're to marry Mr. Glover. Today."

"What!" She'd leapt from the bed. "But I accepted Mr. Torrington's offer! Publicly!"

Her uncle was delusional if he thought to force her hand. Finish packing she would, but only because she refused to ever spend another night under his roof. A room at Claridge's it would be. Her every move would be studied and analyzed by hotel staff and the wealthy, outspoken American girls who had traveled overseas to bag and drag a British peer to the altar, but at least she would be free to come and go as she pleased.

The only setback had been getting there, as her uncle had forbidden the steam staff to remove her possessions to a cart until she'd signed a marriage certificate and settlement both binding her to Mr. Glover *and* granting him control of the Craigieburn estate. An event that would never come to pass. She'd been about to leave the townhome with no more than the clothes on her back and a cat sìth in her arms when Nick had arrived.

Midst the chaos that followed, her uncle had abruptly reversed his position, turning against the formerly favored Mr. Glover, and holding out an olive branch to the man *she'd* chosen. Colleen didn't trust it, not for a single second. Nick—or his family—had something her uncle wanted. Badly. But what?

A knock sounded on the bedroom door, and she turned away from the window.

"Your trunk, Lady Stewart." Hopsworth waved in a steam footman, then followed to place a tray upon the floor. "Cream and tuna. All further feline meals will be left outside in the hall as requested. Is there anything else you need?"

"Thank you, no." She promptly locked the door leading to the hallway after the steambots had exited. Placing the carrier before the cream, she unfastened the buckles that held the wicker lid shut. While Sorcha considered her new surroundings, Colleen set about unpacking a few essentials.

In anticipation of Dr. Farquhar's interrogation and the effluvium of a prison cell, subtle adjustments to her attire were in order. There was nothing to do about her corset or the multiple petticoats or the form-fitting bodice until the rest of her luggage arrived. But she could remove impediments to movement. And boots laced to the knee—not the silk slippers she wore—were better suited to tromping through halls that led to—she very much hoped—a dank and rat-infested prison cell.

She slipped her dirk into the sheath sewn into said boots and replaced the thin chain that held her purse with her thick leather belt, one that not only held a number of essential items, but provided D-loops allowing her to hike her heavy skirts.

With nothing left to do save wait, Colleen began to explore the room, avoiding, for now, the bed. Beside a leather armchair, a small side table groaned beneath a lamp and a stack of weighty tomes. She lifted one. *Diseases of the Heart.* Anatomy was not a topic she'd spent much time investigating but, when he wasn't running about on Queen's errands, such was how Nick spent his time. Given she was about to join him on his current quest, it might be wise to educate herself about matters concerning the human heart.

She gave the Lucifer lamp a good shake, plopped down into the chair and cracked open the text.

~~~

"The Scottish girl is a sneak thief?" His father's expression—no, his entire body—was so stiff, his face so tight that the lightest tap might shatter him, sending pieces crashing to the floor.

Much like an unrepentant cat, Nick couldn't help swatting at the delicate bauble. "She works to fund her own future. Much as I do. And she is properly addressed as Lady Stewart," he corrected his father. "The Much Honored Colleen Stewart of Craigieburn. A landholder
~~~

in her own right." In two short days, she would control the property in its entirety. "Common knowledge, yet no one—for all their insistence upon propriety—bothers to address her correctly."

"It's the eyes," the viscount snapped. "They're not natural." Anything that fell outside a carefully delineated range of human characteristics was unacceptable to the *ton*. "Impossible not to notice them, even behind those odd spectacles. She has the eyes of her sire, the Laird of Craigieburn." His father huffed. "With so many eligible females parading through the ballrooms, you pick the one with nothing to her name but Scottish soil and a decrepit castle. No, not even a castle. It's an aging tower house that will do nothing but drain your bank account to its last shilling. If modernizing it is even a possibility. Don't look at me like that. I made inquiries about her when your mother informed me you'd laid claim to your grandmother's amber ring. Dare I inquire as to why you have brought her *here*? To our family home *before* the wedding?"

Impulse. Instinct. Need. The bone deep knowledge that they belonged together.

"I told you. She's a piece of the puzzle." And... Fine. The image of her reclining in the dark, feet upon a desk and whisky in hand refused to leave his mind. He wanted to peel back the layers and examine what lay beneath. Professionally. Personally. "It's a temporary arrangement," Nick insisted. If Colleen agreed to go forward with a wedding, they certainly wouldn't be spending their honeymoon in his boyhood home. "Her work is much the same as mine." If aimed at private profit, not the public good. "On Anna's behalf, we will be working together. Closely. She refused to stay in her uncle's household, and a hotel is too public." For any number of reasons.

"I'm not interested in funding the Duke of Avesbury's secret missions," his father complained. "Or hosting additional spies." But he lifted his pen and signed a slip of paper authorizing his bank to transfer three thousand pounds to one Mr. Witherspoon, a virtual stranger. Anything for his daughter. "Be sure you fill out the paperwork for reimbursement."

"Of course." Nick rolled his eyes. There was little hope of a refund.

"Now, about your wedding. Your mother claims she knew you and Lady Stewart were destined for each other the first time she saw you share a dance."

Had she? His memory was somewhat different.

He'd been lurking in an alcove, awaiting the arrival of his contact, when a particularly persistent mother began drifting in his direction, her daughter in tow. He'd cursed—and a soft snicker emerged from even deeper in the shadows a moment before Lady Stewart stepped forward.

"May I offer the assistance of an escape dance?" She'd held out her gloved hand. "A brief waltz from here to there? I assure you, I've no interest in being trapped by Lady Delphinia's chatter."

"Most gratefully accepted, my lady." He'd swept her into his arms and onto the dance floor.

She'd been light on her feet, her silk- and boning-encased waist supple beneath his palm. He recalled drawing her closer than was strictly sanctioned, and the sly curve of her lips as she permitted it, a shared moment of mutual collaboration to antagonize their pursuers.

Perhaps he'd taken longer than necessary to traverse the room, but he'd deposited her midst a set of ferns and took his leave with a wink, unquestioning and oblivious to any further depth until they'd met again: at night, atop a roof and behind the concealing bulk of a chimney.

It did not, perhaps, speak well to his instincts as a spy.

"It's too soon to make plans." Though he had no qualms, a bride who wished for a trial engagement wouldn't appreciate such assumptions. "I need Lady Stewart free to work." Whatever heat flared between them in their free moments was an entirely separate affair. "Not attending frivolous social events." He reached for the bank slip with the intent to snatch it and flee.

His father slid it out of reach. "I'll send it by special courier. The funds will be transferred in an hour, perhaps two." The viscount leaned forward. "Now, I don't care what arrangements you've made with your fiancée, you'll not be dragging our family's name through the mud. If she's to stay here, an announcement will be placed in the papers. I will procure a special license while your mother plans—dress fittings, guest lists, a wedding breakfast—all to be held here, with the ceremony in our London parlor, in a few days' time."

"I promised her more time," Nick objected. "And a wedding in Scotland." Would Colleen bolt the moment she learned of the viscount's conditions? She was not a woman to be kept. Such a prospect was as unlikely as keeping the cat sìth in a cage. Were anyone to attempt it, she would slip her tether and there would be hell to pay. "And I agreed to meet with her uncle. I know you don't trust Lord Maynard, but—"

"He wants something, and it's bound to be unpleasant."

Nick agreed, but for the sake of Colleen's relationship with her young aunt, he was willing to try. "Still, I'll meet with him. See what he has in mind."

"For aether's sake, don't agree to *anything* without first consulting me. He's too fond of leading people into legal quagmires. Do you have any idea how many lives he's ruined?"

"Too many to count." All the more reason to lend Colleen his assistance, even if she decided marriage was not to her taste. "I'll be careful. Did you discover anything irregular about the Laird of Craigieburn's will?"

"Nothing," his father admitted. Frustration simmered beneath his carefully starched and ironed collar. "Though the prior Lord Maynard surgically cut his daughter from his life, the family rift was mended after his death. The current Lord Maynard re-established ties, lending his brother-in-law funds and arranging for his niece to have a London Season. My contacts have yet to discover what promises Lord Maynard extracted from *Lady* Stewart's father in exchange for such aid. But I've every confidence they will."

"Given Lord Maynard's sudden attempt to marry her to a business partner, one easily controlled, there must be something." While his father focused upon his youngest son's future, Nick wagered that he could pass along a task that, while necessary, might distract them from pursuing any leads their interrogation of Farquhar produced. "There is one agreed upon condition of my partnership, one separate from any wedding that may or may not occur. In addition to an agreed upon fee, our solicitors must collect all necessary paperwork and documents to return complete and total control of the Craigieburn estate and its properties to Lady Stewart upon her twenty-fifth birthday, two days hence."

"It is with pleasure that I shall rip such papers from her uncle's hands." Only then did his father smirk. "Work fast. Regardless of what we tell your mother, when she learns Lady Stewart possesses land *and* a castle her wedding plans will be in earnest." His voice dropped to a whisper of conspiracy, one that suggested his parents would—as always—be united in their goals. "Those yellow eyes? They bother me not a whit."

Chapter Eleven

Family business attended to, Nick mounted the stairs. He'd take Colleen for a brief visit in the nursery. From there, they'd head upward to the aviary and wait for word from the constabulary or Mr. Witherspoon himself.

While he'd been contemplating how to court Colleen for months now, it was strange to realize how ready his family was to rush him to the proverbial altar. Not that he was opposed. Charles, his oldest brother, had already produced the next heir to the viscountcy and had another child on the way. James, a second son, had married a wealthy American and was the proud father of a sweet, little girl. Only Nick had resisted his mother's every effort to see him settled.

In the hallway, before the closed door of his room, a steambot rolled back and forth, spinning in circles upon the carpet, wielding a dust bin and broom like knights of old, while steam billowed from beneath her skirts. All in an effort to elude capture by the kitchen boy and reach the door handle.

"Sorry, sir." Robby jumped out of range to make a quick bow. "Hopsworth sent me to change her punch card, but Steam Mary is hardwired to clean your room at the top of the hour."

"There's a trick to these older models, if you you'll allow me?"

"Please, sir?"

Nick pulled a short length of hooked wire from his pocket.

"What's that for?" Robby asked.

"Watch." After a few more wild spins, Steam Mary's sensors registered that the path was clear. She lowered her arms and approached the door. "Beneath that ruff of lace and ribbon about where you'd expect a shoulder, lies the clavicular joint. When she reaches for the door handle..."

The steambot's clothing shifted and a chink in her iron housing appeared, exposing wires and tubing. With a strategic swipe, Nick hooked his wire beneath a thick cord of cable and tugged. Steam Mary froze.

The kitchen boy's eyes grew wide. "You broke her!"

"I did not. What kind of trick would that be? Now finish up. Change her programming."

Robby unpinned her apron, flipped open a panel upon her chest, and swapped one punch card for another.

"Now, while you're in there, look deeper." He handed Robby his decilamp. "That cable I yanked will have unplugged from its socket and should be dangling free. Do you see it?"

The boy bent over the steambot, peering into her illuminated innards. "I do!"

"Push it back into the empty receptacle, and she'll reset."

With a whistle, Steam Mary straightened, glanced at her dust bin and broom in confusion and moved on.

"Thank you, sir!" He bounced on his toes, holding out the decilamp.

"Keep it." Nick handed Robby the hooked wire as well. "But try to catch all the other steambots before you have to resort to sabotage."

"Sir! Yes, sir!" And Robby ran off, a grin stretched across his bright face.

His own grin fading, Nick stared at the door. He leaned closer, listening. All was silent. What had he expected to hear? The yowls of a wildcat? No, more like the sounds of a woman unpacking. Then again, she had but a single trunk in her possession. His lips curved. He could only hope it held a few scraps of red silk.

With a yank, he opened his own door, and all the air left his lungs in a single whoosh. For the space of a heartbeat, all he could do was stare at Colleen, lounging in his favorite chair reading by lamplight. Her skirts hiked up by silver chains to fall above her knees, legs dangling over its arm to cross at her booted ankles. She looked up from a thick journal propped upon her lap. But his eyes refused to focus on its title, preferring the hollow of her throat where a soft curl of hair brushed as she toyed with a long strand wrapped about her finger.

He closed the door behind him with a thud. Sorcha—who, peripheral vision informed him—lounged dead center in the middle of the bed, leg in the air, bathing with complete disregard for onlookers, certain she would not be disturbed. And she wouldn't be, for he had no interest in beginning their courtship upon a bed.

Perhaps the chair?

"The basic anatomy of the heart is simple enough." Colleen swung her feet to the ground with a soft thud and nodded at a nearby anatomy textbook. "But you neglected to mention that many of the facts you presented me with during your horseback lecture on heart physiology were drawn from experiments conducted upon the heart of an eel." She shuddered and pulled a face. "An *eel*, Nick."

Nick swallowed, finally realizing that she'd found and read the draft of an article submitted to the *Journal of Physiology* by J.A. MacWilliam in which the scientist detailed his studies conducted upon the heart of eels. "On the Structure and Rhythm of the Heart in Fishes, with especial reference to the Heart of an Eel." He'd wondered where he'd mislaid it.

"It's a fascinating thought," she said. "If hard to wrap the mind about, to reconcile oneself with the idea that the heart is essentially autonomous, that various sections beat at their own pace, speeding or slowing in response to heat and cold."

"You've been busy." Impressive, her willingness and ability to throw herself into the topic at hand. All these years, she'd hidden a spectacular mind from the *ton.* Perhaps there were many such young ladies concealing their intelligence, but only one particular woman had disturbed his dreams last night, leaving his sheets tangled about his waist. He met her eyes. No barrier blocked their gaze, as she'd set aside her smoky glasses to read in the dim light of his room, and her golden eyes gleamed. "And now your grasp of cardiac electrophysiology easily surpasses that of many first year medical students."

"Only after a concerted effort to understand all matters of heart physiology pertaining to our particular case. Information as currency. We do have a galvanist to interview." Tossing aside the paper, Colleen arched her back, stretching her arms above her head before rising onto her feet. Lips curving upward, she stalked across the space separating them and rose up onto her toes, wrapping her arms about his neck. "Dr. MacWilliam seems to have left out one particular stimulus. Or perhaps eels don't possess them?"

"What's that?" Anticipation set his heart pounding as he dropped his hands to her hips.

"Emotions." Her soft breasts pressed against his chest as her fingertips toyed with the fringe of hair that brushed his collar.

Vague thoughts of leaving the room flitted about in his mind, then flew away altogether. His sister and skeet pigeons could wait. "He's a mind as sharp as a scalpel but, no, I don't think he's interested in theory of mind. MacWilliam has, however, begun a systematic investigation into the mammalian heart studying cardiac fibrillation and the possibility that a spark of electricity—carefully timed and applied—might help restore a normal heartbeat."

"Begun." She kissed the corner of his mouth. "But impatience compels you to chase after a scientist who might already have fabricated such a device."

"It does."

"How long until Dr. Farquhar awakens?"

"Another hour at least." He slipped his palms over the smooth satin encasing her waist, drawing her closer still. "We'll bring pen and paper. If he can't pinpoint the location of his device, a composition exercise detailing its features and functions might be in order." He skimmed his lips across the edge of her hairline.

He bent and caught her lips with his own, spinning her off her feet and pinning her against the door. All while plundering her soft, sweet mouth while she mewled her encouragement, wrapping her legs about his and tugging at his cravat.

Nick couldn't recall the last time a woman had driven him to such distraction that he stood on the knife's edge of losing control. Yet his mind constantly returned to a certain sturdy desk, the first time she'd offered herself to him—in a location that flirted with the possibility of discovery. Despite all public appearances, Colleen was a woman who enjoyed flirting with danger and discovery. Indulgences he'd be happy to provide.

He nipped her lower lip, then drew back, tucking a long, silky strand of her hair back into the coil at the base of her neck. "Not here," he murmured. "Someone might come looking for us, and it's too obvious a location."

"So it is." Her legs dropped to the ground, and she straightened his collar, all business, though her amber eyes were still dark with desire.

He swallowed. Hard. "Introduce me, formally, to Sorcha. Then we've things to do," he slid her a knowing glance and a smile, "before we can carve out a moment to play. Some place a bit more… exotic."

~~~

Colleen's breath caught in her throat. She'd been smothering her disappointment that Nick had failed to do more than kiss her against the wall, but at his words, her pulse jumped anew. The sooner necessary tasks were behind them…

"Sorcha?" She approached the bed—hand extended—where the cat sìth sat, enthroned. "Might I?"

The feline returned Colleen's request with a long, steady gaze, then rose onto her feet, tail lifted, and approached, arching her back as Colleen stroked a palm down her soft, sleek pelt.

A quick scan of the shaved patch of skin upon her shoulder informed her that the small incision remained uninfected. Thank aether Dr. Farquhar hadn't had a chance to do further damage. "Allow me to present
~~~

Mr. Torrington, the gentleman who led me to your prison."

"She's quite majestic." His lips quirked. "If the male of her species is a king, does this make her a queen?"

"On par with Queen Victoria herself, yes."

Smiling, he bowed. Then extended his own hand, fingers curled.

Sorcha sniffed, her whiskers twitching as she considered his offer of friendship, then accepted a brief chin scratch before padding to the head of the bed to select a pillow for her nap.

"Quite at home," Nick commented. He slid open a bedside table drawer, slipping something from its recesses into his pocket. "Much like you've made yourself."

"A compliment," Colleen replied, leaning backward against the thick and solid carved bedpost that reached toward the ceiling. "I love the darkness of your room. The rich wood, heavy curtains, worn leather and the whorls of vines that twist across the forest green wallpaper. So much better than the light, the airy, and the ruffled that's forever thrust upon women."

"The dark suits you."

She lifted her chin toward the window where raindrops pelted the panes and ran in rivulets down the glass. "Rain suits me as well, though it makes the rooftops treacherous."

"So it does." They shared a knowing glance, spy to burglar. "Come, let's stop by the nursery. We'll visit Anna and I'll introduce you to my niece, Clara."

He reached for her, tugging her from the room. Had a man ever held her hand in such a manner? She had no memory of anyone save her father, but that was years in the past. Every inch of her skin delighted in the feel of his palm sliding against her own with a roughness that came from gripping stone walls, drain pipes, and ropes. It created a delightful friction that she couldn't wait to feel brushed across the rest of her skin.

She blinked, then focused on the moment. "Your sister is among those family members who know?"

"That I'm a spy?" Nick closed the door behind him, then led her up a flight of stairs. "Yes. She and my parents are aware, not so much my brothers. It would have been impossible to hide my odd comings and goings from this house, given I often stay here when she's feeling poorly. Anna is fully aware that I've also been making more private inquiries on her behalf, but all of them know better than to press for details about the tasks I carry out for the Queen."

Carefully, quietly, Nick opened the door. Inside, Anna—a woman with the heart-shaped face of an angel—sat in a rocking chair beside a fire, cuddling an adorable baby. Three months? It had been years since Colleen had held an infant. Her heart gave a twist. The price of refusing to consider any London gentlemen. She glanced at Nick. What kind of father would he make?

"She rarely leaves my niece alone," he whispered. Colleen understood. With an uncertain lifespan, precious moments must be savored. "But both of them have an aid, should help be required." At the far end of the room, one nurse's face lifted from the sewing she held in her lap, while the other glanced up from a book. At Nick's wave, both nodded respectfully, then dropped their gazes back to their occupations.

"Shh." Anna held a finger to her lips. "Clara has only just fallen asleep."

They tiptoed across a soft carpet to Anna's side. The room was dim, but the low light hid nothing from Colleen's eyes. Behind Nick's sister, a large, disturbing machine hulked and hummed in the corner. Dials and buttons and switches covered its surface. A long wire extended—tentacle-like—from its side, its end screwed into a sharp, pointed metal rod. One designed to pierce the skin and touch the heart to deliver a life-saving bolt of electricity? A shudder of terror ran over Colleen. The thought of wielding such a device turned her insides to custard.

"Anna, allow me to introduce Lady Colleen Stewart," Nick whispered. "She'll be working as my partner while posing as my fiancée. We've unearthed some promising information about a new device."

They politely greeted each other with a nod.

"We've met, though briefly." Colleen kept her voice to a murmur.

"A fiancée?" Anna's eyebrows rose.

She felt awful, letting his family wonder about the depth of their involvement. "Your brother has proposed. I'm considering his offer but, like him, I also possess a flair for prying into affairs that men and women prefer to keep hidden."

From the corner of her eye, she saw Nick struggle to control his shock, followed by a subtle straightening of the shoulders as satisfaction settled upon them.

"Ah, I see." A knowing grin stretched his sister's face. "I won't turn down a miracle or a new sister-in-law. Either or both would be more than welcome."

Nick lifted the sleeping infant from his sister's arm with practiced expertise, and warmth spread through Colleen's chest at the sight. Gentleman, scientist, spy. Devoted brother. Quite probably he'd make a most excellent husband and father.

Marrying him would be the adventure of a lifetime, but it would also bind her to London. What of her responsibilities in Scotland? As laird, people depended upon her, and she'd been absent far too long.

He turned and passed the baby into Colleen's arms, smiling at her shocked expression. "If you don't mind. Anna has spoiled her. To the point she rarely sleeps unless held, and I want to listen to her mother's heart."

"Of course." Colleen gathered the precious bundle close, and found herself gently swaying. She pressed a kiss to the fine, silky curls upon the baby's head—inhaling her soft, sweet scent—and caught a small waving fist as she stirred, all while marveling at the perfect, tiny, pink bow of her lips.

When she thought to glance up, Nick—eyes closed—held a stethoscope to his sister's narrow chest. Only then did Colleen note the bluish tinge of Anna's fingertips and the heavy woolen rug draped over her knees despite the warmth of the room. She'd taken a risk, bearing a child, and regretted nothing. Impossible not to admire a woman who'd reached out and grabbed what she most desired despite all advice to the contrary. Colleen resolved to do the same.

"Are you still experiencing occasional numbness in your hands and face?" Nick asked, moving his fingers to Anna's wrist, taking note of her pulse. A careful blankness clung to his face. "A feeling of being out of breath? Damp palms?"

"Yes, yes, and yes," Anna answered. "Along with all the usual symptoms. Fatigue, chest pain, dizziness, and shortness of breath. But only one seizure in the past week."

As Nick straightened, pain and a hint of helplessness flickered in his eyes, but quickly resolved into steely determination. No stone would be left unturned, no scientist left unquestioned. He shifted, impatient and keen to take action. "When Mother returns, do try to keep her contained."

His sister laughed softly. "You ask the impossible."

Resignation tightened his mouth, and he lifted his gaze to Colleen. "Time to visit the aviary. We've a message to send."

Indeed, Mr. Witherspoon could be counted upon to act quickly once funds reached him. "And one to watch for."

As she slid the swaddled baby back into her mother's arms—somewhat reluctant to part with the soft weight, Anna whispered, "I've been away from society, but don't think I never noticed the sparks that fly whenever the two of you are together. It's easy to see you've captured my brother's... regard and have the look of a woman about to lead him on an adventure. I heartily approve. He needs a partner..." She glanced at Colleen's skirt hikes, then gave her an impish wink. "And a distraction."

A slow burn crept across her cheeks. She'd certainly offered him one. Repeatedly. But the man was determined to torture her with searing kisses and teasing promises. He'd best deliver, and soon.

Chapter Twelve

The narrow, metal staircase leading to the aviary folded back upon itself several times before it reached the roof. A hatch opened to reveal a low wall supporting an arch of iron and glass that protected the message-carrying skeet pigeons—and them—from the afternoon's soft, misty rain. At one end, a glass door. At the other, a square window—propped open—allowed the clockwork birds entry and exit. A corner of the space had been appropriated for more than birds. Warmed by the sun's occasional appearance, a small potted garden of purslane, rosemary and fennel thrived upon a low bench.

Steadying herself on the iron railing she climbed into a different world where, through grit and soot-smudged panes of glass, all of London stretched before her. High overhead, silver dirigibles dotted the sky. Slate roof-tiles glistened in the dim light while smoke rose in billows from thousands of chimneys. Thousands of windows glowed—some yellow with oil, some a brighter white with gas, and a few with the blue tinge of bioluminescence.

Colleen pressed her palms against the cool glass. In this vast city, rooftops meant freedom. Exploring the possibilities that lay above London had saved her mind from the gloom that descended following the loss of her parents, of her forced relocation. "So breathtaking. Always." And in the raincloud-muted light, her spectacles were unnecessary. She tucked them away and turned to watch Nick.

He was all brisk business and impatience, examining the legs of the six skeet pigeons who perched upon the aviary's interior ledge. For years they'd circled each other—beneath both the glow of chandeliers and the twinkle of starlight—sharing casual flirtations. Light touches. Pointed, knowing glances. And details of their lives not meant for anyone else. Never quite daring to fully enter the other's orbit. Until now.

"No message yet from the constabulary," he reported, selecting a dispatch canister from a metal box and inserting a tightly rolled scroll. "Funds are being transferred to your employer as we speak. I assume you keep a punch card with his location near at hand?" He lifted a bird from its perch, fastening the canister to its ankle.

Mr. Witherspoon hadn't been pleased at her request. Though he'd agreed to reveal the buyer's name for a hefty sum, the skeet pigeon hadn't contained a return token. A clear message that—had she not retired—her employment would have been terminated. But Mr. Witherspoon knew Colleen kept a backup punch card, permitting her to contact him by bird one last time. Not that she wished to return to his employ. Not after what she'd found in that burnt-out shell of a laboratory.

Pushing all dark thoughts aside, she smiled. Nick would like this.

"I do." Lifting her fingers to the first button beneath her chin, she turned to face him as she unfastened her bodice, letting silk panels fall open to expose the lacy trim of her chemise.

His eyes brightened and the corner of his mouth lifted. Silent, but keenly attentive, Nick raised an eyebrow and waited.

With the edge of her underbust corset revealed—along with a generous bit of cleavage—she extracted a pen knife from the pouch at her waist and slit the half-dozen threads that held shut a tiny pocket sewn into its hem. She extracted a punched address card and pressed it into his palm. "It's my last token."

The pulse at his neck jumped. "Don't move." He pointed at her. "Not so much as a single extra button." With deft fingers, he slid the punch card into its slot, then quickly wound the skeet pigeon's mechanism. Wings flapping, Nick tossed the bird into the gray London sky before turning the full force of his intense gaze upon her.

"Does a rooftop aviary qualify as exotic?" She hoped so. For once they were alone with no one in pursuit and nowhere else they needed to be. A brief window of time open to them before a message arrived.

He glanced at her, swallowed, then flipped the hatch closed, kicking a bar across it to ensure there would be no interruptions from below. "Do you want it to?" Desire darkened his eyes as he closed the gap between them.

"Desperately." She tugged at his cravat, urging him closer.

He gripped the edge of her jaw, tipping her face upward, searching her eyes for any objection. "Anyone might catch a glimpse."

She shrugged a shoulder. "In this weather? Unlikely, but they *might*. Will that stop you?"

"Not a chance." The dam broke and his mouth crashed down upon hers. Their tongues tangled and plundered as spikes of pleasure zinged though her body. She tightened her hands upon his coat, anchoring herself upright as her world tilted off center and plunged her into a kiss so deep it stole her every last breath.

He pulled back, nipping at her lip. "More?"

"You need to ask?" Her voice was huff of frustration.

Impatient fingers fell upon the buttons of her bodice, finishing the task, pushing the silk from her shoulders and down her arms until the garment fell away. He tossed it over the railing, then froze. All his attention focused upon her as she tugged the drawstring of her chemise loose and slid the straps down her shoulders. The lacy-edges caught upon the swell of her breasts.

"All the way," he ordered, his voice hoarse.

"As you wish." A cold, damp breeze drifted across her bare breasts, peaking her nipples. She arched her back and dragged a fingertip over their swell, a clear invitation.

His eyes flashed, but he spun a finger in the air, denying her. "Turn around. Hands against the glass."

This was new. And most definitely exciting. She complied, bracing herself. In front of her, all of London glittered with light and swirled with fog. She might miss the countryside, but the city held such an interesting variety of secrets within its many nooks and crannies. Including—the corners of her mouth curved upward—rooftop trysts.

Hands skimmed over the boning at her waist, over the metal fastenings that held her corset closed. But made no effort to free them. Instead, his broad, warm palms moved upward, cupping and caressing her breasts as his mouth sank against the skin at the nape of her neck. A soft bite that spoke to primitive desires, electrifying every nerve ending and sending her heart racing.

"Is this what you want? A touch of danger?"

She rocked back against him—against the stiff evidence of his arousal—and groaned at the sensation. Need built to a fever pitch.

He nipped her earlobe. "Say it," he whispered over the skin beneath her ear.

"Yes," she breathed. "Don't stop." This moment—atop and apart—far exceeded anything her imagination had dared to conjure.

For too many years, she'd dreamed of ending their flirtatious dances by dragging him from the ballroom onto a dark balcony to steal a kiss. But with a reputation to maintain, propriety had always won. No more. At last he was hers, and she intended to make the most of it.

With a groan, he nudged her forward, pressing her bare breasts against the cool, smooth glass and her hips to the low, brick wall. His body was hot and hard at her back, crushing her with just the right pressure as his warm, demanding mouth explored the curve of her neck.

She let her head fall backward onto his shoulder. Every touch fanned the flames that licked across her skin as a wet heat gathered between her legs. Was this really her, tossing all inhibitions aside to give in to every wanton desire? It was. Her only regret was that they'd wasted so much time denying each other.

His fingers caught at her skirts, hiking them higher still, settling them about her hips. "Yes," she breathed, rocking her head sideways to nip at his neck. Waiting with sweet anticipation.

He eased back, giving himself room to touch her. To run his fingers across the top edge of her stocking, to discover she wore no knickers. Abandoned in his room, they lay among the last vestiges of her inclinations to follow society's rules. "Aether," he whispered. "I'd thought to find red silk."

"Last night you would have." She pushed backward. "Disappointed?"

"Not at all." His hand shifted and dipped between her legs to stroke her. Gentle yet firm, extracting the maximum of pleasure. Her hips flexed, eyes drifting shut as need coiled and twisted, tighter and tighter and—

Rough, calloused hands gripped her bare hips and spun her about, lifting her, propping her on the edge of the low wall. "Wait for me," he growled.

Feet dangling, she grabbed at his shoulders to brace herself. Her lungs dragged in a ragged breath. "Hurry."

"Foot on the railing behind me." He tore at his waistband, as desperate for her as she was for him.

He was going to take her—back to the glass—where discovery was a distant, but real possibility. No gentle, careful explorations in the dark. Rather a raw, primal coupling. Perfect. She lifted a leg, catching the heel of her boot upon the steel bar, watching as his cock fell free, thick and heavy.

"My turn to touch." She caught his length in her hand—smooth, hard, hot—and stroked from tip to base. Aether, she wanted him deep inside her.

From his coat pocket, he drew forth a wrapped sheath and pressed it into her palm. Another first. Never had a man placed so much control in her hands. Without letting go, she tore the paper with her teeth, covered him, then lifted her gaze to his.

Dark with arousal, his eyes stared down at her, hazy with lust and... something more. His gaze pierced straight through her heart. "Have you any idea how many times I've imagined this?" His voice was a growl. "At the end of a shadowy garden path. Behind a rooftop chimney?"

"Atop a sturdy desk in a stranger's study? I've lost count." She clawed at his cravat, pulling his lips down to hers. As his mouth devoured hers, she unfastened the buttons of his waistcoat, of his shirt. At last, the warm, firm skin of his chest and stomach met her hands. Skin she wanted to feel against her own. Wrapping hands about the mounds of his tight buttocks, she tugged him closer. "Stop wasting time."

Again, his hands slid up her thighs, shoving aside layers of skirts and parting her legs before him. He touched her center and—finding her wet and ready—entered her with one hard thrust. "Yes!" Lightning ran up her spine and shot through her limbs as he claimed her, and she gasped at the sensation of him filling her.

Slowly, he began to move, his long length sending darts of pleasure radiating through her. Heart pounding, she panted, digging the tips of her nails into his skin, urging him deeper still.

His intense thrusts came faster now. She closed her eyes and mewled her pleasure as the smooth glass at her back grew warm, as the rough brick beneath her dug into her soft flesh, as the rough scattering of hairs upon his chest brushed across the sensitive tips of her breasts. So many sensations, all of them building as he drove into her again and again and again pushing her ever closer to her peak.

"Nick!" The tension snapped and pleasure exploded in repeated waves of pleasure.

Once, twice more he plunged into her, stiffening as the spasms of his own release overtook him.

Braced against rough and smooth, Colleen wrapped her arms around his hot and heaving chest, hanging on as her world tilted, as she rearranged every expectation she'd ever had for a husband. Nick had shattered them all and the pieces no longer fit together. Worse, the tender feeling tugging at her heart would need to be ruthlessly leashed and caged, lest he glimpse the emotions roiling through her mind. She needed to think about this, about how—a mere two days from freedom—a man had managed to steal a piece of her soul.

She rested her head against his chest and listened to the steady beat of his heart.

~~~

Was it possible to see stars in a cloud-covered sky? Nick closed his eyes and found the celestial bodies still dancing before them, a lingering euphoria unlike anything he'd ever experienced. In his arms, Colleen's soft curves melted against him, mere moments after she'd come apart, screaming his name. A wildcat in... well, not in bed. On a wall.

He grinned, entirely too self-satisfied for such a brief encounter. With the pent-up passion of days, weeks, no, months of flirtation finally released, might they manage to take things slower next time?

Next time.

Hot and sweaty, their bodies were still fused. His skin touched hers at all the right points, and he was reluctant to part, to let so much as a thin layer of cool air rush between them. He'd been a fool not to act sooner.

He'd kept his past affairs simple, short and sweet. Much like their own flirtations had begun. But with
~~~

each passing interaction, words shared between them had grown richer with meaning, as he'd caught glimpses inside her curious and exceptional mind. She'd wormed her way into his heart, and he could think of nothing he wanted more than to call one Lady Colleen Stewart his wife.

As her fingertips traced cords of muscle up and down his back beneath the linen of his shirt, an unsettling twist buried itself deep in his gut. He'd managed to make her his fiancée, but would two days be long enough to convince her they ought to stay together?

Fiancée. *Shit.* He'd meant to tell Colleen about the very real wedding plans that might even now be taking place several stories beneath their feet, but when she'd sliced that punch card from the edge of her corset, his mind had short circuited, leaving behind only the most basic of thoughts.

He would warn her. In a moment. After he'd stolen a few more seconds to revel in the glory of finally holding the only woman to ever steal his sleep and invade his dreams. He brushed his lips over the skin of her neck and felt her shiver beneath his touch. "Walls and desks and chairs are all well and good, but I want more." More than rooftop trysts. "I want to stretch you out fireside so that I might peel away and examine all your layers. Slowly. One by one."

Her head lifted and a cool rush of air invaded the space between them. "Likewise." She pressed an open-mouthed kiss to the hollow of his throat. "But as we're trapped here on the roof, we might move to the bench and explore other options." Eyeing the rosy tips of her nipples, he stirred inside her, and she laughed, throaty and low. "Or we could stay here." She flexed her hips. "That works for me."

"Vixen." He caught her face in his hands and brushed a thumb over her swollen lips, grateful fate had landed them both on the same roof—chimney side—one particularly dark night.

Her fingers slid down his backside, urging him—

Crack.

A dull crunching sounded against a glass window pane. Their gazes caught, then turned toward the noise. A rusty skeet pigeon jerked and slipped upon the rooftop, dragging a broken wing as its internal programming insisted upon reaching the final, preprogrammed destination. Not far away, an overlarge black cat crouched, tail twitching.

"Is that… Sorcha?"

"It is." She sighed at the interruption. "It's rather a habit of hers, I'm afraid."

"That makes two wildcats on my roof." He grinned against her skin. "It appears we must postpone our activities. Work calls."

"Flaps," she amended, her lips curving upward as she tugged the two halves of his shirt together. "No worries about the message, she'll drag it inside in a moment."

He relaxed his grip on her hips, pulling free as he lowered her onto the rooftop and silently cursed the resilience of one particular mad scientist. "The constabulary prefers boots on the ground and the element of surprise—the better to read a guilty expression—and sees no reason to invest in maintaining a flock." A poor investment, his coin. The bobby had done no more than pocket it. "When forced to send a skeet pigeon, they snatch up the closest bird. One that is clearly no match for an interested feline." He tucked himself away as she drew her chemise back into place and reached for her bodice.

"Indeed. I, for one, want to look into Dr. Farquhar's eyes while I ask my questions." Anticipation lit a flame in her eyes. "Before we're done with him, I'll want to know who supplied him with a cat sìth. Fairy tale or not, such cats are rare and ought not be stolen away from their homes."

"Not only that, but I want to know who was funding his research. And why." He held her gaze, even when guilt urged him to look away. She needed to know. Now. "About our engagement—my father insisted upon a few slight alterations to our plans."

Chapter Thirteen

"Setting a date is not slight." Had her uncle known the Viscount Stafford would also insist upon a prompt ceremony? Without doubt. Foolish of her to act as if she would be free from society's expectations the moment she vacated her uncle's property. A touch of panic swirled in her stomach. Everything was happening so fast, and she was being pressured to make life-altering decisions without enough time to consider all the possible outcomes. A verbal promise was one thing, but a signature upon a marriage license? That was binding. "This is all very... rushed."

She tore her eyes away to focus upon the clockwork bird as it turned itself about and hopped toward the door of the aviary. Behind the skeet pigeon stalked Sorcha, alert and fully prepared to keep the contraption from taking wing. Colleen opened the door and snatched up the beady-eyed bird, focusing upon unfastening the message canister all while willing away the slight tremble of her fingers.

"I'm sorry." Nick took the still-twitching clockwork pigeon from her hands, smoothing its wing back into place and turning it off before setting it beside the others. "If you'd prefer, I can escort you to a hotel."

Sorcha, with the skeet pigeon no longer an item of interest, turned her back upon them with an air of nonchalance and returned to watch for a new victim.

"No." She pushed her worries aside, focusing upon another emotion that thrummed though her body: yearning. "Your family only wants what's best for you. As they should." Her own parents would have guarded and protected her so. She missed it. "I'm staying."

Nick stroked a finger down the side of her cheek. "If you change your mind..."

"I'm not opposed." Her heart tripped as she spoke the words. "But I won't walk blindly into such a commitment. Might we discuss expectations later... fireside?"

"Done." He dipped his head and pressed a soft kiss to her lips. "Make a list of your demands." A provocative smile curved his lips. "I look forward to experiencing your persuasive techniques."

Did he mean... Her mind began to consider various possibilities, rendering her mute. And slow. For Nick snatched the paper scroll from her fingers with a laugh. "But don't think I won't exploit your every weakness in return."

Grinning, she smacked his arm, then leaned close. "That trick will only work once."

"We'll see." He read the note aloud, his voice sobering.

Apologies, sir. Your man was removed from my custody without explanation. Carted away, while only semiconscious and muttering about hearts and worms. I objected and demanded an explanation from my supervisor, but was told the Queen's agents had no business interfering in private matters.

"Damn it." Nick crumpled the message in his fist.

"Private matters?" Colleen's eyebrows drew together. "Might it be time for your long, complicated story about Queen's agent's business?"

He pinched the bridge of his nose. "He's the missing connection, Dr. Farquhar."

"Missing being the operative term." Colleen crossed her arms. Ice crystalized on her next words. "I can't help if I don't have all the relevant details."

"My hunt for the cardio-pacing device began when a stray comment crossed my path. A laboratory technician glanced at MacWilliam's paper."

"The one I read?"

"One and the same. Though the technician couldn't recall details, he remembered that the Lister Institute had once considered hiring someone whose work had reached similar conclusions. That there'd been talk of constructing a device that might supersede or alter the automatic pacing of a heart. But that nothing had come of it."

Colleen wrapped her hand about his fist and squeezed.

"I took my questions to Lord Aldridge, a board member of the Lister Institute."

She drew in a deep breath as all became clear. "*That's* why you were in his study in the dead of night?"

Another nod. "I've no proof he's involved in anything. Nothing but the slightest of hesitations when I inquired about past cardiac electrophysiology applicants."

Hesitations could mean something—or nothing. But Nick's instincts had pointed him in the direction of decidedly suspicious research activity. "And, like a cat with a mouse, you couldn't stop toying with the idea."

He threw her a twisted smile, then opened his fist and caught her hand in his, lifting it to his lips. His eyes were two deep pools that might hide any number of secrets. "Would a business partner and fiancée agree that any secrets a Queen's agent shares are sacrosanct?"

Warmth spread through her chest, driving back the frost. "She would. Tell me what this has to do with Sorcha."

"We're not old enough to remember when it began, but there was a time when biologists scoffed at the mention of such creatures as kraken and pteryformes, but now—"

"They darken our skies and choke the Thames."

"And cryptozoology is an established science." He took a deep breath. "There are rumors of a shadow committee known as CEAP, the Committee for the Exploration of Anthropomorphic Peculiarities."

"Anthropomorphic," she repeated. "Ascribing human characteristics to nonhuman creatures?" The ice crept back.

"Selkies, for example. Seals who can turn into humans. There have been reports of them on the northwest coast of Scotland."

Her eyes widened. "Are you telling me *selkies* are real?"

"No. But neither am I saying they aren't. Someone else is tracking down those sightings." He drew her hand to his heart and caught her gaze. "Within CEAP are individuals who are also interested in humans with animal characteristics. Men who would like nothing better than to capture and study such humans with an eye toward exploiting their unique skills. They've no interest in protecting even the most basic of individual rights and are not to be trusted."

Humans with unique skills. "Such as myself," she whispered. A woman who might once have been burned at the stake for suspicions of cavorting with the devil beneath the moonlight. Colleen struggled to keep her breathing steady. That mad scientist had stared at her, not with fear, but with amazement. And far too much interest.

"If you keep working with me, if a member of this CEAP committee is watching, it may well draw his attention to—"

"My distinctive eyes," she spoke on a soft exhalation. Caged within her ribs, her heart began to pace. "My uncanny athletic abilities. But it's too late. Dr. Farquhar has already taken note of my eyes. That explains his spellbound stare before he turned tail and ran."

Nick swore.

Precious few cat sìth roamed the woods of her family's Scottish estate. The same could be said of the men, women and children who also possessed golden eyes. Sorcha had been snatched from the streets of London, but now that Dr. Farquhar had made the link from the cat sìth to her, it was only a matter of time until someone connected her to Craigieburn and its unique occupants.

Knees weak, she sank to the floor, leaning against the low wall at her back.

Nick crouched beside her. "Colleen?" Concern filled his voice, but throughout it threaded a note of curiosity. "I have to ask. Are there any truths to the myths surrounding the cat sìth?"

"Truths?" She took a deep breath and looked into the eyes of the only man to ever treat her as an equal. "I've the eyes of a cat—as did my father and his mother before him. A number of families who live on or near my land can name at least one member—past or present—with eyes such as mine."

"A tapetum lucidum, a reflective layer of the retina allowing an animal—"

She winced.

"Or the rare human," he squeezed her hand, "to see in the dark."

"In low light," she corrected. "A candle. A spark. A thin ray of moonlight. But there must be at least a glimmer light for them to reflect, for me to see."

"And your spectacles?" Nick gathered her to his side.

"Bright light tends to blur my vision, hence the tinted lenses." She waved a hand at the arch of glass above them. The rain had stopped and rivulets no longer ran down the glass panes in long streams. "But fog, clouds, rain. Soot. Anything that turns London bleak and gray brings the world into sharp focus."

"Enhancing your nighttime prowling abilities." He kissed the tip of her nose. "And what of Sorcha's devotion, do you have a unique attachment to her?"

"My familiar?" The term once used with lighthearted humor had lost its appeal.

"I didn't mean—"

"But perhaps it's true. Cat sìth are rumored to be drawn to those who share my eyes." She shrugged. "We've an affinity of sorts, an ability to understand their thoughts when others sometimes struggle. Nothing unnatural, but I can easily deduce from the sound of their cries, the tension or position of their bodies, the intensity of their stares, what they want or need. More so than most. What seems a bit exceptional is that a cat sìth who has attached itself to a human will carry out tasks on their behalf. Sorcha occasionally assists me. Fetching an item from a top shelf, for example. Yowling if another prowler approaches while I'm working. And she's learned to carry messages home to Isabella, a precaution in the event I ever needed help extracting myself from a sticky situation."

"And has that ever happened?"

She smiled. "Not yet."

"Nonetheless, we have circled back to the cat sìth and the origin of one particular myth."

"Or, in other words, am I a witch with nine lives?" Her laugh was rueful. "If only. I can't shape-shift, and I assure you, were I to fall from a rooftop or lose my grip on the cornice, I might land on my feet, but the impact would kill me, same as it would you." Sadness swept through her. "Death, after all, stole away my father, as it did my mother and every other life on that ill-fated train."

She'd told him once of the Tay Bridge disaster, when a violent storm had caused the bridge to collapse as a train ran across it, plunging all aboard into the river. Over seventy lives lost that night and not one survivor.

His thumb brushed a tear from her cheek. "I'm sorry."

"It's five years in the past." And was a tragedy that had altered the course of her life, but did not define her. "It may have stolen away my parents and my home, but I intend to recover the latter. I won't sit idly by if there's a threat to those like me, to the cat sìth."

"Spoken like a woman with sharp claws."

"Who is ready to prowl."

They both laughed.

Smack. Crunch. Four soft paws dropped back onto the slate roof, and Sorcha proudly carried in a freshly crushed skeet pigeon. The thin, overlapping plates of the bird's irises stared blankly, all input terminated. The cat sìth deposited the newly arrived mechanical bird at Colleen's feet. A gift. Dropping onto her haunches, the cat awaited the praise that was her due.

"Thank ye." As Colleen stroked her hand down the feline's sleek back, Sorcha closed her eyes, quite pleased with herself. "Your assistance is noted and appreciated."

Beside her, Nick smothered a snort and reached for the message canister.

"My turn." She batted his hand away to unfurl this new scroll sent to them by none other than her former employer, Mr. Witherspoon. "Cornelius Pierpont," she read the scrawled name aloud. "It sounds familiar, but I can't quite place it. Is he anyone you know?"

"No. I am, however, curious to discover if one particular individual might find it familiar." Nick stood and held out a hand. "A steam carriage collects Lord Aldridge from the Lister Institute promptly every evening. The rain has stopped, and his house—with the mews behind it—is only a few rooftops away, while beneath us lies nothing but trouble."

She let him pull her to her feet. "In the form of dress fittings, guest lists and menus."

"And my mother." Nick tugged her close. "Who is certain to be overenthusiastic to the point where she might already have browbeaten my father into procuring a special license."

Colleen lifted an eyebrow. "Not much chance of stretching out before a fire to conduct our... discussion?"

"Not without interruption." He lowered his mouth to hers, savoring a slow and sultry kiss that ended all too soon. "We'll have better luck as the midnight hour approaches. I've climbed that trellis too many times to count. Leave the window open. In the meantime, shall we interrogate Lord Aldridge?"

Chapter Fourteen

From the roof of the mews, Nick kept his eyes on the activity of the stable hands in the alleyway below them, waiting for Lord Aldridge's distinctive steam carriage to emerge from the carriage house. Clockwork horses mixed with the living beasts, an increasing rarity in the city. Most vehicles housed in the stables that backed against the terraced homes of Mayfair were of the steam-driven variety, though a few crank-wagons were kept close for the sake of convenience.

"You're certain Lord Aldridge won't have us thrown behind bars?" Skirts hiked, Colleen crouched beside him. As did Sorcha. The cat sìth had followed them across the rooftops. Not closely, but behind them. Occasionally in full view, but the feline often disappeared behind rooflines and chimneys and aviaries.

It was all he could do not to let his gaze wander to Colleen's ankles, to admire the boots snugged against her calves, to note the shape of her stockinged knees. *Later.* There would be time later to contemplate how easily the woman he hoped to call his wife transformed from a lady into a thief. Perhaps he ought not feel so deeply satisfied that she hadn't so much as hesitated when he suggested they sidestep propriety to invade a gentleman's private conveyance and demand answers, yet he was nonetheless.

"For the minor transgression of a brief ride in his steam carriage?" Nick smirked. "He ought to appreciate the discretion with which we approach this matter. He was asked—directly—by a Queen's agent to provide information that would inform a course of action—"

"To be fair, you were prying into matters for personal gain, not in the service of the Crown." She rolled her eyes. "Are you not his employee?"

"Debatable. The Lister Institute's board supervises the medical school and all research conducted under its roof. Some of us, including Lord Aldridge, also answer to the Duke of Avesbury. His will supersedes all."

She cocked an eyebrow. "Does it now? There seems to be some debate about that, given his daughter, Lady Amanda, somehow managed to enroll in medical school. And I hear Lady Olivia was involved recently in some kind of scandal? Though both seem happily married now."

"Indeed." He wasn't privy to all the details, but the whispers he'd heard were fascinating. "Marry me, and

I'll introduce you to them. Perhaps you can pry free their secrets."

She gave an amused snort. "Are you attempting to lure me to the altar with the promise of gossip?"

"Among other things. Have you ever thought of becoming a Queen's agent yourself? Not all of us are scientists." He winked. "I could be persuaded to put in a good word." She laughed, and it occurred to him he'd never asked. "What exactly precipitated your appearance in Lord Aldridge's study?"

"I snatched his daughter from the jaws of a harsh future. What?" She smacked his arm. "Don't look so disappointed. You know I worked to set wrongs to right, not to relieve the wealthy of their family jewels or stock holdings."

True. "An ethical sneak thief, so rare." He grinned. "You've never been tempted to snatch a necklace, a ring, stock certificates? By now you could have built a hoard that even a dragon would envy."

"Temptation at every turn. But no. None of my activities could ever be traced back to me."

"Ah, but they could," Nick disagreed. "If an interested party presented Mr. Witherspoon a number with enough zeros."

"With all I know?" Her lip curled. "I doubt it."

"Bedtime stories?" he teased.

"None that would lull you to sleep. The peerage, for all its talk of honor, has a dark underbelly."

That it did. "Not a problem," he said. "I've no real interest in using a bed for sleep. Not if you're in it."

Her cheeks flushed, and he debated teasing her with a few possibilities for passing the small hours of the night, but a belch of black smoke curled about the roof's edge, and a moment later, Lord Aldridge's steam carriage jerked and rattled onto the cobblestones. It was time.

"Ready?"

Her eyes—muted behind the dark lenses once again propped upon her nose—swept their surroundings once more. Satisfied, she nodded. "Let's go."

The scratch of a phosphorus match across the roof slate ignited a flame that he touched to the short wick of a loud firecracker. He lobbed it to the cobblestones below.

Bang!

A cloud of smoke billowed upward, and shouts rang out as stable hands turned about, searching for a miscreant guttersnipe who laughed at their expense. But he and Colleen had already leapt to the ground and slipped inside the earl's steam carriage.

None of them paid any attention to the cat who followed, disappearing beneath the vehicle, no doubt finding a handy cubby in which to secrete herself.

A well-appointed interior surrounded them. A Lucifer lamp for light. An iron box filled with hot coals for heat. And velvet upholstery for comfort. But even better was the view. Perched on the seat opposite him, Colleen unhooked her skirts from their hikes to smooth them over booted ankles. He squeezed his eyes shut and tried not to dwell on the memory of them wrapped about his hips, braced on the railing while he—

"Straighten that cravat of yours," she chided.

His eyes snapped open, the dream shattered.

Colleen's eyes glittered in the lamplight. She knew *exactly* where his mind had wandered. "And tuck in your shirt. Or Lord Aldridge will think we commandeered his carriage for entirely different purposes."

Such a plan inked itself onto his mind. A private carriage on the streets of London. He'd see it happen. And soon. "Not helping." His voice was strangled.

She laughed. "While I have to admit I rather like that hungry look on your face, you need to make yourself respectable."

While he did his best to repair his attire, his eyes were fixed upon Colleen's own transformation. It was like watching a butterfly crawl back into its cocoon. Loose locks of hair were ruthlessly pinned in place. Her spectacles adjusted upon the bridge of her nose. Elbow-length gloves—over which she carefully slid her ring—appeared from inside a pocket slit into her skirt. All of this followed by a small hat and a glinting hatpin to position it at a jaunty angle upon her sleek, dark hair. By the time the steam carriage jerked into motion, she looked every inch a lady while he—hatless, gloveless and rumpled—still very much resembled a profligate rogue.

"Tell me I'm the only one to ever watch such a transformation."

"The only *man*." She leaned forward to trail a single gloved fingertip down the edge of his face while the ghost of a tease clung to her lips. "Isabella, working to stall or divert my discovery, has caught glimpses."

Two days, he reflected as the steam carriage chuffed, clattered and swayed toward the Lister Institute, was not going to be enough time with this woman. He wanted to look into those golden eyes of hers and speak vows. "How set are you on returning to Scotland?"

She blinked at the sudden change in topics. "Extremely." Colleen glanced out the window, worrying the stone of the amber ring with her thumb. "I've long-neglected responsibilities to shoulder."

"The University of Aberdeen, complete with research facilities, is a short dirigible ride away from Craigieburn Castle," he answered, initiating negotiations.

"Are you offering to relocate?" She glanced at him from the corner of her eyes.

"I am. Not all Queen's agents are located in London year-round. If a position were to open, might there be any chance you would allow me to build a landing platform upon its roof?"

"Were there a roof to build upon." His mouth fell open while she recounted a story of irresponsible boys and a fiery crash—and the reason behind her participation in the obfuscation chain involving the rosewood box. "Now is the perfect time to incorporate such an upgrade. But are you certain you wish to leave London?"

"Do I detect a slight note of regret?" he asked. "Could it be you'll miss the city? Do you worry you might tire of land management and home repairs?"

She pressed her lips together. "It's true. The city, though overcrowded and grimy, is bursting with innovations and activity of all sorts."

An interesting tangle. "Married female agents are not unheard of. Many work on a case by case basis. Any interest?"

"You'd permit a wife of yours—"

He leapt across the space separating them to sit beside her. "Not permit." He growled in her ear before nipping the lobe. "Encourage."

Her breath caught. "Perhaps we could split our time between country and city."

"A perfect compromise." He nibbled at the corner of her jaw as he spoke.

Alas, the carriage chose that moment to rattle to a stop. Outside, there were thuds as feet landed upon the ground.

"I suppose that might depend upon the outcome of this interview. You might find yourself summarily dismissed from employ." She batted at his leg, and her voice took on a haughty tone. "Now place a respectable distance between us, that I might cling to the few remaining shreds of my reputation." As the carriage door swung open, Colleen folded her hands and dropped her gaze, once again assuming the mantle of the demure, lusterless young lady she was anything but.

Nick drew himself straighter. He was about to step onto thin ice with little knowledge of what clawed tentacles might lurk beneath, ready to snag his career at Lister Institute into an abyss from which he might not escape.

"Torrington?" Lord Aldridge gaped for a brief moment before his bushy eyebrows slammed down. He pointed a silver-capped walking stick at Nick. "What cause have you to invade my carriage? If it's about that—" He caught sight of Colleen and recoiled. "You."

Interesting.

"And you would criticize my manners?" Nick reproached. "May I presume a prior acquaintance with Lady Stewart?"

Lord Aldridge pressed his lips into a flat, bloodless line.

"Join us," Nick waved, inviting the man into his own vehicle. "We need to discuss the whereabouts of one Dr. Farquhar."

"Sir?" The guard holding the door—for that was his role despite his braid-embroidered livery—possessed an unusual amount of muscle. A single word from Lord Aldridge and he would empty the carriage of uninvited guests.

His graying mustache twitched. Lord Aldridge knew something. "No worries," he told his guard before climbing into the carriage. The ease of his movements suggested a wiry strength, identifying his walking stick as a weapon, not a support.

The door closed behind them and, a moment later, the carriage lurched into movement.

"The scientist is mad," Lord Aldridge stated. "His whereabouts do not concern me."

"And yet he might be the only hope of my sister surviving her third decade. Would you decline to answer my questions knowing that you might deprive an infant of her mother?"

"You'd let a mad man experiment upon your own sister?" Lord Aldridge growled back through clenched teeth. "Like as not, he'd kill her."

"Genius is often mistaken for insanity," Nick countered. "I *am* a trained physician and scientist, capable of evaluating any treatment he's developed. He was in custody not two hours ago. I'd prefer not to cause a scene at the local station house, but if he's my only lead..."

Not for the first time, Lord Aldridge's gaze darted to Colleen who sat still and silent beside him. "Is it?"

Telling, that glance. Had it to do with the reason she'd been in his study, a fact he didn't care to hear spoken aloud? Or was there yet more?

"I'm not here on behalf of Witherspoon and Associates, my lord. Blackmail is not a service he provides."

Nick snorted. He'd beg to disagree.

But Colleen's voice continued, eerily calm and professional. "I would, however, consider it a personal favor were you to provide us with information about Dr. Farquhar. A favor you might call upon should your—shall we say—willful daughter fall prey to any *further* indiscretions."

Oh? Was Lady Sophia not quite the demure debutant she appeared? Had she been caught with a man? Impressed with the currency Colleen offered, Nick watched the exchange, pride swelling in his chest.

"Done." The lord snapped up the bait all too quickly. Was anyone in the *ton* as they seemed? Certainly not

Lady Sophia's father, for intensity darkened his gaze. "A few years past, the board offered Dr. Farquhar a research position despite my concerns about his mental stability." His gaze shifted to Nick. "Documents were drawn up. Laboratory space was assigned. But he declined in favor of private funding." Lord Aldridge narrowed his eyes. "He threw away a promising career to chase after feral cats."

Colleen stiffened, then carefully framed her question. "What have feral cats to do with studies of the heart?"

"An excellent question, Lady Stewart." Sarcasm laced his voice. "Some are rumored to have nine lives. Perhaps that makes them a more robust experimental subject?"

All vestiges of good humor burned away as Nick scowled. "You knew of his connection to a shadow board and said nothing? Knowing my role as a Queen's agent, knowing the smallest of connections sometimes matter most?"

"Your questions were of a personal bent. It was time you set aside your futile pursuits to focus on your career. And how dare you bring *her* into this," Lord Aldridge hissed. "Such information is only for the ears of—"

"I've also informed her about the existence of CEAP." Nick leaned forward. "Her involvement is directly relevant. My personal concerns and the Crown's interests are one and the same. Tell me—us—what you know." Had Lord Aldridge seen fit to share, Dr. Farquhar's activities might have been unearthed months ago.

Lord Aldridge turned his glare upon Colleen. "I always wondered if your uncle's ostensible acceptance of you in his household possessed a mercenary bent."

Unhooking the wire of her spectacles from behind one ear, she tugged them free and tipped her chin upward in challenge. Her eyes caught the light of the Lucifer lamp affixed to the carriage wall and flashed a brilliant green-gold.

"Impressive, my dear," he commented, his voice bland, for after five years in London Colleen's unusual eyes surprised no one in the *ton*. "But I'm not prey to such superstitions. Animals shape-shifting to take human form is a ridiculous proposition. As is the reverse. Stuff and nonsense. Now, concerning your eyes, were one to propose a hypothesis involving descent with modification as an adaptation to a more nocturnal environment, we might be able to apply scientific reasoning to discuss the possibilities by which such an unusual feature might arise."

His words—highbrow and clipped—were betrayed by a white-knuckled grip upon his cane, as if he feared the docile Lady Stewart might lunge without warning. A claw to the cravat? A bite to the neck? Yes, she was entirely capable of such actions, but as her fiancé, he would have to insist she confine such activities to one man.

"Don't dodge the question," Nick said. "Did Dr. Farquhar's interests catch the attention of anyone suspected to be a member of CEAP?"

The gentleman's gaze did not waver, but stayed locked upon Colleen. "Despite efforts to uncover these reputed shadow committees, no such organizations have yet been found to exist. As to rogue scientists managing something resembling loose organization?" Lord Aldridge offered Colleen a smile brimming with pity. "When your uncle became your guardian, the trappings of his lifestyle improved. Tell me, how much do you know about the goings-on at your estate?"

"It's been some five years since I have set foot upon Scottish soil. I do, however, exchange frequent correspondence with my estate manager who—" Colleen's mouth snapped shut. Anger vibrated off her in waves.

Eyebrows lifted, Lord Aldridge finished. "Makes frequent requests for funds? My dear, it appears Lord Maynard has fashioned himself a villain while ostensibly acting as a guardian." He turned his attention back to Nick. "If you're looking to connect Dr. Farquhar, feral cats, and Lady Stewart to a purported shadow committee, may I offer advice as old as dirt? Follow the money." He raised his cane and thumped upon the roof, indicating their interview had reached an end. The steam carriage came to a stop. "Be careful not to misstep, Torrington. Lord Maynard has extensive connections."

Nick refused to be dismissed. "One last question."

Lord Aldridge sighed heavily. "One."

"We need to speak with one Cornelius Pierpont. Can you provide an introduction?"

"No. I've never heard of the man." The carriage door swung open. From the tone of his voice, Lord Aldridge was clearly at the end of his rope. "Out. Both of you."

Chapter Fifteen

Reeling from Lord Aldridge's revelations, Colleen gripped Nick's arm as they approached his family's townhome. Though she wished to storm her uncle's study and demand answers, unsubstantiated accusations and ravings about fairy cats would see her delivered to the mad house.

Had her uncle been abusing his position as her trustee to turn a profit? If so, then her estate manager, Watts, was corrupt. He'd been sending her reports for years, and it made her ill to think how many thousands of pounds she had transferred into his care. Had he pocketed the money? Funneled it back to her uncle? What was the true state of Craigieburn and its lands? Was the roof truly damaged, or was it a ruse designed to keep her dashing about the shadows of London, turning a profit with her skills? *Gah!* If so, then all these years he'd *known* she was a sneak thief.

Worse still, had he used those earnings to fund a mad man's research? Had her uncle himself placed Sorcha in Dr. Farquhar's hands? She recalled the charred bodies in the burned-out basement laboratory. Exactly how many other cat sìth had been sacrificed to this lunacy? Did cryptid hunters roam her land, unchallenged, collecting the cats to sell to others who believed them capable of magic? And what of those men, women and children who possessed golden eyes? Might such attention incite a modern witch hunt?

Bilious twistings escaped the pit of her stomach and spread upward, constricting her throat.

Not that the repercussions ended there. Though the imprisonment and torment of cat sìth made her blood boil, any good that might have come of it—a possible treatment for heart block—had slipped through her own fingers.

"I'm of a mind to gather a few supplies and head directly to your uncle's door," Nick said.

"As am I." Colleen entertained a brief fantasy of doing exactly that. With Nick at her side, they could— She shook her head. "But he won't tell you anything, and he certainly won't admit to any underhanded dealings." Her feet slowed. "There is, however, a dinner party he's attending this evening."

"You think he's involved."

"I do. In so many ways."

"And you want to break into his home, his study, and rifle through his papers for answers and evidence. Before we confront him about Dr. Farquhar's whereabouts. Properly, over tea and whisky. And perhaps the sights of my TTX pistol."

"You know me so well." She managed a faint smile. The brilliant orange sun hung low over London, casting the jagged line of rooftops into a dark profile and setting the low-hanging clouds aglow. Chimney pots spouted smoke, warming homes as the city quieted, hunkering down for the night. "I'll contact Isabella, make certain she and my uncle still plan to attend the dinner party. I'm certain they do. He'll want to keep up appearances."

His face was all business, yet she knew revenge and justice lurked beneath the surface. "A few hours from now, then, we'll go. Together."

"Agreed." They stopped upon the pavement before the entrance of his family townhome. A few feet behind them, Sorcha brushed against a scrolled iron railing, watching. Lights blazed in every window. Not once had Colleen left by roof to return by door, lest she find herself floundering for an explanation before her uncle. Not, apparently, that it had mattered.

She pulled free her dark spectacles and perched them upon her nose.

"No worries." Nick led her up the stairs. "They're accustomed to my odd comings and goings. They'll adjust to the cat."

The door swung open. Hopsworth lifted haughty wire eyebrows, but said nothing as they entered the foyer, an overlarge black cat trailing in their wake.

"Where have the two of you been?" Lady Stafford cried as she rushed down the staircase and past Hopsworth, the train of her shimmering gold tea gown rustling as it swept behind her. Ruffles edged in daring black lace framed her face, circled her wrists, and cascaded to the floor. "No—" She lifted a hand, palm outward. "I've changed my mind. *Do not* tell me what you've been about. It will only color my nightmares. Nicholas, you look a fright. Please change into more appropriate attire. Lady Stewart," the viscountess held out her arm, waggling her fingers, "do come with me. I managed to persuade the modiste with the loosest tongue in all of London to abandon her other clients and transport her wares to our parlor, but we must make haste if we're to have a gown ready in four days' time."

Colleen blinked at the rush of words.

"Mother—" Nick objected.

"I'm aware of the terms and conditions of your fiancée's presence, Nicholas," the viscountess said. "Wedding or not, maintaining appearances means providing society with the finer details of Lady Stewart's wedding preparations, down to the beads upon her bodice and the embroidery upon her sleeves. Invitations must be engraved. A wedding breakfast planned. And so on and so forth."

"Your mother is correct." Colleen found her voice. "A closely chaperoned young woman in the throes of frantic wedding plans is unlikely to have time for other pursuits." She cast him a significant glance. There were several hours before her uncle's house would grow quiet.

"While we coo over silk and lace, you might best use the time to investigate the positions of other players upon the board."

Nick hesitated. Furrows of worry lined his brow. "There are individuals I must contact. You've no objections if I leave you in my mother's care?"

"None." On the contrary. Lady Stafford presented a curious mix of co-conspirator and managing mother, and Colleen was curious about which direction the balance tipped.

Within minutes, she stood upon a stool in her undergarments while a seamstress affecting a French accent poked, prodded and measured, calling orders to her two young assistants while eyeing Sorcha—who crouched before the fireplace, front paws tucked beneath the flare of white upon her chest—with deep mistrust. When cats and rustling cloth mixed, the fabric was always trounced.

"Is it possible to remove *le chat noir*?"

"Entirely possible," Colleen answered, stepping down. En route to the cat sìth, she snatched up a stray bit of string, tied three knots—a code—then looped it about Sorcha's neck as she carried the feline to the window. "Tae Isabella," Colleen whispered. *To Isabella.* Then cracked the window. "A sasser o cream fin ye return." *A saucer of cream when you return.*

With a twitch of her whiskers, the cat sìth leapt free.

She turned to find two partially finished gowns held up for her approval. "Perhaps the silk moiré?" It rippled and flowed beautifully beneath the flickering gaslight.

"An excellent choice, my lady," the seamstress agreed. Pins and needles flew, securing swaths of heavy silk about her hips, slipping sleeves with raw edges over her arms while her assistant's needle flashed as she basted panels together. Moments later, a mirror was placed before her, and the modiste gathered her assistants and moved to the far end of the room, giving their patron and her future daughter-in-law a moment's privacy.

Lifting a shaking hand to her chest, Colleen touched a row of filigree-set amber buttons hastily tacked in place to embellish the simple, unfinished bodice. Sparks of light flashed off the stone inclusions embedded in the ancient resin.

"They match the ring." First an heirloom of sentimental value, now this. The thought and consideration Nick and his mother had showered upon her was almost too much. She blinked back the tears that threatened.

"And your eyes." Anna's voice was breathy. Waif-thin and pale, she made her way across the room. Behind her, an attendant wheeled the bulky, quietly-humming, yet truly terrifying machine into the room, doing her best to be unobtrusive. The name of the device, P.C. Hutchinson's Magneto-Shock Machine, was embossed across its side. Did Anna go nowhere without it? Anna and her mother shared a conspiratorial look. "What are the odds you'll stand with my brother before clergy?"

Colleen's mouth opened. Then closed. This was no hastily arranged fitting. It was a planned ambush.

"From the look upon her face?" Lady Stafford's smile was rather smug. "Higher than I'd hoped. Nicholas brought her home dusty and rumpled, but smiling. Given those boots laced to her knees and the knife they *almost* conceal, I think my son might finally have found his match."

"Agreed," Anna said. "Only a wife predisposed to similar clandestine activities will ever truly understand him."

Colleen's heart constricted. Never could she have predicted such a warm welcome. She'd reconciled herself to abandoning her career and returning alone to Craigieburn, but with Nick waving temptation before her in all its forms, she was reassessing her decision. Thoughts of becoming his wife, of becoming a member of his family filled her with warmth and happiness. "How long ago did he ask for his grandmother's ring?"

"Months ago, before his most recent, unexpected disappearance." Nick's mother clasped her hands to her chest. "I do hope you'll forgive our attempts to convince you to become a more permanent member of our family."

The modiste cleared her throat, impatient.

"Ah, we mustn't keep her waiting." The viscountess winked. "She's a gown to finish and rumors to spread."

Released from the heavy fabric and handed a robe, Colleen pulled Anna aside while the seamstress consulted with the Lady Stafford about details such as seed pearls and knife pleats and the necessity of trim. Choices she was happy to cede to another.

"I can't believe this is happening," Colleen murmured. It was a struggle to follow the various strings knotted together in her mind. A welcome marriage proposal. A quest to improve Anna's declining health. The discovery of a mad scientist with designs upon cat sìth. The manipulations and involvement of her uncle.

"And why not?" Anna pressed a hand to Colleen's arm. "Admittedly, I do not often attend *ton* events, but did you think I never noticed the dances you and my brother shared?"

"It could have been no more than pity for a dull wallflower in a plain vase set high upon a dusty shelf." Their first dance had been one shared for mutual convenience, an exercise in moving from one point to another in a manner least likely to draw comment.

"Perhaps at first." Anna tipped her head. "But I've long suspected you might share more than dances."

As they had. But only out of the public eye and well-hidden in the shadows. A blush crept across her cheeks.

"Ever since that first waltz, every woman we've pushed, shoved or dragged into his path has been summarily rejected. So if you think we'll let you escape without a fight—"

"There are, of course, complications," Colleen interrupted even as she fought back a smile. "I've my own responsibilities—and desires—that lay in Scotland. And your brother has his. To the Crown, to—"

"Me," Anna finished on a sigh. "He can be a fool, my brother. He drives himself too hard and neglects his own interests. I know very well he's on a quest to heal my heart, to fix what he did not break. I appreciate his efforts. I truly do, but he should not put the entirety of his life on hold."

"Listen," Colleen caught up Anna's cool, gaunt hands, unwilling to admit aloud that Nick's devotion to his sister might well drive a wedge between them no matter how hard they worked to find middle ground. Until they located Dr. Farquhar, Cornelius Pierpont and the contents of a certain rosewood box, deciding upon their future would have to wait.

"I can't and won't make you promises about the likelihood that the device we seek—one I've yet to lay eyes upon—will offer you any solutions. But we will find it." She thought of Sorcha locked in a cage. Of the morbid contents within the other wire cages of Dr. Farquhar's charred laboratory. Was it possible another cat sìth had undergone some kind of testing *and survived*? "If there's any hope of its success, we'll do our best to— Anna?"

Anna crumpled to the floor, and Colleen lunged, managing to catch her about the waist, softening an otherwise hard landing. "Help!" she cried.

"Anna!" The viscountess dropped a length of fabric as both she and the attendant nurse rushed forward to drop to their knees besides Anna's convulsing form.

The nurse lifted her wrist. "Respiration steady. Pulse absent." Standing, the nurse pressed a pocket watch into Lady Stafford's hand. "Mark the time. Three minutes, no more." She hurried back toward P.C. Hutchinson's Magneto-Shock Machine, flipping a lever that made the contraption hum and crackle as she pushed it to Anna's side.

"Fifteen seconds." The viscountess encircled her daughter's wrist, searching for a pulse. A tear ran down her cheek.

In two minutes and forty-five seconds they would… what?

Her own heart hammering against her ribcage, Colleen cradled Anna's head while the nurse ripped open the loose bodice fitted about her narrow chest and swiftly unbuttoned the camisole that lay beneath, exposing the pale expanse of her torso to begin chest compressions.

"Thirty." The viscountess's breaths came in short bursts. Her face was ashen and bloodless as she detached a sharp and glinting probe from the instrument's side.

Every instinct screamed at Colleen to stop this madness. But Anna herself—and her mother and Nick—must approve, for they'd installed both the nurse and the device.

A treatment acceptable only in the face of certain death.

"Forty-five." A tear splashed onto the viscountess's cheek.

The whine from the device grew louder.

Crack! Colleen jumped as a blinding flash of white light arced between the point of the metal rod and the device itself. The machine fell silent. A puff of acrid smoke rose from its innards.

Lady Harrington let out a deep wail and began to frantically bang on the device, flipping switches and spinning dials. But to no avail.

~~~
~~~

While Colleen was swept up the stairs and into a room filled with flowing lengths of white silk, lace and other assorted trims, Nick fled into the study where he scratched out a quick note to Jackson requesting help. Friend and fellow agent, the man was tasked with keeping an eye on foreigners looking to turn a profit by absconding with British ingenuity. Perhaps Cornelius Pierpont was one such individual. Moreover, Jackson was a damned good agent. They'd worked together in the past and, given today's revelations, backup would be welcome, particularly if he and Colleen found hard evidence upon examining the contents of her uncle's safe. He dashed up the stairs to the aviary—his new favorite location—and sent the message on its way.

Task done, he tugged his pocket watch from his waistcoat. Seven o'clock. Given Colleen's presence, would his family insist upon a formal evening meal? Months of flirtation had crystalized into the oddest of courtships, and he hated to leave her in his family's clutches for even a short length of time while their future was still on uncertain ground. He didn't keep much clothing in his old wardrobe, but he'd make do rather than return to his bachelor quarters.

He started down the stairs toward his old room.

Distress at Lord Aldridge's revelations that her uncle and estate might well fund Dr. Farquhar's studies of the cat sìth had tensed Colleen's supple frame and stiffened her resolve to see their quest through to the finish line. Cryptid hunters were a blight upon their nation's natural resources and, if they'd been turned loose at Craigieburn, there was no telling the damage her uncle had wrought upon her inheritance and its inhabitants. The anger such thoughts engendered curled his hands into fists, ones which he'd like nothing better than to wrap around the man's throat. He would see the man pay. Any connection to CEAP needed to be severed and quickly, before men without inconvenient moral scruples used the existence of cat sìth as an excuse to study human oddities in the name of scientific advancement. With her reflective eyes, Colleen—and others like her—might well end up as unwilling research subjects. He'd not let that happen, not to any of them.

As his list of tasks grew longer, they'd begun to circle back upon each other, winding tighter with each revelation. Save his sister. Assist the woman he wished to marry. Locate a mad scientist and his device. Shut down a shadow committee by ripping control of his fiancée's estate from her guardian's hands. All while wondering at the ethics of employing a life-saving contraption that tainted money had financed.

Life had grown immeasurably complicated these past few days.

Screams echoed up the stairwell. Shouts followed. As he ran down the steps, he could feel the hum of electricity as P.C. Hutchinson's Magneto-Shock Machine came to life. A loud *pop* sounded and his mother cried out. He burst into the parlor, trampling silk in his rush to reach his sister's side where the nurse administered percussive pacing and chest compressions.

Anna's eyes flew open and she dragged in a great, horrible and stertorous breath. Her face flushed red as blood began to flow through her veins and arteries, her heart once again condescending to continue its labors.

"It happened again?" his sister whispered, staring up at her brother.

"It did, darling." His mother wrapped her arms about her daughter, ignoring the tears that still trickled over her cheeks. "For about one minute and thirty seconds."

The nurse nodded, confirming his worst fears. "And the device short-circuited. I'll send for the technician."

Colleen, eyes wide, looked at him.

"Longer than before." He answered her unspoken question as the sound of his own heartbeat thrashing in his ears faded.

"She'll recover?" Colleen's voice was a whisper.

He nodded. *This time.*

Only then did he glance at the Magneto-Shock Machine. A faint wisp of smoke rose from deep inside its mechanisms. So much for its usefulness. He was almost grateful, and yet, had his sister not revived, a functioning device—horrible though it was—might well have saved her.

"How are you feeling?" he asked, turning his attention to his sister, ever careful to maintain a calm, clinical pretense after each attack, watching closely as color returned to her face.

"Fine." She rubbed her chest. There would be bruises. "Mostly."

"Is there anything more that can be done?" Colleen pushed a loose lock of hair behind her ear with a shaking hand.

He shook his head. "These episodes come on without warning and don't seem to cluster, though she'll be watched closely."

"As always," Anna sighed. She threw Colleen a wan smile. "Privacy is in short supply when your heart can't be relied upon."

"It's necessary," he commented. "Come. I'll carry you to bed."

"In the nursery," Anna insisted.

Nick knew better than to argue that point. He scooped his sister into his arms and turned to leave the room. "Where you will let me listen to your heart." To be certain he could detect no further progression of the damage. He gave Colleen a speaking look. "Don't... take any actions without me."

"I'll wait," Colleen assured him. "In your—my—room."

Where there was a fire, a bed, and a few hours until they could take once more to the roofs.

Anna snickered softly. "Convenient," she muttered under her breath, just loud enough for her brother to hear.

He gave her arm a pinch. "Hush, lest I accidentally drop you." He wouldn't, but light-hearted sibling sparring always brought a grin to her face.

"Let me see the modiste out." His mother pressed a kiss to Anna's cheek. "I'll be with you directly."

"Of course." As their mother hurried to the flustered dressmaker and her assistants, Anna dropped her head against Nick's chest. "I'll be fine. Well, as fine as I ever am. I'll feel even better if the 'actions' you have planned for tonight have to do with that miracle mentioned earlier?"

"They do." If they didn't find answers inside Lord Maynard's safe, he'd hunt the man down himself and drag forth the whereabouts of Dr. Farquhar in a most ungentlemanly manner. "We've a new lead to chase down."

"Progress?" Her eyes held a cautious hope.

"Perhaps," he warned.

"I won't keep him long." Anna caught Colleen by the sleeve of her dressing gown. "There's nothing he can do that my nurse isn't equally capable of—save hunt down whichever scientist is jealously guarding this secret you seek. Promise you'll come visit me tomorrow and tell stories about your toe-curling adventures?"

"They're more of a scandalous nature." Colleen gave his sister a wink. "I can't—and won't—tell you *all* the details, but you *might* ask me questions about the gossip rags, and we'll see what I can confirm or deny."

"Excellent." His sister's cheeks were pale, but maintaining a healthy glow. "I've a full year of missed ballroom scandals to inquire about." She released Colleen. "Let's go, brother."

Colleen turned away to gather her things, and Nick began the climb to the nursery. "I hate to leave you so soon after an attack."

"But you will," Anna answered him. "Go find this device you've been carrying on about and, while you're at it, convince Lady Stewart to marry you. I'd like nothing more than to attend your wedding before—"

"Don't say it," Nick stopped her, frowning. "I've every confidence you will live to hold your grandchildren."

She slapped him lightly on the chest. "So long as it's not at the expense of being able to hold your own. You have an hour, no more, before I toss you from the nursery."

Chapter Sixteen

Colleen arrived at her—Nick's—door to find a small boy bent at the waist and peering through the keyhole while balancing a tray.

"Something of interest?" she asked.

He jumped backward, nearly upsetting the saucer of milk, and looked up at her with wide eyes. "That's a really large, *black* cat. Aren't black cats supposed to be bad luck?"

"Only if you treat them badly," she said. "But since you come bearing food, she'll likely be predisposed in your favor. Would you like to meet Sorcha?"

"It's yours?" The boy gaped.

"Some might say so, but one never *owns* a cat." Colleen opened the door while the child lifted the tray. "*She* chose *me*. Sorcha, meet—" She raised an eyebrow.

"Robby," the boy supplied, setting down the tray.

"Hold your hand out for her to sniff."

Tail held high, Sorcha strolled over. Though her attention was focused upon dinner, the feline recognized an in-house ally, permitting Robby to run his hand over her back as she lapped up the cream.

"There's a string about her neck," he said, examining the twine. "And a message!" His eyes blinked up at her. "You trained a *cat*?"

Trained? No. Frequently bribed was a more appropriate description. But none of the feral cats that prowled the streets of London could ever be coaxed to her aid, making the cat sìth a far superior species. "Sorcha is no ordinary feline." She held out her hand, and he dropped the paper scroll into her palm.

She unfurled Isabella's message.

Our evening proceeds according to plan, but take every precaution. After your departure, your uncle was called away on urgent business. He returned white-faced and shaking with rage. I suffered a pointed stare of suspicion that bodes nothing but ill. Tonight, we most both walk upon eggshells.

Had her uncle been the one to free Dr. Farquhar from his prison cell? Try as she might, Colleen could not imagine him passing down the halls of a station house. No, one of his minions would have been sent to fetch the mad scientist.

But he *would* know where the man had been deposited.

And might well know this Cornelius Pierpont. The name continued to niggle at her mind. She'd heard it before. Somewhere.

"Are you going to save Lady Anna?" Robby broke into her thoughts.

"We're going to do all we can, starting later tonight." She hesitated, then decided this interval of time must not be squandered. "Can I count upon you to wake me in two hours' time? With a tea tray fit for a human?"

He jumped up. "Anything to support the mission." Grinning, the boy exited the room.

Though her nerves were still wound tight—would she ever forget such a moment of watching a woman's heart stop… then start again as if nothing at all was amiss?—she could feel the edge of exhaustion dulling her mind, her reflexes. The rest of the household would be doting upon Anna, as they should. She looked at the mattress with longing. A short nap, a light tea, and she'd be ready to hunt down Cornelius Pierpont and the contents of a particular rosewood box. A task that needed to be accomplished tonight. Ferreting out Dr. Farquhar's location was another goal, though wading through his madness to extract the specifications of the device was a far less appealing—though potentially viable—option.

Alone, Colleen unlaced her boots and tugged them from her feet. There was no point in unlacing a corset only to struggle with it in a few hours. She pulled a few pins from her hair, letting it tumble free. Tossing the dressing gown aside, she crawled beneath the covers and lay her head down upon the soft pillow with a sigh.

Years of late nights had trained her to sink swiftly into a deep sleep. In moments sweet oblivion claimed her.

Some time later, the mattress shifted. A displacement of far more weight than that of an overlarge cat. Her heart slammed against her chest and her eyes flew open, every nerve ending alive and alert.

“Shh.” Nick’s voice was a whisper as he stretched out beside her atop the covers wearing nothing but his trousers and shirtsleeves. “Go back to sleep.”

Unlikely. Not when the tips of her fingers were tingling with the desire to touch the rough stubble that had begun to shadow his face. Or while her elevated pulse flooded her body with heat and desire. Even his scent teased, leather and spice and something decidedly male.

With so many other bedrooms from which he might choose, he’d come to her. Her heart flipped in her chest, and her mind agreed: sleep was not what he had in mind. Still, she willed herself motionless for she’d not deprive Nick of his own chance for rest. Except his eyes didn’t close. Instead, after several long minutes, they still stared at the ceiling while heavy thoughts weighed down his mind.

“How is your sister?” She rolled onto her side, propping her head upon her hand.

“Resting.” He sighed. “Save for the trauma of the attack itself, there is little in the way of aftereffects, save a bit of fatigue.”

"With little to be done save fret and worry about when the next will occur and what the outcome will be?" The clock upon the mantle informed her there was plenty of time yet before her aunt and uncle would depart from their townhome.

"In a nutshell." He rolled to face her, and a faint, suggestive gleam kindled in his eyes. "The door is locked." He winked. "And I've clean shirts in the wardrobe."

"Oh?" She let a knowing smile touch her lips. "And you wish for me to… help you dress?"

"I rather thought you might help me undress. It's such an inconvenience to work these small buttons of my shirt by myself. What with the door locked, there's no one else to assist."

Colleen pushed herself upright, tossed aside the covers, and reached to pop free the button directly beneath his chin. "Such troublesome things, buttons." Her mouth watered at the sight of the hollow of his neck. She freed another button and trailed a fingertip over the dark curls of hair she'd exposed before unfastening a third, a fourth.

A rumble of approval sounded deep in his chest. "They are."

"If I'm to set myself to such an onerous task, you must loosen my laces. I find this task takes my breath away." The last buttons fell free and she spread the placket wide. Leaning forward, she ran her palm over the firm muscles of his chest that flexed beneath her touch, then traced the trail of hair leading downward between the ridges of his stomach. Her finger caught at his waistband. "You're certain you only wish to change your shirt? These trousers?" She clucked, her hand hovering above the obvious bulge of his erection. "They're a bit... dirty."

"So they are." His hands fell on her shoulders and pulled, dropping her crosswise over his bare chest and crushing her breasts against him. Only a wisp of silk and an underbust corset separated them. Too much. She kissed the hollow of his throat while his frantic fingers worked the laces of her corset until it fell loose. "Sit back, Colleen, and extricate yourself from that garment so that I can see you breathe freely."

Laughing, she pushed back onto her knees to unhook the corset and toss it aside. "And?" She pulled her chemise over her head.

The look he gave her sent a shiver down her spine.

"Perfect." His hand ran up the side of her ribcage until it came to rest, cupping her breast. "In every way." His thumb brushed over its tip, slow and languid, sending a new flood of warmth between her legs. "But come closer. Finish what you proposed to start."

"Enjoying all the attention, are you?"

"And the view." His eyes filled with a gratifying, lust-crazed interest as his hands fell to her hips, urging her closer.

Bare, save for her stockings, she straddled him and leaned forward to lightly kiss his lips, dragging the sensitive tips of her nipples over the coarse hairs that sprinkled his chest. Her own breath caught as fire crawled across her skin.

He groaned and opened his mouth, inviting her in.

"Not yet." She nipped at his lip and backed away, swatting at his wandering hands to focus upon a task that grew more urgent by the minute. She caught at his waistband, unfastening its closure.

"Torture?" He all but strangled on the word. "Is that what you have planned?"

"A touch." Nick began to sit upright, but she pushed him back onto the pillow. "This time, I'm in charge. Stay." Crawling backward, she dragged his trousers to his knees. A most impressive erection sprang free.

Reversing course, she slid her hands up the firm, strong muscles of his legs. As she reached their apex, she dipped her head to taste the hard length of his cock, reveling in the faint saltiness that met her tongue.

Nick's fingers threaded into her hair as if he would guide her to the very tip of his erection. She obliged, pulling as much of his length into her mouth as she could manage, toying with him, enjoying the groan that tore free from his lungs.

But this was not how she intended to finish what he'd started. Not today. Crawling back up the bed, she pulled open his bedside drawer, plucking forth a sheath and dropping it on his chest. "Suit up."

He grinned, tearing the paper and covering himself. "Caught that move earlier?"

"You'll find it's hard to hide anything from me." Once again, she straddled him, guiding the thick, blunt tip of his cock to her weeping entrance. Then, ever so slowly, she sank onto him, inch by sweet inch as he stretched her, filling her completely with a glorious pressure. "Aether," she breathed. He was so perfect. Too perfect.

He nudged upward, and she gasped as his hips pressed snug to hers.

She began to rock her hips, shifting him inside her ever so slightly as a delicious tension built while hundreds of thousands of nerves all cried out at the delightful friction. She met his gaze and saw wonder and lust and something she thought might be love all twisting and surging across his face.

Aether, she'd lost more than a small piece of her heart to this man.

"Kiss me, Colleen," Nick pleaded.

And she fell forward, dropping her hands to his shoulders and sliding them beneath the linen of his shirt. Parting her lips, she tangled her tongue with his, all while the slow motion of their hips continued their sensual dance. Push, pull. Push, pull.

Until she needed more. His fingers tightened on her hips as he tore his mouth away, giving voice to the same thoughts that ran through her head. "Harder," he begged. "Please."

Colleen rose up onto her knees, letting him all but slip free. Then dropped as he rose, thrusting deep into her. She mewled her pleasure aloud as his fingers dug into her flesh pushing her away, then pulling her tight against his hips. "Is this what you want?"

"Yes," she cried, clutching his shoulders and spreading her thighs wider even as she rose for the next fall. "More!"

Nick thrust harder still.

Again and again their hips slapped together as coils of pleasure wound themselves tight. "Come for me, Colleen."

Already teetering on the edge, his words sent a frisson of electricity arcing through her body, and she threw her head backward, crying out her pleasure. Nick stiffened and surged upward, slamming into her as he yelled his own release.

As the world about them once again came into focus, she collapsed onto his chest. He wrapped his arms about her waist. "Next time," his voice was husky, "all the clothes come off."

"All," she promised, laughing softly against his neck as her stockinged feet brushed over his trouser-clad calves. Wondrously boneless, she rolled free.

~~~

How he could still move after such amazing sex, Nick was uncertain. But he managed to clean himself, then shuck the remainder of his clothing before crawling back onto the bed and gathering Colleen close. He pulled the blanket over them both, wondering at how he'd managed to fall head over boots in love with such an amazing woman. "Now," he began, "about our future." He lifted her amber-clad hand to his mouth and pressed a kiss to the inside of her wrist. "Have you given any thought to becoming a Queen's agent? I've a contact, a married
~~~

woman, who might provide you with insight that I cannot if you'd like to speak with her."

"I'd like that." Brushing a lock of hair from her face, Colleen drew breath. "While you were with Anna, Sorcha returned. About her neck—"

Bang. Bang. Bang.

Colleen froze.

He closed his eyes. *Dammit.* Ignoring *any* summons this evening was an impossibility.

Bang. Bang. Bang.

He lifted an eyebrow and tipped his head at the door. She *was* the only one who ought to be present in his room.

"Who is it?" Colleen called out. "I did ask for a light tea," she informed him under her breath.

"Robby, miss," the kitchen boy answered. "Is Mr. Torrington about?"

She pulled the sheet to her chin when an eyeball appeared at the keyhole. "Er."

Nick sighed. He'd have to speak with the boy about that bad habit. "Present," he called.

So much for a perception of privacy.

A brief moment of silence followed before Robby spoke again. "I've been sent to let you know there's a package, sir. One marked 'urgent'. Hopsworth placed it upon a table in the library. He's rather upset. It's leaking, sir."

"Leaking?" Colleen whispered. Her eyebrows drew together.

His thoughts echoed hers. "This can't be good." He forced himself to his feet. "I'll be down momentarily, Robby."

"Shall I bring that tea now, miss?"

"Yes," Colleen called, though feebly and with color high upon her cheekbones. She glanced at him. "I've not eaten since breakfast."

"Nor have I. Save me a bite." He threw open the wardrobe and yanked out a clean shirt and a pair of trousers. A glance at the mantle clock informed him it was just past ten o'clock. A bit late for parcel deliveries.

Colleen also slid from the bed and began to dress, pulling on dark trousers, a shirt and a corded cincher—not a corset—to gather in the excess cloth. Clothing better suited to leaping across rooftops than her earlier skirts.

She caught his glance. "Don't worry. I won't leave without you. Go see about this package."

"So much for any pretense of propriety beneath my parents' roof." He pulled on a waistcoat, shrugged on his holster and TTX pistol and shoved his feet into his boots. "If Hopsworth knows we're both in here, the rest of the household is certain to have their suspicions as well." Perhaps they should have made an effort to muffle their cries, but he found it hard to regret her moans of pleasure.

Her lips parted, and Nick saw a hint of anxiety creep onto her face. "I can't—"

"I'm not pressuring you, merely pointing out the obvious." He tipped her chin up. "And the reason I'll not be bothering with the trellis in the future. Remember, it doesn't matter what my family wants. Or yours. What's between us is ours alone to decide." He dipped his head and kissed her, pouring devotion into it, hoping their dreams for the future would align. His heart gave a great thud when she rose onto her toes and returned the kiss with an equal amount of passion.

"Mr. Torrington?" This time the interruption was accompanied by a huff of impatience outside the door, then a light rapping began. Hopsworth himself had arrived outside their door. The matter must truly be urgent. "I intercepted the kitchen boy who insisted you ordered tea. I really must stress that this is a pressing matter, not one that can be addressed at leisure."

"A moment, Hopsworth," Nick called. With a sigh, he dropped his hand from her face and stepped back. "I'd best see what is wrong with this package before our steam butler begins to ding with impatience and stirs up the entire household."

"Please do," she said. "I'm not at all certain Hopsworth can be convinced to overlook our indiscretions or the presence of a cat sìth."

"If we marry, we'll be certain to acquire steam staff that can be customized to *our* specific and unique needs."

"Go." She swatted at him, but he caught the hint of a smile. "We'll speak about such things later. For now, we have work."

~~~
~~~

"Has my father returned from his club?" Nick asked. They would need to take to the roofs within the hour, and he hated to leave his mother alone in the townhouse so soon after an attack. Not that there was anything to be done save to offer moral support by patting her hand while she sat by Anna's bedside in a silent vigil.

"He's been sent for, sir. Expected at any moment." Hopsworth rushed past Nick down the hall, wheels clacking, intent upon fulfilling his duties, lest the entire British hierarchy crumble because a gentleman opened a door before his butler. "Many, many apologies for the," gears grated in the steam butler's throat, "interruption. The package arrived by human courier. He insisted it be brought to your attention as a time sensitive issue."

"Let me know when my father returns," Nick said. "That will be all, Hopsworth."

The door closed softly behind him as he advanced, eyeing the paper-wrapped package bound up with coarse string upon the library's table. A dark stain spread outward from a lower corner. Not a promising sign. A tight band of dread wrapped about his chest, ratcheting tighter as he slid free the folded note tucked beneath its knotted bow.

The message was sealed with red wax and imprinted with a triangle. *No.* The Greek letter delta, the symbol for change. Had he been contacted by CEAP? Possible. *Someone* had taken note of his activities and wished to convey a message.

Bile crept into his throat as he broke the seal.

Your interest in our organization has been brought to my attention. Though our methods are unorthodox, they facilitate the acquisition of knowledge that would otherwise remain shrouded by myth and dismissed as superstition.

One of our members has recently been demoted for failing to properly secure his research and findings. Should you accept this invitation to fill his position, you will be privy to the specifics of his work. Though a procedure still in the experimental phase, we have what you seek. Not a treatment, but a cure.

An interview, should you choose to proceed, has been arranged. A carriage awaits. Come alone. Come immediately. Tell no one.

Should you choose to decline, cease your inquiries. Outside interference is not tolerated.

Damn it. He should never have trusted Dr. Farquhar to the constabulary. By snatching him off the street, he'd done nothing but hand him back to his vengeful overlords. The mad scientist *did* possess what Nick sought, what Anna needed.

A cure.

Was it not an electrical pacer the man had developed, but something more? Something better? Whatever discovery the mad scientist had made, at the heart of it were the cat sìth. What biological truth hid behind the myth of a shape-shifting feline said to possess nine lives? This shadow committee knew. Dr. Farquhar knew. And presumably one Mr. Cornelius Pierpont knew.

Clenching his jaw, he pulled a penknife from his pocket and cut through the string. With the tip of his knife, he unwrapped the box and flipped open the lid.

Shock rippled through him at the stark warning that lay before him. A human heart rested on a bed of bloodied tissue paper. One freshly removed. Glistening dark red with bands of whitish fat, veins threaded across its surface, branching and wrapping across the muscular tissue on their—former—mission to deliver blood. At its crown, the attached blood vessels—the aortic and pulmonary trunks, the venae cavae—had been roughly cut, hacked from the chest of—

Dr. Farquhar? A cold sweat gathered between his shoulder blades. No. The note had mentioned outside interference. Did this heart belong to the man's wife?

Either way, this was a cold-blooded and calculated murder. The need to report this "warning" warred with the advice contained within its accompanying message. If he delivered this to his superiors, CEAP was certain to retaliate. Neither, however, could he contact the local authorities with ramblings about a scientific committee making inquiries into the possibilities of shape-shifting. He himself had been tasked with infiltrating this very sub-committee, and such suspicions were to remain confidential.

Shock shifted to anger, and blood began to pound and roar in his ears. All he wished to do was provide his sister with a better—and longer—life. To stop the exploitation of rare animals—and perhaps humans. He'd long known it would eventually require him to walk into the midst of a predatory community of individuals who had the temerity to call themselves scientists and who thought nothing of lives lost, rare animals poached, or patients denied access to secret medical advances.

Unacceptable.

The moment to act had finally arrived.

A scream rent the air.

Nick jerked his head up to stare at the heavily curtained window that faced the street, listening. A second outcry followed the first. More shouts, each joining the next, grew louder by the second. His stomach twisted. The timing could be no accident. Was the grisly parcel not enough?

With a curse, he dropped the lid and loosely wrapped the paper about the box. Yanking open the drawer of a nearby cabinet, he hid the stained package and message within, lest another member of the household stumble across it. He slammed the drawer shut at the very moment the library door banged open.

Steam billowed from under Hopsworth's collar as he rolled across the rug at a furious clip, flapping his articulated hands. "Sir, come quick!" He careened back toward the door. "A catastrophe of immense proportions has landed upon our doorstep!"

Nick ran past Hopsworth into the foyer and heaved open the front door. He froze at the sight before him. His second guess as to the origin of the heart had been on the mark.

A pool of light cast by the streetlamp highlighted what remained of Mrs. Farquhar impaled upon the iron spikes of the fence before his home. Back arched, arms out-flung, her sightless eyes stared upward. Gray skirts and long, dark hair fluttered in the wind, her chest a gaping, raw and *empty* cavity.

A bold and public statement drawing much unwanted attention to his family home... within which the woman's heart lay, wrapped and hidden.

Shit. Shit. Shit.

"...fell from the sky!"

"A dirigible..."

"...swooped low and someone shoved..."

His eyes swept the scene before him. The engines of steam carriages idled and the gears of crank hacks clacked as onlookers paused to stare, those on foot edging ever closer to the gruesome tableau before them. Crime the likes of which was never visited upon Mayfair. A well-dressed lady had collapsed upon the pavement at the sight, and her weeping daughter waved smelling salts beneath her nose. A gentleman brandished his cane in the air while yelling for the constabulary.

On the far side of the road sat a richly appointed clockwork horse-drawn carriage. The man perched upon the driver's seat boldly met Nick's stare, his expression expectant. A slight tip of his head was all the invitation Nick received.

The damning evidence in his possession was meant to make it impossible to decline. He returned the nod, lifted a finger, then turned to climb back into the house—a moment too late to spare his mother.

"Nicholas?" She appeared in the door, craning her neck to look behind him. "What is going—?" Her hands flew her mouth, stifling a scream.

Colleen, eyes wide, stood directly behind his mother. "Is that—?"

"It is." Arms wide, Nick forced them both back into the foyer. "Hopsworth," he called. "My coat and hat."

"Yes, sir!" Still wobbling on his wheels, the steam butler zipped off to the cloakroom.

He turned back to the women. "I need to leave. Immediately. Work calls."

"But there's a body!" His mother's hands flapped. "What am I supposed to *do*? Your father isn't home yet."

"He'll be here soon. In the meantime, cooperate fully with the police. Make my excuses. It will look bad, my absence, but it can't be helped. Invent a medical emergency." He kissed his mother's forehead. "I can't explain. But, please, for Anna's sake."

His mother's face grew stony, but she nodded.

"Work?" Colleen repeated flatly. "Has this anything to do with—"

"Yes." He cut her off, catching her wrist and tugging her aside. Fully dressed and geared up—though a dressing gown was strategically wrapped about her to conceal her non-traditional attire—she was ready to leap across rooftops to her uncle's home. He leaned close to whisper in her ear. "In the library is a cabinet filled with drawers. Third to the right, second from the bottom is a box that holds what can only be Mrs. Farquhar's heart along with the message accompanying it. Read it, then burn it." A risk to share such information, but she deserved to know.

The blood drained from her face. "CEAP?"

"Perhaps. Either way I've received an ultimatum." The clock ticked, counting each second that passed. How long would the driver wait? Another such opportunity would not present itself. "I'm not supposed to speak with anyone about it, but I need your help. Please dispose of the contents of that drawer; they cannot be found in my—or my family's—possession." Rifling through his pockets, he turned up a punch card and pressed it into her hand. "This is the address of a colleague, a Mr. Jackson. He's aware of my assignment. Write to him before you go... out," he added, for her face informed him she would not be waiting for his return. Her uncle's safe would be cracked open and searched this very night. It worried him, and yet such was the very reason he'd been so determined to win her hand. "Explain our situation. Stress the need for urgency." Not caring who watched, he dipped his head and caught her lips with a quick kiss. "Be careful."

Hopsworth was back, frowning. "Sir—"

But Nick had no time for protestations. He grabbed his hat and coat—and was gone.

Chapter Seventeen

The note that lay beside the blood-tinged box was written in her uncle's hand. Proof that he was mixed up in the group Nick sought to infiltrate. He might be the very man conducting this "interview".

Heart in her throat, she dashed to the window and flung the curtain aside, ready to throw open the sash and call a warning, but there was no trace of the carriage that had waited across the street for Nick, its driver noticeably detached from the frenzy upon the doorstep. Combined with Isabella's warning, it could mean only one thing.

Her uncle *knew* of their presence at the burned-out building. Had the scientist himself identified them? Had the body on the doorstep been his wife?

It didn't matter; her uncle's message was clear.

A cold frost settled over her. All these years, she'd known he was a merciless reptile, but she hadn't thought him so barbaric as to order a woman's heart ripped from her chest. For there was no chance a man who prized neatness and order had wielded the knife. A minion with no such misgivings had been set to the task of the woman's execution and disposal.

Who was her uncle to judge another when he'd spent the past few years stealing *her* hard-earned money, poaching upon *her* property, sacrificing the hapless cat sìth who roamed free in *her* woods all to fund Dr. Farquhar's research so that he might... what?

She glanced again at the note.

A cure? Her mind struggled with the concept. A cure implied there was a way to return Anna's heart to full working order. No device could accomplish that. Which meant that whatever was in that rosewood box was *not* an electrical pacing device. But what could restore a damaged heart's ability to beat? What exactly had she transported beneath her bustle?

Her mind recalled the broken, smoke-stained shards of glass that had littered the floor of the charred basement laboratory, the pools of liquid, the threadlike material that floated, curling and twisting within the liquid, and she shuddered. They'd missed a key clue, but she couldn't begin to fathom what it was.

Sorcha leapt onto the table and sniffed the distasteful package. She pulled back her lips and gave it a baleful stare.

"Agreed," Colleen said. "Tonight, we put an end to my uncle's crimes. And then there are others who must pay." The memory of scorched skulls lining the charred shelves of Dr. Farquhar's laboratory could never be erased. "We must also locate the mad scientist and drag forth answers." Perhaps some good might be yet salvaged on Anna's behalf. "After which we take back my lands and your forest. I'll not allow another cat sìth to be harmed to serve my uncle's selfishness and arrogance."

The Queen's agents might expect Nick to play the long game, to infiltrate this shadow committee and trace its many tentacles, but his sister was running out of time. Faster to break into her uncle's safe, retrieve any relevant papers that lay within—suspicious property deeds, accountings of funds paid to mysterious men, documents relevant to her inheritance—and drag them into the light of day before he had the chance to destroy any evidence linking him to illegal activities.

Tossing the letter into the small fire burning upon the grate, she scribbled a quick note to Mr. Jackson letting him know the particulars of their situation. Thinking of what Nick might face alone made her stomach churn, no matter how many times reason reminded her that he was a trained Queen's agent. She too would face risks creeping into her uncle's study. What if someone was stationed inside, waiting? But if he could trust her to handle herself alone, she could return the favor.

Wrapped in bloodstained paper and cardboard, the cold, still heart weighed heavily in her hands as she began to climb the stairs toward the aviary. She had to try. Tonight might be the only night such an opportunity presented itself. A man who would order the murder of another man's wife might easily turn upon his own, particularly now that her uncle had guessed—or at least suspected—his own wife's collusion. Isabella was no longer safe. There'd be no leaving London before this serpent had been slain. Time to breach her uncle's study and discover exactly what he was about before he slithered home.

Tucking away her tinted spectacles, she cracked open the hatch and climbed into the aviary, happy to have Sorcha shadowing her once more. She plucked a skeet pigeon from its roost and inserted the message into an ankle canister. *Snap*, the punch card with Mr. Jackson's address clicked into place. She wound the bird's mechanism and tossed it through the window, watching as it took to the night air.

She set aside the dressing gown and checked her tool belt one last time. Lock picks, Rapunzel rope, pouches of various other items, and her precious Keller stethoscope—audiologically enhanced at great personal expense—all securely hooked. She'd yet to lay fingers upon her uncle's personal safe, but she'd seen the strongbox delivered and knew precisely where it lay.

There was no more avoiding the horrid package. Sliding it into a cloth sack, she tied it about her hips. She might have burned the letter, but she had other plans for Mrs. Farquhar's heart. Over her shoulder, she slung a map case, one she'd found in Nick's study that would allow her to carry away any important or incriminating documents. With her dirk in her boot and her hooded cape about her shoulders, it was time to take to the rooftops.

Overhead, a dark shadow passed—a hungry pteryform soaring toward the Thames, ready to fish out a kraken or two for breakfast, their preference for the cephalopods the only reason the city council did not launch an armed force to terminate their presence in the city. Stars struggled to shine through the haze that filled the nighttime London sky, and the running lights of several Sparrow-class personal dirigibles fared little better. Those who could afford them—like her uncle—risked their own safety to discreetly travel to evening activities.

Colleen stepped from the aviary onto the roof and slid her hands into a powder-filled pouch. She dusted her hands and lifted her face to the cool night air, sensing the direction of the gentle breeze that blew through London. Taking a deep breath, she stretched, reveling in the anticipation of freedom that always accompanied a long, complex rooftop run.

"Riggit?" she asked Sorcha. *Ready?*

The cat sìth crouched, braced to spring forward.

Colleen took off at a running start along the ridges of the roofs, leaping onto, over and around row after row of chimney pots that delineated one terraced home from the next. Tail held high, Sorcha shadowed her every move.

A controlled slide down the sharp slope of a slate-tiled roof… a fast run along the edge… a dash past a heated rooftop greenhouse. Over and again until she reached a corner tower. Crouching, she gripped the eaves of the roof to drop onto a narrow balcony.

A deep breath. An assessment. Then she continued. Corbel to cornice to lintel, she dropped toward the street, jumping off the rounded finial of an iron fence onto the pavement. The cat sìth followed. Lifting her hood and dodging lamplight, Colleen darted through traffic with Sorcha at her heels. A few quick steps and she was down a narrow passageway—one with a drainpipe. She paused, letting Sorcha leap onto her shoulder before she began to climb. In seconds, both of them were safe upon the rooftops, once again leaping across slate tiles and clay chimney pots.

And finally arrived at her uncle's rooftop where the dirigible stood upon the landing pad. Wary, she crept closer and peered inside. A hasty attempt to wipe blood from the jump seat had been made, but there was no mistaking the rusty-brown stain that clung to the upholstery's stitching. Though she could prove nothing, there was no doubt in her mind that this very dirigible had been used to drop Mrs. Farquhar's body onto the Stafford's doorstep. Mr. Vanderburn might have piloted, but who had assisted? And did they now patrol the interior of her uncle's home?

Her stomach gave a slight twist. Never before had she taken a job where she might encounter deadly force.

But, she reminded herself, Mr. Vanderburn—and his assistant—were employees of her uncle's. They wouldn't kill her simply for being caught in his home, would they? Still, she would take extra care.

There could be no creeping through its halls; she'd have to make a direct entry. Thankful her uncle's study faced the back of the house, she pulled on her leather gloves, then looped the Rapunzel rope about a chimney and secured its other end to her belt. Lowering herself onto her stomach, she slid—feet first—down the pitch of the roof, dangling from the eaves and waiting until Sorcha climbed onto her shoulders. Slowly, she dropped them both down the rope until they hung outside the window of her uncle's study. Smart, to have installed a lock, but it was no match for her picks, not even while she was hanging like a spider from a thread and working the lock one-handed. She pried open the window, glanced inside to be certain no one was about, then nodded to the cat sìth. Sorcha leapt into a room lit only by the fading glow of a single Lucifer lamp. Colleen swung in behind her, dropping noiselessly into a crouch upon the floor, listening.

The room was empty but for a mechanical brush—now with an overlarge feline riding upon it—that whirred its way back and forth across the room, grooming the carpet.

Reassured by Sorcha's nonchalance, she took a step forward, but the small hairs on the back of her neck lifted.

The house was eerily quiet.

Suspiciously quiet.

There ought to be a low-level hum of *human* activity, but all she heard was the *thrum* and *chuff* of the steam servants.

She sniffed the air and caught the faint scent of warm sugar and dried currants—spotted dick and custard—along with the fragrance of bergamot-laced tea, a favorite. Had the servants gathered in the kitchen for a late tea of their own volition? Or had they been confined there?

Likely the later, increasing the odds that Mr. Vanderburn walked a patrol by one hundred percent. Were this any other mission, she would have turned back, but she refused to leave. Not until she'd plundered her uncle's safe and dragged the proof of his misdeeds into the moonlight.

Not once had she entered this inner sanctum without a summons; she'd had no wish to tip her hand inside her own home. But all too often she'd been called to stand before his desk to be berated for her behavior or, of late, for her refusal to consider a particular suitor. Over the years, she'd taken note of wear patterns, observed which ornaments shifted upon her uncle's shelves. And which did not.

Though a relic of times long past, not once had the medieval helmet of a distant ancestor acquired the tiniest speck of dust. She flipped up the visor and rolled her eyes at the predictable lever concealed within. Grasping it, she pulled… and the bookshelf swung open—silent upon well-oiled hinges—to reveal the Crypt Safe. A smile turned up the corners of her mouth. Advertised as unbreakable, not one had been breached. Or so they claimed. Colleen had cracked two.

Time to scour the depths of her uncle's safe.

She pressed the thin membrane stretched across the Keller stethoscope's bell to the cold, steel door and focused on the faint sounds of the lock wheels as they each clicked into place. Even with her many talents, catching and identifying all ten numbers in order was a challenge. But in the end, the safe gave up its secrets.

The heavy door swung open and there, in pride of place upon the top shelf, sat the rosewood box. Her jaw dropped. How was it possible? Had he tracked down the buyer himself to snatch back that which had been stolen from him?

Though her fingers itched to peer inside, piles of documents awaited. She forced herself to rifle through them, looking for cold, hard evidence of his wrongdoings. And she found it. A stack of papers signed by none other than Cornelius Pierpont agreeing to the sale of a cure for "sluggish hearts" to a number of prominent gentlemen.

But why would such documents be in her uncle's possession?

She squinted at the scrawled signature—and gasped. It was her uncle's handwriting.

If Lord Maynard and Cornelius Pierpont were one and the same, *that* meant he'd stolen from the very shadow committee he chaired, deliberately plotting to profit from the death and suffering of others. He'd bought the "cure" from the scientist's wife, framed her to take the blame, then conveniently murdered her to send a "message". All the while the "cure" sat securely within his own safe.

The betrayal struck her hard in the chest, making her heartbeat stumble and her lungs struggle for breath.

Over and over men had demonstrated there were profits to be made selling snake oil and sham cures to desperate individuals. But the value of a working cure selectively distributed only to those with deep pockets? Priceless. And therefore irresistible.

Her uncle was a despicable man.

She'd carried that rosewood box through a step on the obfuscation chain, all on his behalf. The thought that she'd aided her uncle burned with the heat of a thousand suns. How could Mr. Witherspoon have agreed to such a task? Had he not known? Did that excuse him from complicity? She'd consider the moral implications later for, as fast as righteous anger had flared, it quickly cooled, turning to terror. If her uncle was so quick to order murder, what might become of her, were she caught rifling through his safe?

She picked up her pace, locating the property deed to Craigieburn and the documents naming her uncle as guardian and trustee. Quickly, she rolled them together with the most damning of contracts signed in Pierpont's name and stuffed them into the map tube.

Then, unhooking the burlap sack from her belt, she swapped the blood-stained cardboard box for the one of carved rosewood. Like Pandora's box, it was impossible not to look inside. She lifted the lid. Upon a padded velvet cushion rested a glass vial filled with a clear fluid and a tangle of white threads.

No. Not threads. Threads didn't move.

She dropped the vial with a sharp yelp, then clamped her hand over her mouth as the last meal she'd eaten curdled in her stomach.

Worms. Her uncle was peddling *worms*?

How was this a cure for anything? She'd heard of tapeworm eggs swallowed by women unhappy with their girth, but never of the radical step producing positive results. If anything, reports were negative, when women found their bodily organs riddled with cysts.

Remembering the worms from the fire, she shuddered.

Somewhere in the bowels of the Lister Institute a parasitologist must exist, hunched over a microscope, studying distasteful organisms of all kinds. He—or she—would wish to study this.

Colleen took a deep breath. Swallowed. Then retrieved the vial, skin crawling, and dropped it into the burlap sack before tying it to her belt. She gave a shudder, thinking of the distasteful items she carried about this evening. Shoving the wriggling creatures from her mind, she reached for a velvet pouch that sat deep within the safe.

Sorcha hissed a warning and leapt from the carpet sweeper. Colleen was out of time. Slamming the safe closed, she spun the dial and yanked on the lever. As she turned to follow Sorcha to the window, the bookcase closed behind her.

The door banged open. "Stop right there, Colleen."

The cat sìth—fur standing on end—let out a yowl that scraped every nerve ending raw, then leapt to freedom.

Mr. Glover? Mr. Glover was her uncle's minion? Regrets and recriminations could wait until later. She didn't turn her head to look, but reached for the window frame, seconds from freedom, when—

Bang!

Sharp daggers of glass rained down upon her, and her hand slipped as a strange numbness washed over her right arm. She leapt onto the sill, pulling with her other arm, about to jump blindly, when a rough hand grabbed her hair and dragged her back into the study.

With a twist and a shove, he tossed her to the ground. There was a faint click. "Don't move." A revolver appeared before her face and, behind it, Mr. Glover's enraged face.

She clutched at her limp arm as a tight pressure built. She'd been shot by an ex-lover? *Aether.* She wouldn't have thought he had the nerve. But her burning arm, the hot and wet sleeve beneath her palm, informed her otherwise. She was bleeding. Bleeding badly.

"You wouldn't," she challenged, rolling onto her side and curling her knees to her chest. No need to feign the agony she felt. She slid the palm of her good arm over her trousers, wiping the blood free before reaching for the dirk concealed in her boot. Shaking fingers found its hilt and clutched at its leather-wrapped handle. Years had passed since her father trained her in its use, and she'd never before needed the blade. Excellent reflexes, keen senses and speed had kept her from any direct confrontations on the job. But she always wore the blade, because she'd be damned if men like Mr. Glover would ever win.

"Why not? It isn't as if I'd marry you now that you've welcomed another man into your bed."

"Fool." She slid the blade free and slashed his ankle. "Did you think you were the first?"

Mr. Glover screamed—anger or agony, she couldn't tell—as she scrambled onto her feet, but Colleen hadn't taken more than one step when he launched himself at her, bodily slamming her to the ground, knocking the air from her lungs and sending her dirk skittering across the floor.

She rolled, clawing at his eyes.

He caught her wrists and pinned them to the ground, holding her down with the weight of his body. "I should have been the last," he growled. "You were promised to me. All I had to do was—"

Another man, gasping, ran into the room. In his hand was a long, metal rod. It hummed. Ominously. "Enough!" he yelled, his eyes wild. A shock of white hair rose from his head. "We need her. Stick with the plan."

"You!" It was Dr. Farquhar, the man who'd tried to rip Sorcha's carrier from her hands. Her last lover might be a possessive, jealous man sewn together by a thin thread of incipient madness, but Dr. Farquhar had long ago fallen down the rabbit hole of insanity.

Grudgingly, Mr. Glover stood, yanking Colleen onto her feet. Blood dripped from her fingertips. So much blood. But she would fight to the end. And the stupid man had no idea how close they were to the shelves. Ignoring the pain, she reached behind her. A book met her hand. She smashed it into Mr. Glover's face, and his hand flew open, releasing her.

"Witch!" he yelled, lunging.

But she slipped away and lifted the tome over her head, struggling against the numbness. Blood ran down her wounded arm and dripped onto the rug as her heart pounded. Escape was impossible. Still, she had to try. Whatever the two of them had planned for her couldn't be pleasant. "Out of my way! Both of you!"

But the scientist only stared back at her, his head tipped. A demented light glittered in his eyes, and a shadow of a smile touched his lips. "Such spectacular eyes. All this time, he kept you from me. All of them did. Only when they witness it for themselves will they believe."

"Quit your rambling, old man!" Mr. Glover limped across the room and ripped the humming rod from the scientist's hands. "If you had married me, Colleen, I would have protected you from this."

"From what, exactly?" she spat. Her arm began to shake with the effort of holding the book aloft. She stood no chance against an electrified weapon.

"From becoming a laboratory rat." He pointed the strange rod directly at her.

Her eyebrows drew together, struggling to process his words. They intended to... Dr. Farquhar was to be allowed to... stop her heart? The room began to spin. If she could make the front door, fling herself into the street, perhaps the good will of strangers might save her. With a war cry worthy of Boudicca herself, Colleen heaved the book at Mr. Glover and ran for the door.

But as she passed, the humming weapon met her side and a loud buzzing filled her ears. Every muscle tensed, then she felt herself falling toward the floor.

Chapter Eighteen

Nick ground his teeth and muttered to himself as the carriage wound its way—slowly, painfully—though the chaos of humanity and technology that thronged the evening streets of London. Banging on the roof of the carriage had done nothing to quicken its pace, and he suspected the driver had been given specific orders not to arrive before an appointed hour. The vehicle came to a stop before a familiar passageway in Hatton Garden at precisely ten o'clock.

This was London's jewelry quarter, famous for its underground tunnels, vaults, and rooms. But in its darker recesses lurked other infamous locations. Tucked away down this particular dark, narrow and dimly lit path lay The Three-Eyed Bat. An outwardly respectable pub during business hours, it became a den of iniquity when the sun fell. Years ago, when he was a new, untried agent, he'd chased a man down this very alleyway nearly losing his life when the criminal turned on him with a knife, striking for his neck. If he looked, would there still be a gouge in the brick wall?

The door swung open, and Mr. Vanderburn stood before him, blocking his exit. It gave Nick no pleasure to see his worst suspicions confirmed, that Lord Maynard did indeed control this shadow committee.

"Before we proceed, Mr. Torrington," the henchman said, "I have orders to confiscate your weapons."

Nick bristled. "Unacceptable."

"Very well," Vanderburn said, his voice flat. "The driver will see you home. I will convey your regrets to Miss Stewart. Best wishes for your sister's continued health." He began to close the door.

Nick thrust out his hand, holding it open. The cold wind blew shards of ice beneath his collar, freezing the air in his lungs. How was it possible? "Lady Stewart is here?"

"She is expected shortly." Vanderburn's dead eyes gave away nothing, but it was clear the man could read his. "You think to wait, but it will do you no good. They will divert her elsewhere."

His hackles rose. Duty might forbid he comply, but love insisted. He could no sooner leave Colleen to her uncle's schemes than he could stop breathing. Nor could he turn away from anything that might help heal his sister's heart. Gritting his teeth, he drew his TTX pistol from its holster and handed it over. Down this path lay disaster.

Vanderburn turned the unique weapon over in his hands before sliding it into his coat pocket. Nick caught a glimpse of a holster containing a standard revolver. "Blades as well."

He growled. One knife followed another, each clattering to the ground as a small pile grew at the henchman's feet. "Satisfied?"

"For now." Vanderburn made no attempt to collect them. "This way, Mr. Torrington." He turned.

Between the cobblestones beneath Nick's feet, a sluggish fluid oozed, glowing with a faint bluish light and leading the way to the old pub. There, small panes of wavy glass emitted the warm glow of oil lanterns and coal fires. A cast iron bracket held aloft the winged sign, as it flapped and creaked in the night wind. Every so often, the bat's gilded eyes caught a stray beam of light, flashing gold. His stomach tied itself another knot. Only for Colleen and his family would he violate every instinct that screamed "Trap!"

"If you'll take a seat, I'll let Lord Maynard know you've arrived." Vanderburn tugged on the worn, brass handle and waved Nick inside.

The dark, paneled room was filled with smoke and gentlemen of dubious morality. He ignored the server behind the bar, made his way to a heavy oak table near the fireplace, and sat beneath a low ceiling held up by rough-hewn beams. The pub was rumored to date to the reign of King George the First and, from appearances, had not once been updated. As he waited, the room closed in on him.

Colleen would have left immediately for the aviary, to send the message before leaping across roofs to reach her uncle's house. But it was a move her uncle had been expecting. Nick glared at the fire. The bloody package had been a diversion, designed to separate them. He should have anticipated such a move. Wrapped up in emotions from lust and love to disgust and fear, they'd both missed it. She'd been caught, and now an entirely different evening would unfold. This meeting was less interview than it was a hostage negotiation, and Nick wouldn't like the terms.

A gust of cold air set the flames dancing as Lord Maynard entered the pub. Vanderburn lurked beside the door while the earl joined Nick, lowering himself into a chair. His eyes were irritated, impatient and set in a face that appeared all too capable of plotting a woman's demise.

"Interesting gifts you've sent." Nick felt no need for pretense. Neither, however, could he afford to antagonize the gentleman now in control of both his fiancée and a potential cure for his sister. And so he suppressed his anger and kept his words benign. Any chance Nick had at convincing Maynard to admit him to the inner circle relied upon him keeping his personal feelings about the man and his project locked inside a chained box and buried fifty feet deep. "Original. Well-designed to catch the attention of a man you wish to offer employment."

"I thought as much." Colleen's uncle tapped his fingers on the table between them, sizing up the man before him. "Mrs. Farquhar failed the simplest of tests, betraying years of her husband's work for a sum that netted her very little in the way of funds. I considered letting her run free but, alas, she knew too much. It took her husband years to unearth the secret of those curious cats' longevity, and I won't chance that information falling into other hands."

Failed a test. Maynard himself had arranged the opportunity for his scientist's wife to betray herself? Were the earl and Pierpont one and the same? When Nick had stormed the man's office to lay claim to his niece, had he stood—as before—mere feet away from a particular rosewood box? He struggled to keep his face impassive. "Hence the warning that arrived with your offer of a position."

"Interview," Maynard reminded him. His eyes narrowed. "You were sighted at the scene of the fire, and yet are so much more than an inconvenient witness of which I might easily dispose."

"Trained in cardiophysiology. Sworn to uphold the law. Engaged to your niece." Nick leaned forward. "Hence your decision to recruit me."

"As we're being blunt, yes." Maynard smirked. "The fire, though distressing to a certain organization, presents me—and therefore you—with a unique opportunity to strike out on our own. I alone have access to the cure."

Did he? Colleen might have been captured in his study, but there was no chance the earl himself had captured her. Nor did Vanderburn have his fiancée in his grips. If she had managed to breach her uncle's safe before she was apprehended—and there was, as yet, no proof that she'd been caught—this purported cure might now be in another's hands. But whose? Two particular men came to mind. A mad scientist and the man who'd campaigned to marry Colleen, despite his obvious hatred of her.

"What about the minions who carry out your orders?"

"They answer to me. Like you, they've little option but to accept my terms." The earl's words were bold, but a tremor of uncertainty ran beneath them. Were the reins slipping from his fingers?

"Is that so?" It was time to begin negotiations, to lull the man into believing Nick was willing to collaborate for the right compensation. "Farquhar's work might be dependent upon your funds, but why would you expect Glover's continued loyalty? He expected to become family, to gain control of Craigieburn, of its lands… of its inhabitants. At last glimpse, he was not handling disappointment well."

Maynard's lips twisted. "There will be profit for all. If he cannot accept a new role…" *Then he'd be the next example.* No need to speak the words aloud. "Work with me, Torrington, and you'll be a rich man. No need to rely upon your father or," his lip curled, "a government position to pay your debts. You'd be surprised what a man will pay for an exclusive and limited remedy to keep his heart beating."

Profiting on the sick and desperate. Lovely.

"I have investments," Nick countered. "Money alone is insufficient inducement."

The earl glowered. "How many more heart seizures will your sister survive? Ten? Two? Or will the next one snuff out that fragile spark of life?"

Beneath the table, Nick balled his hand into a fist and resisted an urge to throttle the man. "Your scientist appears mad, attempting to rip your niece's pet cat from her arms. What could possibly induce me to allow him to lay a single finger upon my sister?"

"Ah, but the creature is so much more than a mere house cat." The earl cocked his head. "I'd no idea my sister had stumbled into such a windfall when she ran away with a Scottish laird." His lips pressed together. "Glover proved himself a sluggard when he chose to hand over Colleen's particular beast to Farquhar rather than make another trip north. But not wrong. Those cats hold the key."

Another reason to hate the man. "What could a cat possibly possess that would cure my sister?" Speaking the words aloud, watching the earl's face as he said them, was the confirmation he needed. There was no electrical pacer. The cure was biological. But what? And how?

Movement beyond the pub's windows caught Vanderburn's attention—and Nick's—but when the guard dismissed it with a glance and settled back to his post, Nick forced his full attention back to Maynard's arrogant face.

"I don't think so, Torrington." The earl puffed out his chest. "I'll not be sharing any details until we've reached an agreement. But wipe the doubts from your mind. Dr. Farquhar may dance at the edge of sanity, but he's proven his life-saving technique again and again. I witnessed one such experiment with my own eyes. It works."

"On cats?" Nick lifted an eyebrow in challenge. He hadn't missed the animal cages or their unfortunate contents.

"And dogs. We've also managed to revive a fox, a weasel and a badger. Most notably, a monkey acquired from the London Zoo. Human trials are the next logical step."

Of course they were. And a man who thought nothing of murder and arson wouldn't let the question of medical consent stand in his way.

"But Farquhar needs closer supervision and direction. Of late, his mind has taken a maddening turn, veering from the scientific toward the realm of fantasy. I'm in need of a scientific-minded man with a clear head."

"Who has connections to the scientific and medical community." Nick crossed his arms, leaning back in his chair. "You're proposing a partnership?"

"No." Maynard's eyebrows slammed together. "The cure is in *my* possession, the knowledge under *my* control. It is *my* funds that will pay to establish and outfit a new laboratory."

"That may be," Nick said. "But recall that I am engaged to *your* niece. Not only will you and I soon be family, but in two days, she will control the Scottish property upon which you rely."

The man's eyes narrowed and his lips pressed into a thin line.

Damnit. The cure *was* reliant upon the cat sìth. "I expect convincing my future wife to look past your questionable land management will require much work on my part." It was an impossible task. "But for equal terms, I'm willing to convince her." He wasn't. "She might find it curious to learn her uncle is so keen to profit off her lands. Is the coffer nearly empty?"

Maynard glared at him.

Beyond the ripples of the pub's glass windows, two men passed carrying a large, rolled carpet upon their shoulders. One of a length and width that might accommodate the form of a woman. His heart began to pound. Was this how Colleen was *expected* to arrive?

Nick shoved his chair back and began to rise.

"Sit," Maynard commanded. "You'll not make it past the door."

A glance at the door informed him the earl was correct. In Vanderburn's hand was Nick's TTX pistol. The man's eyes dared him to make a move.

"If she's injured..." Nick began, then realized his mistake.

"Care for her, do you?" The earl shook his head. "A shame you let that chink in the armor show. You ought to be more careful. Sentimentality is a weakness, and Colleen has been mine. A final tie to my sister that I ought to sever, but I've found it curious to observe her preternatural sight and reflexes as she's busied herself about London's nightscape, working to fund this very enterprise."

Nick held still, for a predator's stare was upon him. *Follow the money.* Lord Aldridge's speculation had had the precision of a kraken sharpshooter. If only they'd known her uncle ought to be considered a target.

"I find myself facing a curious dilemma," Maynard continued, annoyingly smug. "I can't have her marrying someone upright and honorable, someone who might take objection to my project. I'm not at all certain either of you can be controlled." The earl tapped his fingers on the table, then rose. Vanderburn crossed the room, snatched up a lantern, and disappeared into a room behind the bar. "But I'll give you one last chance to prove your worth. Follow my assistant."

~~~

The cellars of The Three-Eyed Bat twisted beneath the ground, a labyrinthine tangle of corridors, stairways and storage vaults filled with stacks of barrels and crates, broken and discarded furniture, crockery and rusty machinery. Without breadcrumbs or string, Nick was quickly lost. Not that there would be any turning back, not with Maynard at his back.

Long minutes of following the bob and weave of Vanderburn's lantern led them to a room fitted with a rusty iron door and a strikingly shiny brass padlock. Not the best for keeping people out, but effective at keeping
~~~

them *in.* The space was lined with riveted sheets of metal, and beneath the raised threshold ran two copper pipes. His eyes traced the path of those pipes down the hallway to a Linde's Ice Machine, a vapor-compression artificial refrigeration system. It squatted in the hallway, silent.

Activated, however, it would cool the space and turn the entire room into a refrigeration unit, into a cold storage room. Memories of the cat sìth beneath the fume hood and a bucket of water sprang to mind. Ice was used by cardiac electrophysiologists to slow—and stop—the heart.

Nothing good could happen here.

The door hung ajar.

Nick heard faint groan of pain, feminine and familiar. Any hope that Colleen's capture was a bluff disintegrated. An aching hollow took root inside his chest. He pushed past Vanderburn, yanking on the door, and found Colleen stretched out upon a carpet. Her dark shirt was torn and bloody, a rent in the garment exposing pale skin where a raw bullet wound to her upper arm oozed. Used rags littered the metal floor, and a bloody bullet rested in a bowl beside a pair of tweezers. Dr. Farquhar bent over her arm with a needle and thread, muttering to himself.

Glover stood over her, holding a voltaic prod, one that—turned to the highest setting—could drop a charging rhino. He leveled the humming weapon at Nick, but nodded to Colleen. "By all means, tend to your whore. Farquhar's a bit out of practice with his human doctoring skills. Too much time with the cats." Laughter with an edge of anger met Nick's ears. "Then again, maybe he's the perfect man for the job."

Rage gripped him as he rushed forward, dropping to his knees beside Colleen. He pushed the mad scientist's unsteady hands aside. Colleen's eyes were hazy and unfocused. Eyeing the color of her skin, he pressed his finders to the pulse at her wrist. Steady and strong, an excellent sign. No major blood vessel damage. "What did you give her?"

"Laudanum for the pain," Farquhar answered, his eyes filled with an awe that confused Nick. As did his next words. "I'm so very sorry, sir. Had I known why you sought to join us—"

Glover cuffed him. "Let the man work. On with it, Torrington."

"I *told* you not to hurt her," Maynard bellowed.

"It was necessary," Glover snapped. "She was too quiet, too fast. But even she couldn't outrun a bullet. We stopped her, but not before she broke into your safe."

"*My* safe?" Disbelief colored Maynard's voice. So many strongboxes advertised as uncrackable, but none of them truly were. Yet all the gentlemen believed.

"Colleen." Nick grasped her limp fingers. "It's me."

Her head rolled to meet his gaze. "It hurts."

Vanderburn hung his lamp from a hook fastened to the ceiling.

"I imagine so." And he would see Glover pay for it. "You've been shot in the arm. Can you squeeze my hand?" Her fingers flexed. "Harder. Ignore the pain. Crush my fingers like you're hanging from a ledge fifty feet above the ground."

She squeezed, crying out at the pain, but her fingers pressed against his with nearly full strength. Good, there was no nerve damage.

"You'll need a few stitches," he warned. "But you'll heal." Assuming he could find a way for them to escape this windowless, underground space. Not a soul—save those present—knew where they were. "I need alcohol to clean the wound."

"Er." Confused, Farquhar turned about as if he might find a bottle conveniently resting nearby in the empty room.

"We're beneath a pub!" Nick snapped. "Whisky. Vodka. Find some."

Vanderburn sighed and reached into his pocket. "Here." He held out a flask. "Vodka."

It would have to do. Nick splashed a measure over Colleen's wound, over the needle and thread, then carefully drew the edges of her flesh back together.

"Your niece may be an unpleasant aberration," Glover said. "But she is talented. Came in the window of your study, not the door. We almost missed her. A minute later, and she'd have been out the window behind that damned cat." He shifted, and Nick noted the man favored his left leg. He hoped Colleen was the cause of his injury.

While they argued, Nick leaned close to Colleen's ear. He needed to ask even if questioning her while using a sharp implement to pierce her flesh felt akin to torture. "Did you find anything of note?"

"Worms," she half-gasped, half-whispered.

Though he'd known the answers wouldn't involve wires or batteries, any other words would have made more sense than... "Worms? The creeping invertebrates one digs out of the dirt?" Another stitch.

"More the wriggling kind that infest an animal's intestines. Threadlike and alive."

Revulsion twisted and writhed at the back of his throat. He resisted an urge to glare at Maynard. Cure? The man was as insane as Farquhar. The needle plunged, the thread pulled. "You found them... in the safe?"

Confusion tumbled inside her amber eyes as she nodded her confirmation while gritting her teeth against the pain. "In the rosewood box," she whispered. "Nothing else, save the vial in which they floated."

Around them, the argument grew heated. He tied a knot, snipped the thread, and quickly bandaged her arm.

"Fine!" Maynard barked. "It doesn't matter. We have her, and she'll serve as our first human test subject."

Ice ran through Nick's veins. "What? No!" He'd not allow these worms to...

"You will if you wish to leave this basement alive," the earl snarled. "As discussed, you'll oversee the transplant, accurately recording *human* data, all while ensuring my niece cooperates." He waved a hand at Farquhar. "I don't trust a man who mutters like a loon about transmutation."

"Both questions can be answered at once," Farquhar defended weakly.

"I don't think so," Glover barked back, ignoring the mad scientist. "Not after you let him," a hand slashed in Nick's direction, "waltz out your front door with *my* fiancée!"

"No!" Colleen's voice warbled as she struggled to sit up, to focus through an opium-laced haze. "I refuse."

Nick tensed, sweeping his gaze about the room, hunting for anything that would make a suitable weapon.

"Everyone settle down," Vanderburn said. He pointed Nick's own TTX pistol at him. "Back up. We've time enough to wait for the lady to recover."

Hands in the air, Nick complied.

"I care not who weds my niece," the earl barked.

"But I do!" Glover yelled back. "Whoever controls the property, controls the profits. That cat sìth is replaceable, as is the witch herself. What cannot be replicated are the legal documents, conveniently inked with your own hand, and the marriage certificate, valid but for her signature. Imagine how pleased I was to find such documents *and* a certain vial all in her possession."

Vanderburn met Nick's gaze and slowly shook his head. Between the TTX pistol and the voltaic prod that hummed and crackled in Glover's hands, Nick wouldn't stand a chance.

"Fine," the earl spat. "You marry her."

"I will," Glover said. "But I no longer trust you, a man who exploits his own niece's inheritance, offered my fiancée to another, and lured Farquhar's wife into stealing his hard-earned findings. All so you could quietly sell them for profit." His lips pulled back. "For there's no other explanation for the missing vial of worms in her possession, is there?"

"I meant to—"

"Betrayal after betrayal. Enough." Glover rushed at the earl, ramming the humming weapon he held into the man's stomach.

"Wha—" But the cry died in Maynard's throat with a crackle as the Galvanic prod discharged, sending bolts of electricity shooting through the earl's body and dropping him to the floor.

Colleen screamed and Nick grabbed the opportunity to kick out, landing a solid blow to Glover's damaged leg. The man screamed as he fell, and the Galvanic prod skittered across the floor, useless until it recharged.

"Stop!" Vanderburn squeezed the trigger of the TTX pistol, discharging all ammunition at once. *Crack! Ping! Thwack!* The first dart went wide, glancing off the metal wall, but the second and third caught Nick in the arm and wrist.

Shit. He had mere seconds before unconsciousness.

He yanked them out and threw them to the floor, hoping not all of the toxin had discharged, then fell on Glover with balled fists. An uppercut to the jaw made a satisfying crunch, whipping his head to the side. Blood erupted from Glover's mouth. But he felt nothing for his hand was already numb. A second punch to his abdomen doubled Glover over into a howling ball of pain.

Bang!

Nick twisted about.

"I said stop!" Smoke curled up from the standard revolver Vanderburn held in his hand, one now pointed at Nick. He froze, stunned. At his feet, the earl lay in a rapidly spreading pool of blood, a gunshot wound to his head. Dead. "A man wants to be protected, he should pay his employees. The way I see it, the less people involved, the more profit there will be to share. I'm willing to reserve judgment, Torrington, but I'm not at all certain you've anything to contribute to our project, so don't test me."

As if he could. The numbness spread up his arm and outward. Into his chest. Across his face. He swayed as his legs began to give out.

"Nick?" Colleen's distant voice was at his ear, but he couldn't answer her. He could barely feel her arms wrap about him as, together, they collapsed. The floor rushed up at him, but—completely numb—he never felt it hit.

Chapter Nineteen

"Let me go!" Colleen screamed and clawed at her uncle's henchman as he dragged her away from Nick. A desperate act, as the man's body was three times the size of hers and comprised of nothing but thick, ropy muscle.

Nick lay motionless on the cold, metal floor. His wide and unblinking eyes gave no indication that he could see her. But for the faint pulse at his throat and the shallow rise and fall of his chest, he appeared dead. And might well be if the toxin overtook him. How many darts had struck him? *Not enough to kill him.* And that thought alone gave her hope, one she clung to. A tear trickled down her cheek. For the thought of living in a world without him brought far too much pain. Had she fallen in love?

She'd loved her parents, and now Isabella. Her bond with Sorcha was deep and unbreakable. But Nick? He was a friend, a colleague, a lover... and so much more. Love and marriage were scary prospects, for his thoughts, opinions and decisions would—necessarily—influence hers. As hers would impact his. Was this a weakness or a strength? She rather thought it might be the latter. And she was tired of being so very, very alone.

One thing she knew with certainty: she'd never loved her uncle. That cold, selfish, arrogant man was dead. Blood oozed from the hole in his forehead, spreading in a widening pool beneath his skull. Grotesque, horrifying, but she felt only detached relief. And a twinge of happiness. Not so much for her, but for Isabella. If Colleen didn't survive this, at least her aunt would be free.

Beaten and bloody, Mr. Glover rose from the floor. He pressed his hand to his mouth, checking for broken or loose teeth. She spat at his feet, happy to see Nick had managed to bloody Mr. Glover before he'd fallen. "I hope you've lost several. You're no better than the brutes you employ."

Mr. Vanderburn's hands tightened on her arms.

"And entirely capable of murder," Mr. Glover agreed, eyes narrow. "Keep that in mind." His nostrils flared as he glared at her. "Get what you need, Farquhar," he ordered. "Take this chance while you can, before I end her myself."

Here? This subterranean room was to serve as the man's laboratory? But how? There was no equipment, no instruments. Only the blood-stained rug beneath her feet and a doctor's bag that contained only the most basic of supplies.

"Yes, sir!" The mad scientist—who had pressed himself to the wall and cowered behind raised arms when the fighting broke out—tripped across the room, his steps too lively and cheerful midst the miasma of bloodshed and death. "A chair," he muttered. "A chair will do."

A chair?

"But first." Mr. Glover threw her a malicious grin, and Colleen was glad to note his jaw continued to swell and that he had at least one broken tooth. "About our wedding."

"I refuse." She lifted her chin.

"Do you?" Vicious rage contorted his face and, though a limp hitched his step, he managed to deliver a swift kick to Nick's ribcage. "Let me know when you change your mind. Quickly, if you wish to spare him a punctured lung." A second. A third.

"Stop!" Wretched despair twisted her heart. "I'll sign it! I'll sign it!" Did Nick still breathe?

She told herself a marriage certificate was as worthless as the tree pulp upon which it was printed, provided she could set a match to its corner before it was recorded at the registry. And if it saved Nick's life...

Dr. Farquhar returned with a chair and placed it upon the rug before her. Rope hung over his shoulder. "If you'll sit, my dear."

"In a moment," Mr. Glover snapped. "We've a few legalities to attend to first." He slid the horrid slip from her map case, a pen from his pocket, and slapped them both onto the chair before her. "Sign."

Tears ran down her cheeks as she struggled to lift her throbbing arm, to scrawl her name in ink. "There."

They were married. She snuck a glance at Nick and was relieved to see the gentle rise and fall of his chest.

"Again." Another sheet of paper dropped before her. "Don't even think of refusing. Remember, Torrington's life depends upon it, and forging your signature is always a possibility."

While Mr. Vanderburn kept a tight hand on her upper arm, she signed away control of Craigieburn and its lands. Then threw the pen at Mr. Glover's face. Ink spattered everywhere, mixing with the blood still drying upon his lips. "Satisfied?"

"Not even close." He folded the documents away, then pulled a handkerchief from his pocket and began to wipe away the streaks of blood and ink that marred his face. "Profits, however, those will make me very satisfied indeed. Bedding you, an abomination, was only a necessary exertion to be endured. An experience I doubt I'll be inclined to repeat even if you do survive." He looked over her shoulder and pointed at the chair. "You may proceed."

Mr. Vanderburn spun Colleen about, forcing her to sit.

"Survive?" she asked.

"Please," Mr. Glover said. "The cure must first be tested on a healthy individual. Preferably one that is expendable. But don't worry, Mr. Torrington's sister will be next."

Mr. Vanderburn's grip about her wrist was tight and, though she resisted, the laudanum had weakened her. The rough fibers of a rope bit into her skin as he bound her to the chair.

"I shouldn't worry too much," Mr. Glover went on. "His last few experiments have been wildly successful and, with all the traits you share with your familiar, I'm nearly certain this first test will proceed without incident. If not?" She recoiled as his hot breath brushed across her ear. "As your husband I'll inherit. Cryptid hunters will pay well for a cat sìth. One particular feline is sure to turn up eventually. We'll test the market with your very own familiar, witch."

"No!" She hated the pleading in her voice.

"No?" Mr. Glover shrugged, then gagged her with his bloody handkerchief by stuffing it into her mouth. "Well, then, we could always harvest the cure from its heart. Turn the pelt into a stole for you to wear about your neck. It did, after all, take Dr. Farquhar several cat sìth to suss out the reason for their longevity. Might as well make use of the remains."

Her outraged cry was muffled by the rag.

"Time to let Dr. Farquhar have his fun." He straightened. "Imagine if it works... We'd have to offer a package deal. One cat and one witch." His laughter raked knives down her back.

"I'm nearly certain it will be so." Dr. Farquhar approached with scissors. He cut through her shirt, peeling the linen away to bare her right shoulder while she swallowed back her tears, trying not to choke. "We can preserve your modesty for now, my dear," the doctor crooned in a sing-song voice. "Particularly as there's no need to shave the incision site." He swabbed her skin with cold alcohol. "Given conservation of mass, there must be an additional concept I'm missing. Perhaps energy? After we witness your transformation, I'll adjust my calculations."

Her stomach churned and bile rose into her throat. The scientist really was insane. She could not transform into a cat any more than a cat could turn human. What had addled his brain to believe so?

"It must be exothermic," he muttered, strapping surgical goggles to his forehead and adjusting the magnification. "Might be I should have attempted an endothermic reaction to shift the cat sìth into human form? But I expect cold would do the trick in this case. If not, I'll need to reconsider my approach."

"Enough blathering," Mr. Glover snapped. "Save it for your journal article. On with it."

Icy tentacles wrapped themselves about her spine and squeezed. Dr. Farquhar truly expected her to transform into a cat? Into a cat sìth? How?

No!

The room had metal walls and a metal floor. From the ceiling protruded a number of meat hooks and eye bolts. Giant sheets of iron riveted together—her lungs started to heave—it was one large refrigeration unit. Not running at the moment but—

She screamed into the gag and tensed her body against the ropes, ignoring the throbbing pain that was her arm. He intended to freeze her, to stop her heart? To jolt her back to life with... with what? Electricity? All she'd found in her uncle's safe were those... Worms?

"Hold still," the scientist huffed, tracing the path of her collarbone and tapping at the bare skin that lay beneath it. "A percutaneous approach to the subclavian vein is a different procedure for a human. Bipeds differ from quadrupeds, altering the angle. But it provides almost direct access to the right atrium." He glanced up at Vanderburn. "Hold her very, very still."

Mr. Vanderburn's hands pressed her shoulders tight against the chair. "It will go better if you cooperate," he said. "The animals that struggled were... worse off."

Dead, in other words. Tears streamed from her eyes.

It took her every effort to keep breathing slowly, steadily. If—when—she survived this, they would *all* pay. Nick would help her. She didn't dare turn her head to look at him. He'd been breathing. He was going to be fine. Absolutely fine.

Dr. Farquhar lifted a gleaming hollow needle—one that more resembled a tiny tube—with a sharp point before his eyes. "We begin with a blind puncture at the junction of the clavicle and the first rib."

A sharp pain pieced her chest and a warm rivulet of blood trickled down across her breast. She whimpered, but didn't dare move. Breathing also seemed ill-advised with such a sharp piece of metal implanted in her vein.

"Excellent," Dr. Farquhar congratulated himself. "And on the first try." The scientist's face disappeared. "The nematodes. Where are they?"

"Here," Mr. Glover held out the fluid-filled vial she'd found in the rosewood box.

She shuddered at the horror of it all. Aether, what was he thinking, sending infectious worms directly into her heart? How could this possibly be a cure for *anything*?

"Still!" Mr. Vanderburn commanded.

The mad scientist uncapped the vial, then reached into the glass tube with tweezers, delicately extracting a thin, threadlike strand some four inches long. A single worm wriggled and twisted, glistening as a drop of fluid ran down its body to coalesce and drip onto her shirt.

Mr. Glover made a noise of disgust and turned his face away.

Colleen gagged on the handkerchief.

"Such a lovely, delicate thing." Ever so slowly and carefully, Dr. Farquhar lowered his hand and, against her will, her gaze followed, straining the muscles of her eyes, of her neck, following his movement.

Terror battered her heart against her rib cage. The worm's head—for it must be—lifted. Could it sense blood?

"There you go, little one," the scientist's voice encouraged, as if helping a child to take its first steps. The tapered tip of the creature slid into the blood-slicked opening of the hollow needle, and fresh tears pooled and overflowed from her eyes. "Follow the pathway. Squirm your way home."

The worm disappeared into the tiny, metal tube. Into her vein. Propelled by the very pounding of her heart into the very structure it sought. But no matter the horror, she felt nothing. *Nothing.* The creature had slipped inside, taking up residence within her chest. Preparing to... What?

Tears slid down her cheeks, leaving salt-stained trails behind as they fell from her face, dripping onto her chest. Dark, damp patches upon her linen shirt spread ever wider as the mad scientist lifted another writhing creature from the vial and coaxed it to follow the first. Then another. Five worms in all slipped into her veins.

"Done!" Dr. Farquhar declared. He slipped the needle from her chest and pressed a ball of lint to the puncture wound.

Mr. Vanderburn's hands lifted from her shoulders, but he made no move to loosen the gag that muffled her moans.

"What now?" Mr. Glover asked.

"We wait." A distant, unfocused smile shaped itself onto Dr. Farquhar's face. "The worm is in its final stage of development, ready to implant. Cold speeds the process, encourages the nematode to settle in, to make itself at home. Then we proceed."

"Done," Mr. Glover said. "For now. We've other tasks to see to in the meantime."

"What of Torrington, sir?" Mr. Vanderburn asked, leaning over Nick. "He's still alive."

"Leave him." Mr. Glover's voice held an edge of malice. "He can play nurse to my wife, and I want Maynard's death linked to Mrs. Farquhar's partial evisceration, not his. Besides, if this works, we'll need him to *encourage* his sister to serve as our second patient. If we cure Lady Anna of her heart condition, all afflicted *ton* will beg us to take their money in hopes that such a treatment will reinvigorate their own hearts."

"And the witch might transform," Dr. Farquhar insisted, his focus sharpening. "You promised I could present such findings to the Royal Society."

"Just so." Mr. Glover rolled his eyes as he patted the madman on the shoulder. "Should that come to pass, we'll rearrange all our plans." He looked to Mr. Vanderburn.

"Grab the earl. Our night's not over yet. Decisions, decisions. Do we toss him to the kraken in the Thames? No, I suppose we need him found. We'll dump him on his doorstep, like a cat gifts a mouse. I've no doubt his wife will be glad of a corpse."

A smear of blood streaked across the floor as Mr. Vanderburn dragged her uncle by the collar from the room. Dr. Farquhar unhooked the overhead lamp, snatched up his bag and followed, mumbling about transformative powers of particulate matter. All while Mr. Glover limped away clutching documents to his chest that would twist her future to suit his purposes. All of them ignored her strangled cries.

The iron door clanged shut behind them, plunging the room into darkness.

Chapter Twenty

Bound and gagged and left in the dark with parasites worming their way into her heart, Colleen's muffled cries tore at Nick's soul. He ached to offer her comfort, but all he could do was breathe. One inhalation after another while the increasing cold of the floor beneath his cheek, beneath the entirety of his body, seeped into his bones.

Time passed and Colleen's unsteady breaths smoothed as she fell into a drugged sleep. From time to time, she woke and fought against her bindings, dragging in panicky gasps of air about the gag. But inevitably, the drug dragged her under once more, leaving him alone with his thoughts.

The hellish scene he'd been forced to witness from the floor played out over and over in his mind. Colleen signing a slip of paper that legally bound her to Glover.

Another that handed over her family's lands. A blind vein puncture. A vial of nematodes.

No electrical cardiac pacer existed. No specialized device that could monitor a heart, shocking it back to life when it stilled. Instead, threadlike nematodes—roundworms—would complete the task. But how? Would they burrow through the wall of her heart to lodge in the muscular tissue between the two ventricles? Were their primitive nerve cords capable of conducting an electrical impulse from the top of the heart to the bottom, from atria to ventricles and outwards?

Without evidence, it was impossible to know. Farquhar's mad ramblings about transformations made it impossible to believe any words that fell from his lips. And no proof that this might work existed—not even observational notes that another scientist might examine. All had been destroyed by the fire. Maynard claimed he'd witnessed success, but there would be no questioning the earl. Though it was impossible to mourn the horrid man, his cold-blooded avarice would have been preferable to the emotionally driven ravings of a spurned suitor who only wanted her for her lands, a crazed scientist who thought to turn his fiancée into a cat, and a mercenary guard.

Nick blamed himself for their situation. Distracted by a disembodied heart and certain Colleen would be safe upon the rooftops while her uncle attended a dinner party, he'd both failed to anticipate Maynard as the villain or to anticipate his trap. Keen to infiltrate the shadow committee, Nick had neglected to consider all the angles, including the possibility that she would make both the perfect hostage and the perfect human test subject.

Was there any hope of diverting the outcome of this madness?

His mind ran down a mental list of anti-helminthics that might kill the worm, but any and all vermicidal drugs that sprung to mind were either powerless to act outside the digestive tract or likely to kill a person if injected directly into the bloodstream. Not that it mattered. He could not foresee a future in which he laid his hands upon any such drugs before the creature was lodged in her heart.

At last the effects of the TTX poison began to ebb. Sooner than he'd dared hope, a testament to the thick wool of his coat sleeve and the reflexive instinct to yank the darts from his wrist and arm before the entirety of the toxin had discharged.

He heard Colleen wake with a gasp.

"Steady your breaths," he said with half-numb lips.

Her ragged inhalations steadied. Grew slower.

He filled his lungs again. "No more tears." The rag the bastards had stuffed into her mouth and bound with a length of linen would only become a threat if it began to slide down her throat. "My fingers are tingling. A few minutes more and I'll have you free." With the toxin flushing from his system, his own breaths came more easily.

Light. With Colleen's keen eyesight, the faintest of light would offer a measure of comfort. He flexed his wrist, his biceps, forcing his hand deep into his coat pocket to wrap tingling fingers about his decilamp. *Click.* A reddish light began to glow. He tossed the miniature light source a few feet from his face, casting a faint silhouette of her lithe form onto the far wall.

"I'll be at your side soon." Freeing her, wrapping his arms about her, took precedence above all else.

The room was empty, but for them, the carpet she'd arrived in, an old wooden chair, and the black shadow of pooled blood. When their captors had left, they'd carried away a body and every other loose item that might aid them.

"Look about, Colleen. Hunt for structural weaknesses."

He doubted she'd find any, but she needed a focus and every rivet, every seam must be examined. All they needed was to find a single fault in construction that might be exploited.

He pushed onto his elbows, then shoved himself onto hands and knees, and crawled to her side. Every movement taxed his strength, but his fingers found the rough fibers of the ropes about her booted ankles. The bindings fell away. As yet more strength returned, he lifted onto his knees and freed those about her wrists.

Her hands flew away, yanking the gag from her mouth. She dragged in a deep breath, then dropped onto the rug beside him.

"How bad is it?" he asked.

"The gunshot or puncture wound?" Her cool hands pressed against his cheek and her golden eyes flashed as she searched his face. "And I would ask the same of you."

"Both. And I'm fine. Or, rather, will be." He dropped his gaze to her bare shoulder. To the bandage inexpertly applied to the puncture wound. The men who had done this to her would pay. He'd see them dead or behind bars—or die trying. "But—"

"There's no retrieving them, is there?" She shuddered. "The worms?"

"No." He wished he had a different answer. "And no way to kill it without horrible side effects that would put your very life at risk."

"Perhaps it's not as awful as it seems." She shifted closer, leaning against his side as he wrapped an arm about her shoulder for both comfort and warmth. "The cat sìth are known for being difficult to kill. And there are legends of wild women with amber eyes like my own, known for living alone deep in the woods, women with lifespans that far exceed those that most humans are allotted. If this particular worm somehow resides within their hearts..."

"Nine lives." Nick considered the implications. "A cat with nine lives, and witches who can transform into them. You think the legends might have originated in your woods?"

"They came from somewhere." She shifted. "If there's a truth buried in the myths, what are the odds this could be a cure for your sister?"

"Roundworms do possess a nerve cord, musculature. Though such worms are usually parasitic, they might be able to live within a human in a mutualistic fashion, somehow regulating nerve impulses." He swallowed. "But it's impossible to know." Nick's gut twisted. He hated to offer her false hope. "Not without testing it."

"On a human," she finished. "In this scenario, me." Her face hardened. "Dr. Farquhar plans to stop my heart—much like he did to Sorcha, to all the cat sìth before her—to see if it will restart."

He'd reached the same conclusions. "Making it imperative that we escape. Even if you were willing to risk your life in such a trial, Colleen, I'd not allow it here in such primitive, unsanitary conditions beneath a pub."

"But in a hospital?" She licked her lips, then put on a brave face. "With colleagues that you trust?"

"No." He stilled. Did she think him capable of such an act? "There are no circumstances under which I would agree to test such a thing on an otherwise healthy, young woman."

Maybe over time, if he could independently verify Farquhar's findings and after much consideration of every possible risk such a procedure could involve, he *might* agree to allow a desperate, sick patient on the cusp of death—someone much like his sister—to insert the worms. But he'd never stop a human's heart on purpose, merely to see if such a cure was possible.

She rubbed her chest. "It appears I may have no choice in the matter."

"Unless we manage an escape." He traced a finger down the side of her face. When would he force the words past his lips if not now? "I love you, Lady Colleen Stewart of Craigieburn, and will do everything possible to prevent such an occurrence."

Her mouth fell open, but before she could answer, he kissed her. Was he that afraid of a rejection? Yes. Very much so. He needed to believe they would have a future. Together as man and wife.

Mindful of her bandaged arm, he teased her mouth until both of their hearts beat a rapid staccato. What he wouldn't give for a warm fire and a soft pile of blankets. Alas, there was nothing but cold metal, a stained rug, and a damp woolen coat. Never mind the frigid air. Letting the fantasy fade, he released her. Though still somewhat weakened by the various drugs and toxins that lingered in their veins, it was time to fully assess the grim situation of their current reality.

"Come." He stood and held out a hand, pulling Colleen to her feet.

"About the heart." Pride and concern wrapped about each other and cast a shadow over her face. "I almost made it out the window before they caught me. I found the rosewood box in my uncle's safe along with pages upon pages of signed contracts arranging to sell a 'cure' to a number of prominent gentlemen. Your agency would have a field day, except—"

"Glover tore them to shreds." With the intent to renegotiate. No doubt at a higher price point.

She nodded. "My uncle is—was—Cornelius Pierpont."

There it was. Confirmation. "He bought back his own," for lack of a better word, "product?"

"Worms." She swallowed. Hard. "I took the vial. Directly from that rosewood box. And left my own gift in return. Glover has no idea I left a human heart in my uncle's safe."

A laugh burst forth. "Clever woman." Not at all planned, but it would neatly tie the death of Mrs. Farquhar to the man who was soon to be found upon his own doorstep. Assuming they managed to both find and crack open Maynard's safe. The police would be utterly confounded, but at least no blame could be laid at the feet of his family.

Colleen read his mind. "I imagine when the police swarm my uncle's home, they'll find the incriminating blood stains inside his personal dirigible. Moreover, Dr. Farquhar will soon be a hunted man, and he'll waste no time pointing a finger at my uncle, a man who is conveniently dead." Shivering, she wrapped her arms across her chest and stomped her feet. "Was it so very cold when we first arrived?"

"No." He shrugged his coat from his shoulders and wrapped it about hers. It all but engulfed her. "No objections," he added, when her face told him she was about to do exactly that.

She snapped her mouth shut, then smiled. "Ever the gentleman. Thank you." She pressed her hand against the metal-paneled wall. "There's a faint vibration. And the walls are damp with condensation."

He picked up the decilamp and began to scan the riveted seams of the metal panels. "With the flick of a switch, our captors have activated a Linde's Ice Machine, a vapor-compression artificial refrigeration system, outside in the hallway."

"A refrigeration unit beneath a pub." Her nose wrinkled. "That explains why it smells like soured hops, jellied kraken, and boiled tripe."

"It also explains why they left us alone and unbound." He moved the beam of light along a row of rivets, testing each one in turn. Each and every one was distressingly sound. "Cold saltwater brine is circulating inside the metal panels of this wall through a network of pipes. I expect the temperature will continue to drop, eventually inducing mild hypothermia."

"Making us sluggish and easily controlled."

He nodded. "We need to escape—or disable the pipes—before they return. Our best hope is to find a weak point."

"Where in London, exactly, are we?"

Wounded, drugged and carried through the dank streets inside a rolled carpet, she wouldn't know. "In the labyrinth of storage rooms deep beneath The Three-Eyed Bat." He waited, trailing the faint light across the walls. Was she familiar with its reputation? Her muttered curse informed him she was indeed.

"There." Colleen grasped his wrist and angled the light to shine upon the far wall.

He had to cross the room to see what had caught her eye.

As moisture collected upon the walls, it ran in thin rivulets to form puddles upon the floor. But one particular stream had pooled and caught upon the rust-encrusted bolts of a perforated panel affixed to the wall.

He stepped closer. Holding out the palm of his hand, he detected the slightest air movement. "A ventilation shaft." The panel was only fifteen by eight inches. Not an exit for him, but for Colleen? At the very least, they might snag the attention of someone above it in the pub or on the street… "Is anyone there?" he called.

Silence.

Down this alleyway it surprised him not at all.

Colleen took the light from his hand and peered through the tiny holes. "It's an old coal chute." She winced, then drew in a deep breath. "I can fit through this opening and climb up the chute, but exiting? Standard coal holes come in two varieties. Twelve or fourteen inches in width. I can't fit through the smaller hole, but fourteen inches? That I can squeeze through."

"And find help." Street urchins managed such a maneuver on a regular basis when an unsuspecting homeowner failed to latch the metal plate after a coal delivery. But there was no chance that he, a grown man with wide shoulders, would be exiting from such a hole of any size. He hated the thought of her walking alone through London in the middle of the night, but said nothing. She'd done exactly that for years. "But only if we can remove this grating." He yanked a boot from his foot. "Let's have a try."

"Impressive." She smiled in the dim light as he pried off the heel of his boot to reveal a flat sheet of metal cut to serve as a number of tools.

He held it before the light, triumphant, pleased he had something to offer. Can opener, screwdriver, knife—but most importantly—wrench.

"Glover and Vanderburn were too obsessed with the obvious weapons and missed a few hidden tools," he explained. "I've a wire cord sewn into my waistband. Unfortunately, I should have worn a different coat, one with more options. A lesson to take to heart. You've never thought to hide any weapons within the seams of your clothing?"

"Only punch cards." She smiled. "A short-sighted mistake I intend to rectify." She joined him before the panel, rubbing her hands together.

He fitted the tool to a bolt, twisting. It moved, the slightest of fractions, but it was enough.

Over the next few hours, they took turns as one of them worked at the panel, while the other shouted into the grating or banged on the iron door. But to no avail. Progress was measured by the fall of bolts upon the floor. A few loosened and fell away with relative ease, but those that had rusted presented a greater challenge.

Teeth began to chatter as the temperature within the vault dropped. Slowly but steadily, the cold seeped through their clothing, their skin and into their very bones. The light of the fading decilamp illuminated the frost of their breath and their hands that grew stiff and numb and streaked with blood as they pried at the sharp edges of the panel. By the time the last bolt clattered to the floor, both shivered uncontrollably.

Clang!

The panel dropped to the floor.

Chapter Twenty-One

They both jumped back as the iron grille hit the floor, though not as quickly or as far as they ought. Reflexes and strength were ebbing. The only blessing of the cold was that it dulled the pain in her arm, though a gunshot wound seemed a trivial fact in the face of a greater horror should they fail to escape.

Colleen rubbed her arms, mindful that she wore Nick's coat, leaving him exposed to the chill radiating from the walls. His larger size could only keep him so warm for so long. Overcome by the cold, they were bound to be helpless to resist when Mr. Glover and Dr. Farquhar returned.

Fear and anxiety kept rearing their heads. Trapped, her mind repeated, over and over. As her parents had been when the wind blew their train carriage off the bridge, plunging it into the river below. Had they been killed instantly? Or had there been a frantic scramble to escape before the icy water rushed in? She'd never know.

But here, beneath The Three-Eyed Bat, she had the benefit of time.

And now, the possibility of escape. She dragged in a deep breath and squared her shoulders. Nick loved her. *Her.* A sentiment he'd demonstrated in both words and actions. And, though her heart insisted she felt the same, her mind resisted speaking the words in such a cold, dank space.

Directing the fading light of the decilamp inward, Nick stuck his head into the hole.

"Please," Colleen whispered on a breath of fog and ice. "Tell me there's an 'off' switch."

"Sadly, no. I see shadows of pipes to either side, but even if we managed to break one of them, we'd likely only flood the floor and worsen our sorry state." He stepped back and held out the decilamp. "As to the coal chute, I can make out the original brick wall of the cellars, but the light is too faint for my eyes as it disappears into the darkness above."

Afraid she might drop it, she gripped the light with more force than strictly necessary as she stuck her head into the void. Coal dust stained the narrowing ascent of the shaft. Easy enough to climb, but disappointment waited at the top. "A twelve-inch coal hole." *Not* an escape route. But still an opening onto a street. Buoyed by hope, her heart lifted. Men, women or children might—or might not—pass by, and might or might not be induced to summon help. She backed out. "I'll climb up and try to pass a message."

"Not to the managers of The Three-Eyed Bat," he warned. "At least not until all other options are exhausted. They saw me descend and haven't bothered to come looking. I expect Glover has ensured they've been paid well for the use of this space and their silence. Alerting them would likely only result in our captors' swift return."

"So noted." She shoved her hands deep into the pockets of Nick's coat. They'd stripped her of her belt and with it, all her supplies. "Please tell me you've paper and a pencil somewhere on your person."

With a half-smile, he produced said items from the cuff of his sleeve and the hem of his trousers. The slip of paper was damp, but serviceable. "At your service."

She lifted an eyebrow. "I don't suppose they conveniently overlooked a skeet pigeon you've tucked inside a boot?"

A ghost of a smile touched his lips. "A small mechanical assistant would be quite handy at the moment. Alas, we will need to depend upon the goodwill of drunkards and street urchins. Send as many as you can. Promise them the moon." He blew on his hands and flexed his fingers before tearing the paper into thin strips. "What shall I write and to whom?"

"Begin with a message addressed to my aunt," she directed. "Sorcha might be hanging about in the shadows."

His hand stilled, and Nick lifted his gaze. "Really? Your familiar followed you?"

"She'll sometimes take to the streets on her own business, but when we're out working, not once has she ever left my side. She leapt out the window first, but would have waited. Despite the laudanum forced upon me before they rolled me inside that carpet, I caught glimpses of her trailing behind the crank hack."

"You'll pardon my disbelief, but Sorcha is mostly wild. And a feline. They're not known for being the most cooperative—or trainable—of creatures."

"Agreed." Colleen tore strips of cloth from her damaged sleeve, braiding them together to form a collar, twisting a wider length of the material to form a pouch. "But neither is she a fat house cat accustomed to a life of pampered indulgence. Which is why the promise of a tin of sardines never fails."

Nick made an amused noise.

A small smile twitched her lips. "Isabella and I trained Sorcha to carry messages home to warn my aunt of inevitable delays, so that she might conceal my absence." For all the good that had done. All that time her uncle had known what she was about. "We always knew there might come a day I found myself trapped. This situation certainly qualifies."

Colleen certainly wouldn't suggest they reach out to Mr. Witherspoon. Not after he'd hired her to work an obfuscation chain that helped her own uncle to double-cross his traitorous colleagues in a tangled web of betrayal. If—when—they survived this, she was of a mind to bang on his door and set his ears on fire with a few choice words.

"Worth a try." Nick began to scratch out a message. "I'm asking her to contact my father who, given the dead body dropped upon his stoop, will have noticed our sudden, and now prolonged, absence."

"We only have to pray Isabella is not overly beleaguered with the consequences of her husband's arrival upon the doorstep." By the arrival of constables and Runners. By the morbidly curious. But mostly, by relief. They needed Isabella to retreat to her room and find the cat sìth waiting in time to send help before Dr. Farquhar and Mr. Glover returned with plans for Colleen's death and resurrection.

Nick handed her the slip of paper, then began to compose a few more general pleas for help. Rolling the message into a tight tube, she tucked it into the cloth pouch and knotted it into place. Minutes later, the notes were written, addressed and stashed securely into her cincher.

She caught Nick by the lapel of his waistcoat and rose up on to her toes to press a kiss to his lips. "Thoughts of sitting hearthside with you have never been so appealing." Where she might find the courage to whisper her words of love.

"Sitting?" He forced levity into his tight voice as he caught her waist and let his gaze slide slowly over her ruined shirt and torn cincher. "There'll be no sitting.

Not until we're old and gray. But the sooner we've a fire before us the better. Let me give you a boost."

The opening into the coal chute posed not the slightest problem. Nor—though her cold, raw and much-abused fingers smarted and her arm ached—did the passageway itself. As suspected from the gentle movement of air into the chamber below, the iron plate of the coal hole cover was perforated. Working the latch with frigid fingers proved a challenge, but after a few fumbles, she managed to pop it open. Like a fox emerging from its den, she lifted her head.

Fifty feet away lay the entrance to the pub. Over its dark, wooden door a sign flapped gently in the wind. Inky shadows clung to the street, but the wavy glass of the pub's windows gave off a soft yellow glow despite the hour. She could hear the soft clatter of late night traffic, but The Three-Eye Bat was at the end of a long alleyway, close yet removed from nearby busier streets, and foot traffic was regrettably light. "Sorcha!" she called softly, clicking her tongue against her teeth. "Are ye here?" A shadow detached itself from the gloom, wending its way along the buildings, padding cautiously in her direction upon silent feet. "Div nae worry." *Do not worry.* "It's me, Colleen."

In true feline form, the cat sìth approached in a cautious, roundabout manner. Sorcha sniffed at Colleen's mussed hair with disapproval.

"I'm in need o yer services, fairy cat. Grant me a boon?"

Sorcha sat back upon her haunches, as if contemplating Colleen's quandary. Slowly, she lowered herself back into the hole, hoping the cat sìth's curiosity would draw her closer. It did. The cat sìth peered down into the coal hole, whiskers twitching.

Colleen lifted the braided collar. "Might I?" When Sorcha did not back away, she tied the twisted neckband about the cat sìth's neck, an indignity suffered without complaint. "Ging hame," she said. *Go home.* "Tae Isabella." *To Isabella.*

The cat sìth blinked at Colleen, then turned about and darted across the cobblestones, melting into the shadows.

When she was certain Sorcha was beyond hearing, Colleen began to call for help. "Is anyone there?"

Long minutes passed while she shivered. So close to freedom, yet so very, very far. A drunkard or two staggered from the doors of the pub, oblivious to her beckoning calls. Not until an old, hunch-backed woman turned down the alleyway did a soul turn a face in her direction.

"What's this?" The old woman altered course and crept forward to peer down at Colleen. "In a bit of a pickle are you, young lady?"

"Quite." Colleen lifted a slip of paper beside her face. "I'm trapped inside The Three-Eyed Bat's cellars and desperately in need of help."

"I'd say," the old woman agreed, stroking her hairy chin.

"Please, will you carry a message for me?" Colleen pleaded. "The recipient will pay ten pounds."

"One hundred," she demanded, cackling.

Unease swirled in Colleen's stomach. "Done."

"And what guarantee have I that it will be paid?" The woman made no attempt to reach for the message.

"The recipient will be desperate for news. He holds a seat in Parliament."

"A lord?"

Colleen nodded. "He is."

The old woman took a step back. "What kind of fool do you take me for? A thousand pounds is no use to a dead woman. No one trapped in cellars beneath The Three-Eyed Bat is worth paying the price of drawing the attention of a peer." She straightened. "Now, they do pay their informants well, and that is an effort worth making." The old woman padded to the door of the pub and banged.

"No!" Colleen called. "Please! I'm begging you."

But as the door to the pub cracked open, Colleen ducked beneath the surface, pulling the iron coal hole cover closed and praying those inside The Three-Eyed Bat would dismiss the old woman's tale.

"What is it?" Nick called.

Heart pounding, she slid down the brick shaft. "No amount of money—or so I am informed—is sufficient to purchase assistance. I managed to send a message with Sorcha, but an old woman declined my offer in favor of alerting those inside the pub."

Nick's curses echoed her own thoughts.

She crouched at the bottom of the shaft beside the opening. "What do—"

Bang. Bang. Bang. The sound of a booted foot stomping upon the coal hole, her silent plea denied. "Is that you, Mrs. Glover? I gather the worm has brought about no ill-effects, though by now you ought to be feeling the cold. No? Shimmy back my way so that we might have a word."

"It's Mr. Glover," she hissed. Had he not left the pub? Or had he only just returned?

"Stay still," Nick whispered. "Let him wonder if the old woman lied."

"Quite a lot of trouble you've caused me of late," Mr. Glover called. "Perhaps we shouldn't have skipped so lightly over the marriage vows. I would enjoy hearing you promise obedience." There was a long pause. "Last chance, wife. My patience has grown thinner than a French whore's negligee."

Hatred burned in her chest. She refused to answer him.

"No witty reply?" Mr. Glover said. "Has the chill addled your mind? Excellent. Time to hasten our little experiment. Dr. Farquhar is most anxious to escape to Scotland. Between a burned house and an eviscerated wife, the Metropolitan Police are all too eager to speak with him."

A faint clang sounded above her, the sound of tin scrapping across stone. A second later a deluge of cold water poured down upon her, drenching her hair, her shirt and splashed off the brick, soaking through her trousers and pooling inside her boots. Her lungs dragged in a deep, shuddering breath, but the resulting scream froze in her throat as the entirety of her body began to shake uncontrollably.

"Colleen!" Nick yelled. His hands reached through the metal wall, tugging at her as a second bucket of water rained down.

She slid back into the frigid prison, as Mr. Glover called, his voice twisted by malice. "We won't be much longer, my dear. Inform your lover that if there is any resistance on his part, Lady Anna will not be granted the privilege of a cure while supervised by her most dedicated brother. We will instead dispose of him and consider a more compliant patient with more appreciative family members."

"Bastard!" Nick yelled.

Evil laughter filtered down. "Only a third son, like yourself, looking to secure a future."

Chapter Twenty-Two

Wet and dripping, Colleen fell into his arms. Violent tremors shook her petite body. Not only had the water Glover poured down the coal chute soaked her to the skin, it had splashed onto his own clothes, drenching the front of his waistcoat and trousers. Hypothermia was now a given. At best, they could lessen its severity.

"Hang in there." Nick carried her to the chair as quickly as he could manage. With stiff fingers, he wrung out her long hair, then twisted it into a rough knot and pinned it in place with his pencil to keep the wet from the back of her neck.

"Your sister..." Her teeth chattered, clicking uncontrollably as she spoke. "Is it possible... he has her?"

The thought nagged at him. "Doubtful. She rarely leaves the house and forever has her attendant trailing behind her." And she was in bed. Sleeping deeply after her most recent syncopal episode. Police officers would be swarming the property. Glover could not possibly have Anna in his clutches.

Hanging his wet waistcoat from the back of the chair, he stripped away his coat, then Colleen's cincher and shirt. Tugging off his own shirt, he shoved her cold arms through its sleeves, fingers fumbling to fasten its buttons. Back on went his own waistcoat; when hypothermia threatened, damp clothing was better than no clothing at all.

"But… promise… of a cure."

"With a dead body on our doorstep, I would hope Anna and my parents would be more circumspect about miraculous offers." Off came her boots. He dumped the water pooled within onto the floor and forced her frigid feet back into the damp leather. Stockinged feet were not an option. Not on cold, wet metal. That way led nowhere but to frostbite.

He retrieved her wet shirt from the floor and knotted the garment at the wrist, gathering the bolts within the makeshift pouch. Another knot secured them in place. It was a crude weapon but useful when swung at an enemy. He set it along with the metal grating beside the door. When Glover and his minions arrived, Nick intended to be waiting. He only hoped he'd not be too cold to wield it when the opportunity arose.

When. Not if.

For the deluge of water spoke of impatience, of a desire to push the moment of the cruel experiment sooner.

Lifting Colleen from the chair, he lowered himself onto its seat and settled her upon his lap. Nick tucked her wet head beneath his chin and clasped her against his chest. Shared body heat was their best hope to slow their decent into hypothermia. There'd be no stopping it.

"How are you feeling?" He did his best to ignore the frosty air that billowed about their legs. If the cold drove the nematode into the cardiac muscle of the heart as Farquhar insisted, had it now lodged in her myocardium? "Has your heart skipped a beat? Any sensations of fluttering? Chest pain?"

"No... to all." She touched the bare skin of his arm—a sensation that barely registered. "I'm so cold, Nick. How much longer... before..." A tear slid down her cheek.

"We'll hold out as long as we can," he answered. "Remember, they wish us to live." Farquhar had a mad hypothesis to prove, but Glover only cared to the extent that their—temporary—survival might fill his coffers.

"When this... is over..." A shiver ran through her body, and Colleen tucked her hands beneath her arms. "Ask me again... to marry you. Properly. On one knee."

"Why? Have you finally come to your senses?" The levity in his voice was forced. He rubbed his hands up and down her body, hoping friction might warm her. He'd not win her, only to lose her. "When did you finally realize I was the only man for you?"

Her tremors subsided. Some. In a few moments, he'd insist they stand, move about in an attempt to keep blood flowing through their extremities. Soon. When his own shivering slowed.

She huffed a frosty laugh. "It wasn't one moment. More an accumulation of them. The waltz that first brought us too close. The night we passed an hour with our backs pressed to a chimney stack. Watching you slink through halls. Storm into a room. Seeing you care for your family. Working with you as a partner."

"Let's not forget that desktop kiss. Or time spent in a certain aviary."

"But a thief shouldn't angle for a Queen's agent." Her smile was faint, and if his decilamp could illuminate a full spectrum of colors, he had no doubt her lips would cast a faint blue.

"And yet she caught one." For he was well and truly hooked. "Tell me, if we marry, do I become a laird?" He refused to let morbid thoughts occupy space in his mind. They *would* survive this.

She laughed softly into his neck. "No. That title belongs to the landowner. While a wife is afforded a courtesy title, I do not believe the tradition extends to a husband. Does this third son find himself overly disappointed?"

"Not at all. I've never wished for a title and find myself happy to ponder a future in which I'm a kept man." He kissed her damp hair and tightened his arms about her. "Tell me again about Craigieburn Castle."

"It's styled after a tower house." Her voice grew wistful. "And looks like a miniature castle, stretching straight up toward the sky. No moats. No curtain wall surrounding a courtyard."

"So very disappointing, that. At least it's old."

"If you consider that it dates to the sixteenth century old." She laughed into his shoulder. "And before its heirs depleted the family coffers, they fussed with the architecture adding turrets and balustrades, corbeling and gargoyles."

"What's not to love about a scowling gargoyle?" But though she cherished the castle, he knew the inhabitants of its surrounding lands were ever at the forefront of her mind. "And the countryside?"

"Forests and fields. Most of those who farm the land can lay claim to at least one ancestor with golden eyes, and in the surrounding woods prowl the cat sìth." The faint smile upon her face faded away. "I'm the last Stewart. If I don't return—"

"You will, and I'll escort you there myself." He kissed her cool forehead. "Do tell me there's a massive fireplace in the great hall where we can stretch out before a fire."

"Upon piles of warm blankets woven in the clan tartan." She sighed as her eyelids fluttered shut.

"Such a tease," he quipped. But Colleen's sleepiness worried him. "Time to stand up." He pushed them to their booted feet. "We need to move. Circulate the blood. Frostbite is something potential brides and grooms ought to avoid before a wedding."

Side by side, they moved about the icebox, careful to avoid puddles—be they of blood or water—as they struggled against the deepening freeze.

Time passed. Minutes or hours, he no longer knew. Only when the decilamp flickered and died, only after shaking it failed to reinvigorate the bioluminescent bacteria within, did Nick notice the gray, feeble light filtering down the ventilation coal shaft from some six feet above.

Dawn had arrived. With it came the sounds of iron-shod hooves. Cart wheels clattering over cobblestones. Halloos of workers calling out to each other. Ought they themselves scream from the depths of their prison? Or would it earn them another bucket of water? Did it matter? Yes, they needed to try. Any minute they might succumb to hypothermia.

As their circuit once more drew them near the opening of the ventilation shaft, his ears caught a faint sound. Metal scraping against stone.

"Did you hear that?" Colleen's voice was a thready whisper. "It came from inside the coal chute."

"I did." With Herculean effort, he hastened their progress, but each step required far more effort than it ought and a horrible pounding had begun inside his skull. Each symptom attributable to the onset of hypothermia… save for the jump in his heart rate and an increasing shortness of breath. Something was dreadfully wrong.

Colleen leaned into the opening. "Copper pipe has been threaded through the grating of the coal hole cover." She sniffed. "There's a bite of vinegar and the air feels heavier somehow." Straightening, her eyebrows drew together. "Might they pump some kind of gas down the coal chute?"

All too slowly, his brain churned, and then he swore. "Hypercapnia." That would explain why the pulse at Colleen's throat beat at such a rapid pace. "Carbon dioxide. Easily produced by mixing vinegar and sodium bicarbonate, otherwise known as baking soda."

Aether. He glanced at the bolt-filled sleeve he'd left beside the door. Glover was smarter than Nick had credited him. Their captors wouldn't be entering their prison, not while the occupants were still conscious. Instead, they would send a silent, odorless gas to ease their entry. It was fast becoming a struggle to draw a satisfying breath.

"That sounds... medical. And chemical." She staggered sideways, then sagged against the wall. "Does it explain why the room has begun to spin?"

"Yes." On the floor lay Colleen's damp shirt, minus a sleeve. Snatching it up, he tore the other sleeve loose and pressed it into her hand. His ribs screamed in pain as intercostal muscles contracted with all their might, a futile attempt to provide enough oxygen. "You need to climb into the shaft, Colleen." His words were a desperate plea. "You need to plug the pipe." He pushed her toward the shaft, clumsy as she struggled to climb through the hole. "When its levels become elevated, our blood becomes too acidic. The central nervous system will shut down."

"Can't..." Her foot slipped off the wall, and she fell to the floor even as she reached again for the opening. "Too cold. Too tired."

"No giving up." Catching Colleen beneath her arms, Nick heaved. But she was dead weight and no longer shivering. Her eyelids fell shut. The rag tumbled from her limp fingers.

Shit. Hypothermia. Carbon dioxide poisoning. Both meant death. Air. Fresh air. Door. Crack. He grabbed the collar of her shirt and dragged Colleen across the room. His rib cage ached with the effort of pulling in air. Still, it wasn't enough. The door was tightly sealed.

He'd failed the woman he loved by involving her in this mess. By provoking Glover to such rash behavior. Nick would kill the man at the very first opportunity. As he collapsed beside her, he wrapped his fist about the bolt-filled sleeve, praying he might have a chance to use it. "Sorry. So sorry," he whispered.

A heartbeat before the gas stole the last of his vision, his hearing—both fading with every blink—the door slammed open and two men wearing gas masks burst into the room.

~~~

Cold. So very, very cold. Stiff rubber pressed against her face while warm air filled her lungs. Her body gave a great shudder. Pinpricks of pain needled her fingers and toes as feeling returned. Wet and damp, her clothes stuck to her skin. Soggy boots encased her toes and ankles. But she'd been lifted, transferred to a smooth
~~~

surface. A table of sorts, the kind upon which a mad scientist might dissect his specimens.

Colleen pried open her frozen eyelids, blinking at the bright light that glared overhead. A shock of white hair rose above a beaked mask. Enormous circular eyes ringed in brass stared down at her. From beneath the pointed beak ran a hose, like a giant bird attempting to swallow an equally large worm.

Worm.

"No!" she screamed, her cries muffled as she kicked and thrashed against the iron bands that bound her wrists and ankles. Medical instruments upon a metal tray beside her rattled and shook. "No. NO. NO!"

Memory snapped back. Frozen and gassed, they'd been all but dead. But Mr. Glover and Dr. Farquhar wanted her alive, if only so they could snuff out the last of her life to prove the miracle worked as promised. Try as she might, she couldn't bring herself to believe in the resurrective powers of a heart worm.

Her heart gave a great twist. Nick. Was he still alive? Nick *had* to be alive. Her heart and soul insisted. He *was* still alive, her mind reasoned. Mr. Glover would save him, if only to hold him as a bargaining chip, as a lure to draw Anna into a similar trap.

Colleen fought against the rubber mask the giant avian creature held to her mouth and nose, turning her head.

There! On the floor. A long tube trailed behind another masked birdman, one who hunched over a collapsed form upon the metal floor. Nick. But instead of holding a mask to his mouth, the masked birdman snapped shackles about Nick's wrists and ankles, ones bound to each other via chains, a design used to prevent a convict from spreading his arms, from lifting his hands above his waist.

Which meant Nick was alive.

For now.

The masked man stood, tethering a length of chain to a metal eye loop affixed to the ceiling with a padlock. *Snap.* He turned, then reached behind his head to drag off his mask. Thick-necked and unrepentant, Mr. Vanderburn stared at her with dead eyes. "All secure," he called. "Air acceptable."

The man who stood over her pulled off his beaked mask and handed it to Mr. Vanderburn. "If you'll bring the rest of our supplies," Dr. Farquhar said, "I'd like to take advantage of her near hypothermic state to begin the procedure."

Gathering the masks and hoses, Mr. Vanderburn left the refrigeration unit as Mr. Glover strolled into the frigid chamber, wearing a fur-lined coat and a woolen muffler about his throat. "Rather Arctic in here, isn't it?" He gave a dramatic shiver and patted his arms. "One wonders that you've not already died a time or two, *wife*." He tipped his head. "Or have you, without yet slipping into cat form?"

She growled into the rubber mask.

"No? Well, we'll have a few more tries regardless. We need firm evidence. To lose a Scottish woman with nothing but a courtesy title is one thing. More care must be taken with titled patients."

"Let us go now." Relief swept through her at the sound of Nick's voice. Chains clanged against the metal floor as he stirred. "And I'll consider letting you live. But if you touch Colleen again or dare to lay a finger on my sister..."

Mr. Glover snorted. "Ah, but that is precisely what I intend to do the very minute Farquhar here finishes working out a few pertinent details. Well, *I'll* not touch your precious sister, but the good doctor will. Take heart," he cackled, "the first step of the procedure appears to have done my wife no permanent harm." Mr. Glover turned back to her and patted her cheek. "Did it, wife?"

Colleen snapped her head to the side, dislodging the oxygen mask, and bit his bare hand. A salty tang touched her tongue. She'd drawn blood.

He yanked his hand away, cradling it against his chest. "Witch!"

Silent, she curved her lips into a feral smile. Let him worry what would happen when she survived.

There was a clatter, and Mr. Vanderburn reappeared pushing a machine before him, one that looked exactly like the one Anna's nurse had attempted to use, save this one's wires were not connected to a sharp metal probe. Instead, the leads attached to a jointed metal belt. Humiliation burned as Dr. Farquhar's cold, clinical hands unbuttoned the lower half of Nick's shirt and wrapped the device about her chest. A leather belt cinched it about her ribs, and a buckle held it firmly in place.

Her heart slammed into her ribcage, then took off like a runaway train. "Please," she begged. "Don't do this."

Dr. Farquhar leaned close, eyes dancing. "Know you make history, my dear, for in all the archives I've studied, only one man has witnessed such a forced transition of a witch, but—mired in his pagan belief of magic—failed to discover the scientific underpinnings of such a miracle. An element we will test today."

Swearing, Nick pushed to his knees. Chains clattered as he struggled to stand.

"Scientist or inquisitor, you be the judge." Mr. Glover rolled his eyes. "But know I've every interest in this procedure working and becoming a financial success. Not to mention a *living* wife would help certify the veracity of our marriage. Though, I'll remind you again, with the right solicitor, a grieving widower could easily take control of his lawful property." Mr. Glover tipped his head, uncaring of Nick's attempts to stand. "Torrington, however, presents a problem. For now he lives, but…" A shrug. "I've no qualms about disposing of your lover. We *will* need to point a finger at someone to explain your uncle's death. A thwarted suitor would do nicely." He gave her a sharp, toothy grin. "In the end, it might be the best course of action, allowing me to focus entirely upon you."

"And all I possess," she snapped. With any luck, the bite to his hand would grow septic and bring him the death he so richly deserved.

"All *I* possess," he corrected. "I'm done dancing to your whims. To your uncle's. I did everything he asked of me and more. What did I receive for my troubles? Nothing but contempt and a callous dismissal. From both of you. There will be no bargaining, no deals."

Mr. Vanderburn was back wheeling a new cart stacked tall with bulging oil cloth bags tied with coarse string, and a bucket of ice. Tucked within the bucket, as if a bottle of fine wine, was a glass bottle filled with a clear liquid.

Mr. Glover stepped back. "Today you'll die," he waggled his hand, "eight times? Or just once, if Dr. Farquhar's postulates prove false. I suppose there is also the possibility that you will transform into a fairy cat, in which case there will be much to rethink. Survive," his face contorted into that of a madman as he cackled, "and I shall suffer a witch to live."

"A quick test." Dr. Farquhar fiddled with the knobs and dials of the Magneto-Shock Machine, then pushed a button.

"Ow!" She jumped as a buzz of electricity zipped through her. Or would have jumped, but for the restraints.

"Excellent. The machine appears to be in good working order." Dr. Farquhar cinched the belt tighter still.

“Stop! This is madness.” She twisted, trying to loosen the electrical belt. “Shape-shifting is a physical impossibility.”

“Maybe. Maybe not. We shall see.” Dr. Farquhar’s wild eyes danced. “Behind all myths and legends lie core truths. The cat sìth are special, this is true, but I have established that they do not metamorphose into a human form.”

“How many?” she demanded, seething. “How many fairy cats have met their end beneath your hands?”

“A dozen, maybe more?” Dr. Farquhar answered as if her question was a request for facts, not a furious attempt to point out the harm he’d wrought. “It may well be the felines I’ve been provided are witches forced into a ninth and final transformation, fated to live the remainder of their lives in cat form.”

She gaped, unable to form a response to such insanity.

“You and yours may bear the name Stewart, but in my clan, those with eyes like yours once bore the Kellas name,” he rambled on as if recalling the bedtime stories told to him as a small boy, ones he’d now twisted into a bizarre hypothesis requiring experimental proof. “All but lost now. Finding you was a stroke of luck. All that remains is to test the stories, to determine if—when your life spark flickers and dies—your body will shift into the configuration of a cat. A black cat, I expect, with no white patch of innocence upon your chest.”

“Stop this now, Glover.” Nick stood upright, though he leaned against the wall for support. “Or you’ll end this day in a grave.”

"Ah, Torrington." Glover shrugged. "A man in chains is not much of a threat, is he?"

Mr. Vanderburn picked up an oilcloth bag and lifted an eyebrow.

"Stack them upon her hips, waist, and chest. We need to drop her core temperature yet further." Dr. Farquhar plucked a glass bottle with a nozzle from the ice bucket and hung it from the overhead hook by means of a leather strap before connecting it to a long rubber tube.

When the first bag of ice landed upon her, all the breath left her lungs in one giant rush. Cold. So cold. Another bag of ice landed upon her. And another. The warmth that had begun to seep back into her veins retreated once more. "Please." Tears streamed down her face.

A vision of her own skull placed upon a laboratory shelf beside those of the cat sìth flashed through her mind. All of them cooled until their hearts stopped, never again to prowl the night.

"It's true, I've been labeled insane by my colleagues, but see here?" He waved a hand at the Magneto-Shock Machine. "I took the precaution of insisting they locate and drag this device through the streets of London. Should my hypothesis prove false, should your heart not leap back to life, I will do my best to restart it." He smiled down at her with benevolence in his eyes.

Did he expect her to *thank* him?

Her teeth chattered. She was sinking faster this time, unable to resist the pull of hypothermia. "I love you," she called to Nick, her voice faint. The words wouldn't console him, but she needed to say them nonetheless. Not at all the circumstances under which she'd wished to speak, but at least he would know. Should the worst happen. And she rather thought it might.

She didn't want to die. Not now. Not when everything she'd ever wanted lay within reach. Marriage to the man who had stolen her heart and had done it without demanding she surrender possession or control of Craigieburn or its lands. Nights spent prowling the streets of London together, working side by side on behalf of their country. And, eventually, the possibility of welcoming a child of their own into this world.

"No!" Nick yanked against the iron chains that bound him in a futile struggle to reach her. "Stop this insanity!"

Dr. Farquhar tied a length of rubber tubing about her upper arm, then tapped along the inside of her elbow, hunting for a vein that had not collapsed in fear. "I don't suppose you'll cooperate and hold a thermometer in your mouth, my dear? No. It wouldn't do to have the glass shatter between your clenched teeth. I suppose we'll do without. Hypothermia *is* imminent, but the heart will not cease beating until it reaches approximately seventy degrees Fahrenheit. Chilled saline will hasten internal cooling and speed this process." A ball of cold wet cotton swept across her arm a moment before he produced a needle from the instrument tray beside her. "Mr. Vanderburn, I require precision and our subject refuses to hold her arm perfectly still. Your assistance, please."

Uncaring hands clamped down upon her arms, and the doctor slid the needle into Colleen's arm. The scientist worked quickly, connecting the tube to the needle. Icy fluid burned a path through her veins, and she screamed.

Chapter Twenty-Three

"Excellent. She's slipped into unconsciousness." Dr. Farquhar released Colleen's wrist to slide a thermometer between her lips. "Her heart and respiratory rates are dropping quickly as is her core temperature. A few minutes more and we'll have our answer."

Was that frost on her eyelashes? Aether, her fingernails were blue. After watching it fail during one of his sister's attacks, Nick had little confidence in P.C. Hutchinson's Magneto-Shock Machine, less still in Farquhar's heart worm.

Frantic, his breath hung on the air as he yanked yet again on the chain that tethered him to the ceiling. The eye bolt shifted. Intent on Colleen and ignoring his frantic yells, their captors hadn't noticed Nick's efforts at escape. Losing her wasn't an option, not when he finally *knew* he'd won her heart.

Unable to reach his makeshift weapon, Nick focused his every effort on pulling free. The mortar crumbled, sending another puff of fine dust floating downward, yet still refusing to release the metal ring that held the chain. *Dammit.* But if he couldn't break free, perhaps he could entice a villain closer?

"You lily-livered dowry thief." Nick's jeer sent a bolt of lightning straightening Glover's spine. "Are you so impotent that you must resort to kidnapping and torture to snare a wife?"

The man spun around. Glaring at Nick, he waved a bloody hand, the one into which Colleen had fiercely sunk her teeth. "Gag him," Glover ordered Vanderburn. "We can't have him distracting Dr. Farquhar, and I weary of his blather."

The henchman snatched up a scrap of cloth and stalked toward Nick.

Perfect. He braced his legs.

"Cooperate," Vanderburn said. "Or we do this the hard way."

Sneering, Nick curled a finger, inviting the man to try his worst. "What have I to lose?"

"The hard way it is."

Nick feinted right then jabbed with his left, but the thick-necked guard side-stepped the attack. But Vanderburn had lifted his chin, a faint flinch. Even bound and manacled, the henchman believed Nick had a chance. "Scared?"

"Only that I'll kill you. The boss wants you alive. Me?" He shrugged. "I'm still not convinced of your value."

Nick wrapped his fingers about the chains that bound his wrists together. Readying himself. "More than yours. Hired muscle is cheap and replaceable. It's brains that command a premium."

With a low growl, Vanderburn stomped forward, eyes slitted.

The moment he drew close, Nick jumped, yanking with all his might on the overhead chain, lifting himself into the air as he kicked his feet forward and slammed his boots into the man's chest with a satisfying thud.

Vanderburn staggered backward. "Good try."

Fingers curled into fists, he rushed at Nick, delivering a solid upward blow to his stomach, to his solar plexus, and knocking the wind from his lungs. The pain was awful, the inability to draw breath much worse. For a long moment, his diaphragm spasmed, leaving him groaning in an unmanly manner.

"Not so helpful now, are they, brains?"

Slowly, the ability to draw breath returned, but Nick couldn't take much more.

"For the love of aether," Glover called. "*What* is the problem? He's bound in chains. Use the voltaic prod if you must."

Nick hung from the chain, gasping in great gulps of icy air as he spun, letting his body weight twist the chain. "Weapons? To fight. Me?" His limp body was the very picture of defeat. Poisoned. Frozen. Gassed. He was close. Electrical shock? He would recover, but by then Colleen might no longer be alive. He needed to lure Vanderburn close once more. To make one final—

The bolt screeched and dropped a half inch. He planted his feet beneath him and yanked. Plaster crumbled and the iron ring gave way. With a whoosh and a clatter, the chain fell to the floor. With no time to lose, Nick didn't wait to gauge his attacker's reaction. He wrapped a fist about the chain and, bent double, lurched forward to ram his head into Vanderburn's stomach as he swung the chain upward.

Thwack! Nick struck the guard on the side of his face.

Vanderburn spun sideways, raising a hand to his jaw. A trickle of blood seeped from between his lips. Anger—the only emotion the henchman knew—flared in his eyes, and he rushed at Nick again, fists raised.

Nick swung the loose chain behind the man's legs and caught the free end with his other hand and pulled. Vanderburn toppled like a telegraph pole, straight and stiff. With a sickening crunch, the back of his head slammed against the cold, hard floor and he fell still. With any luck, the man was dead.

Crouching, reduced to functioning like a feral animal, Nick spun the length of iron chain and pivoted toward Glover, ready to forever alter the function of his knee joints.

Click. A pistol's hammer latched into firing position. Slowly, Nick lifted his gaze. Glover held a gun pressed to Colleen's temple.

Glover's irritated voice echoed inside the metal icebox. "Move another inch and I'll end this experiment now."

Farquhar howled. "Absolutely not! We're so very close. Two degrees more and her heart will stop! Shoot *him* instead!" The mad scientist fiddled with the dials of P.C. Hutchinson's Magneto-Shock Machine. Its humming grew louder.

"Don't. Farquhar is right." Nick took a step forward, letting the chain fall slack in his hand, lulling Glover into a false sense of security. "I'm the one you want to shoot." There was a chance Colleen might survive. Slim, but a chance. He'd not steal that from her. Not in exchange for his own life.

Behind him, Vanderburn groaned. "I will kill you, Torrington."

Dammit. Nick couldn't seem to catch a break. Threats before *and* behind him.

"No." The barrel of the gun didn't waver. Glover's response demonstrated more intelligence than Nick would have credited him. "She dies. I inherit. There are more like her we can experiment upon. Your sister, for example."

"You're not going to inherit anything," Nick snarled. "Your death is a foregone conclusion."

"Last warning. Don't take another step forward."

"Success!" Farquhar yelled, clapping his hands. "Her heart has stopped! The moment of truth is upon us!"

Distracted, Glover glanced at Colleen. This would be Nick's last and only chance. He leapt on the opportunity with a feral roar, rushing at Glover, praying the man would turn his weapon back toward Nick.

He did.

Bang! Bang! Bang!

The bullets missed, zinging past Nick's shoulder to strike the metal wall behind him.

Nick slammed into Glover, knocking him to the ground and smashing the iron manacles about his wrists into the man's head. Again and again and again.

Bloody and battered, Glover lay still. Perhaps dead. Nick didn't care.

Behind him, the henchman growled.

As the leather soles of the guard's shoes pounded behind him, Nick snatched up the pistol and rolled, firing a bullet into Vanderburn's head. The henchman dropped to the floor, this time most certainly dead.

Nick staggered onto his feet and turned the weapon on Farquhar. Colleen's chest no longer rose and fell. "Bring her back. Activate the Magneto-Shock Machine."

"She'll turn," the scientist insisted without giving Nick a second glance. "Any second. We must have patience."

"Now!" Nick bellowed. Had the madman not noticed the two men—one dead—at his feet?

Colleen's eyes flew open. A horrible sound—a great and prolonged gasp—ripped from her throat. She was alive!

"Failure!" Farquhar moaned, pressing his hands to either side of his head. His fingers curled into his wild hair, taking hold as if he might rip it from its roots. "I was so very certain it would work." His wide eyes met Nick's gaze, unaware or uncaring of the death that surrounded him. "Perhaps transformation only happens on the final death? On the ninth and final round?" He blinked. "We'll need more ice."

There would be no reasoning with the scientist. They might, however, still have need of him later. Assuming anything logical could be dragged forth from his brain. Nick stalked toward Farquhar and smashed the butt of the pistol into the side of his head, turning away as the man crumpled to the floor.

Colleen's eyes fluttered shut as she sank once more toward cardiopulmonary arrest. She needed warmth, and she needed it now.

Nick shoved the wet, dripping ice bags from her body, then clamped the tubing that fed ice-cold saline into her veins and cut the tubing. He bent, digging through the mad doctor's pockets, yanking out the keys to unlock the iron bands binding her to the metal gurney.

"There'll be a fire upstairs." His fingers felt thick and clumsy and they fumbled his first attempt with the lock. The key nearly jammed with the force of his second effort, but it turned inside the keyhole. *Clang.* The iron band fell to the ground. The second was in his hand.

Yeowl!

The cry of a demon split the air.

Sorcha?

Snatching up the pistol, Nick spun.

Blood dripped from raw gashes upon Glover's face. He'd not had the courtesy to die. Instead, he'd managed to crawl across the floor to retrieve the galvanic prod. It hummed in his hands.

A black shape darted across the room, swiping at Glover's ankles.

Cursing, the man kicked at the cat sìth, then he lowered the galvanic prod, pointing it at Nick.

Their eyes locked.

"Don't." It wasn't a warning. It was a command. Nick hadn't the strength to wrestle Glover, to win control of the galvanic prod. Nor the inclination. Not only would he gladly see the man dead, Colleen needed warmth *now*.

Beside him, Sorcha hissed, arching her back.

But Glover was far beyond reason. His nostrils flared as he rushed forward.

Hiss!

Sorcha slashed at Glover's pant leg as he ran past.

Bang!

Nick fired the last bullet into Glover's chest. Shock and surprise rippled across the man's features. Then he fell. Dead.

Nick felt no remorse. Not the faintest inkling.

He threw aside the weapon and turned back to Colleen. Once her wrists and ankles were free, he yanked off the metal belt, shoved the keys into his pocket and scooped her into his arms. His own shackles could wait.

"Yeowl!" Sorcha looked at him, then ran into the hall.

Nick staggered behind, trailing the cat through the twists and turns of the subterranean cellars of The Three-Eyed Bat, blindly trusting the ever-loyal creature to lead her human to warmth, to safety.

Curled against his chest, Nick could feel the rise and fall of Colleen's chest, the faint thud as her heart beat slowly. Then, without warning, they both stopped.

"No, Colleen." He gave her a great shake, ready to drop to the ground, to pound her upon her chest and insist she revive. "Stay with me!"

Another horrible intake of breath rattled her chest as her heart jolted back to life once more. The heart worm? Could Farquhar have been right about the electrical pulses the nematode could deliver, if not the shape-shifting?

The cat sìth yowled again, looking at Nick insistently.

The distant sound of people yelling met his years. A woman's voice—two—rose above a deeper rumbling. Both warmth and assistance were close at hand.

The feline had not let them down.

Ignoring the snap and groan of his cold joints, Nick struggled onward behind Sorcha who paused at each corner, glancing behind to ensure he followed. A moment later, they arrived at the stairs that led upward into the tavern.

He lifted his foot and heaved them both upward. But Nick's adrenaline-fueled efforts to knock down—kill—their captors had weakened him, making each step a struggle to climb. One. Two. "Help!" he yelled.

A third step.

The voices quieted, then began shouting all at once. "Here!" he called.

A pale face appeared at the top of the stairs. Lady Isabella Maynard peered down the dim staircase. "I found them!"

Footsteps thundered in his direction.

Agent Jackson rushed down the stairs and took Colleen from his arms.

"Fire," Nick ordered. "She needs as much warmth as possible. Immediately."

Jackson nodded. "Of course." He turned and rushed up the stairs.

Another man grasped Nick beneath his arms, pulled him upward and into the warm, fire-lit pub.

~~~

Colleen shifted, burrowing closer to the glorious heat that pressed against her. A soft blanket slipped across her shoulders. Across *bare* shoulders. Beneath one ear was warm skin and the steady thump of a heartbeat. Listening to the soft crackle of a nearby fire, she slid her palm across the rough curls of hair that dusted Nick's chest as they gathered and trailed down his stomach. He'd made good on his promise. A smile formed on her lips—then froze.

Froze.

This wasn't right. She had no memory of—

"Wake up, Colleen," Nick's voice pleaded. His rough hands rubbed up and down her arms beneath the blanket. "Please wake up. We're safe now, I promise."

Her eyes snapped open, and her gaze darted about in confusion. "Where are we?"
~~~

"Thank aether." He pressed a kiss to the top of her head. "Upstairs in the pub. Sorcha reached your aunt, and Isabella mobilized the cavalry, including a number of Queen's agents. When they arrived en masse, everyone but the owner turned tail and fled."

"We're still in The Three-Eyed Bat?" Were she not so chilled, a blush would have crept up onto her cheeks. "We're naked?" The low murmur of nearby voices met her ears. "In a public tavern?"

"Nearly naked. We've a blanket." A low laugh rumbled through his chest. "But no worries, we're not on display." He tipped his head toward a privacy screen that hid them from general view. "Well, except for Sorcha who refuses to let you out of her sight."

She shifted and found the cat sìth seated upon the hearth. "Ach, sweetie," Colleen crooned, slipping a hand from beneath the blanket to stroke her hand down the feline's back. "Thank ye."

Sorcha blinked her two golden eyes slowly. Satisfied her human had rallied, she sank down onto her front feet, tucking them beneath her chest, ever watchful. If the cat sìth wasn't worried, Colleen too could relax.

"What happened? How did we escape? The last thing I can recall is the pain of cold fluid burning through my veins."

"You died," he whispered.

Her jaw dropped as Nick recounted Vanderburn's attack, a pistol held to her head, a mad scientist knocked unconscious, and her miraculous return to the world of the living. "Sorcha, extraordinary creature that she is, arrived in time to alert me of Glover's recovery, of his intent to attack." Nick clenched his jaw. "He didn't survive the second attempt."

"Good." And she meant it. Betrayal had left her bloodthirsty. "I never thought I'd be so happy to find myself a widow."

Nick huffed a laugh. "Sorcha made it back to the pub before our other rescuers, slipping down into the tunnels beneath the building. It was she who led us out through the underground maze while everyone else was above, arguing with the proprietors and organizing a search." Nick squeezed her tight. "You died. At least three times before we reached this room."

"The worms?" She shuddered.

"I suspect they saved your life. Not that it would have needed saving, but for your greedy uncle, a malevolent suitor, and one persistent mad scientist." He slipped his hand from beneath the blanket. Circling his small finger was the amber ring. "My sister found this on the dressing table."

"It catches the light." She reached for her engagement ring. "I didn't want to risk—"

"Shh. You told me to ask again." A gleam lit Nick's eyes from within, and her heart gave a great leap of joy. "I love you, Lady Colleen Stewart of Craigieburn. London or Scotland, running across roofs or restoring family estates, I would be by your side. Will you do me the great honor of becoming my wife?"

"Yes." A tear of happiness escaped the corner of her eye as she took his ring and slid it back onto her finger where it belonged. "Only one man has ever stolen my heart." The corner of her mouth kicked up. "How convenient that I find myself a widow when a date is already set." He opened his mouth, but she pressed a finger to his lips. "And it's fortunate you work for a secret government agency, is it not? I imagine the Duke of Avesbury might be able to make those official papers in Mr. Glover's possession disappear."

"Please," Nick rolled his eyes. "So little faith. While you slept, I dispatched Agent Harrison to Glover's home. He found those pages. So certain of his success, the fool hadn't bothered to secure them, but dropped them atop his desk. The touch of a match to dry paper, and a moment later you were once again an unwed heiress. I'd tell you to abandon your black clothing, but—"

She grinned and kissed his nose. "I've been promised rooftops."

"And I'll see them provided."

"Colleen?" Eyes wide, Isabella peeked around the paneled screen. Her hand was pressed to her chest as if afraid to hope that Colleen had truly rallied. "You're awake! It's been hours. How do you feel?"

"I'm fine. Really." She looked to Nick. "Hours?"

He nodded. "We've all been worried."

Isabella disappeared a moment, then was back, rounding the divider with a tea tray in hand. Depositing it upon the nearest table, she hastily poured a cup of steaming liquid, adding far more sugar than Colleen preferred. "No arguing. You need both the energy and hot liquids."

Dutifully, Colleen cradled the warm cup and sipped.

"After your cryptic note, you can imagine my concern when I returned from the dinner party to find my husband on our doorstep, surrounded by police. A most gruesome sight." Isabella shuddered. "One of those horrid newspaper reporters was dancing about the edge of the crowd, whipped into a frenzy by an earlier death that occurred on—above?—Viscount Stafford's property. All of them firing questions and demanding immediate answers." Her hand fell against her lower abdomen. "Already, like hyenas, they're circling demanding answers. They want to know..."

"Who will inherit," Colleen finished. The watch would be on. Should Isabella's child be male, he would become the next Lord Maynard. Otherwise, a cousin would claim the honorific. But at least her aunt was free.

"I will, of course, wear black, but my husband will not be missed." Her face was tight. "Not by me and certainly not by you. But the burden of his misdeeds will take time to sort, to set to rights. Particularly given what was discovered on the premises. Don't think I didn't see you, Mr. Torrington, passing secrets along to one Mr. Jackson. Soon after, an expert locksmith was sent to my house." She lowered her voice to a whisper. "I'm informed they found a human heart inside the safe!"

"Leave such problems to the Queen's agents," Nick said. "I'll see it sorted."

"Gladly." She glanced from him to Colleen. "In any case, I had to pretend a faint before the police would allow me to rest in my room. Not one minute after I opened that sardine tin, Sorcha was on my window sill and, well," Isabella lifted a hand, "you see the rest."

"I hear voices." Anna rounded the privacy screen and dropped into a free chair. "Receiving guests, are you?" She held up a hand, forestalling Colleen's question. "Yes, they tried to stop me from coming, but I have a vested interest in the outcome of tonight's events." She eyed the ring on Colleen's finger, then glanced at Isabella. "*Is* there to be a wedding after all?"

"Well," her aunt huffed. "It won't be postponed on account of mourning for a murderous, traitorous relative, that's for certain."

"Would a small one disappoint your mother?" Colleen asked.

Anna clapped. "A private ceremony will thrill our mother. She's utterly convinced Nicholas will scare you away before he manages to slip a wedding band on your finger."

"Will you be up to it, Colleen?" Isabella asked. "Lest we forget the trauma of all you've been through this past night."

"There's nothing to be done," Nick added, "but watch and wait."

Colleen snatched up his hand and pressed it to her heart. "I feel absolutely fine. But if you want to delay the wedding..."

"Absolutely not." The sultry look on his face told her everything she needed to know.

"Then all that's left to sort," Anna's haunted face searched Colleen's, "is the matter of... an unconventional treatment for my heart block."

"Anna." Nick's voice warned, though his voice cracked. Desperation warred with logic as he weighed the risks. In the past, charlatans and their false cures had raised the hopes of Anna and her family, one disappointment following another. "It's unproven. There are tests I need to run. People I need to consult, including Dr. Farquhar himself. When they took him into custody, he was spouting all sorts of nonsense. Sorting fact from fantasy will take some time." He pinched the bridge of his nose. "In the meantime, deliberately infecting someone with parasitic nematodes. I—"

"While you were missing," Anna interrupted, her voice soft but firm. The dark shadows beneath her eyes intensified. "I had another attack. Twice in one week. I don't expect to live long enough to watch Clara crawl, to walk, let alone speak her first word. I might not even survive to welcome my husband home."

"Anna," Nick warned. Pain crept over his face.

"It may well be commensal," Colleen reminded him, intent on championing Anna's case. "The cat sìth show no ill effects, but rather live long lives. Remember the women who live in my woods are among the eldest of all Scotland." She tapped his chest. "Three times you watched me revive. With no side effects. If Anna understands the risks, why not let her take the chance?

Those creatures won't survive in a vial indefinitely. If we wait to be certain, they might be all dead—and collecting more? Well, we can hunt for them in the forest, but there's no promise we will we be able to find another infected cat sìth. And if we do, can cysts be acquired from the blood? Or must we examine their very hearts?" It would break hers to face such a choice.

"Please," Anna begged. "No better alternative exists."

Nick's lips pressed together. "You're right," he conceded with a great sigh. "But we do this carefully, in a sterile environment and—as numerous physicians from the Lister Institute will be involved—there will be endless tests involving much poking and prodding."

Anna clasped her hands to her chest as a tear ran down her cheek. "Thank you."

Isabella handed Colleen a fresh cup of tea, then tugged gently at Anna's sleeve. "Let's give them a few more moments of peace. Mr. Torrington? Agent Jackson would have me inform you that there is a duke with many questions. He finds my husband's connection to a 'shadow committee' of some concern. I imagine," she eyed Colleen, "he also requires an explanation for the human remains found in a certain safe. You're both to report to him as soon as possible."

Colleen dropped her head back onto Nick's shoulder, pulling the blanket to their chins. "The Duke of Avesbury himself?" she whispered once they were alone.

"He'll want to know about how you came to be involved." He slid his hand behind her head and kissed her. A long moment later, he added, "There will be no hiding anything from him, but once he hears our story, the duke will realize what a fine Queen's agent you'd make." She closed her eyes as his hand skimmed down her spine, coming to rest upon the small of her back. "Think of all the secrets we could uncover together."

So much had changed in the mere space of two days. "You do realize this is not at all the hearthside encounter you promised me? Next time, I will expect much better."

Nick trailed his fingers along the edge of her jaw, then pressed a soft kiss to her lips. "Recover, sneak thief. As soon as all is settled here in London, we head north to Craigieburn Castle where, a certain laird has assured me, a massive and *private* fireplace is under her command."

Epilogue

"Did you ever think you'd call a castle home?" Colleen walked beneath the raised portcullis to slide the great iron key into the rusty lock of the large oak door, the last barrier between her and her childhood home. She had to use both hands to force the mechanism to give way.

Clank. The lock popped free.

"Never. Especially one with a list of repairs longer than the kraken-infested Thames." Nick winked, then gave the great nail-studded door a shove. It creaked upon rusty hinges as it opened.

The journey to Scotland had been a long one—beginning with a steam train and ending with a clockwork horse-drawn carriage—during which they'd taken every advantage of the private compartments.

Only minutes ago they'd traveled the length of the tree-lined drive, slowly bringing Craigieburn into view. At first, only its turrets peaked above the snow-dusted branches, but then the castle emerged in all its glory, towering above the landscape. A sight she'd yearned to see for far too many years. As they drew closer, her mind grew more critical, noting crumbled plaster, missing shingles and... She squinted. Was that a broken window pane?

The driver of their carriage had dropped them before the castle door and set their trunks beside them. He'd watched Colleen set the cat sìth free, then lifted his gaze to her golden eyes and smiled. "It's a relief to have you return, Lady..." He hesitated, uncertain how to address her now that she'd married. "Will you be staying?"

"Aye," she'd said. "And I'll be setting things to rights, you can count on that."

"Will there be anything else?"

She'd shaken her head. "Nothing. My new husband and I would like to spend the night alone, but let the villagers know that I'll be looking to hire help tomorrow."

Her estate manager, Watts, had indeed been in her uncle's employ. Though not so much as a shilling of her hard-earned money had been invested in caring for Craigieburn or its surroundings, the dirigible crash and resulting fire had been fictitious. All told, simple neglect accounted for the physical damage done to her ancestral estate. Nothing that couldn't be fixed with sufficient funds.

But the cat sìth and those humans in possession of amber eyes? They'd melted into the countryside. Convincing them to return would require quite some effort. Perhaps when news of The Much Honored Colleen Stewart of Craigieburn's homecoming—with a husband, no less—spread through the countryside, a slow and cautious return would begin.

Doffing his hat, the driver had hurried away. Colleen expected that tomorrow would be a very busy day.

Several weeks had passed since their ordeal, ones filled with the joy of their wedding, the anxiety of Anna's treatment, and endless meetings with the Queen's agents, all while a confusion of solicitors dug through the layers of her uncle's misdeeds.

Garbed in the elaborate white gown with amber buttons, Colleen had stood beside Nick in his front parlor and spoken vows. The small and intimate ceremony, however, was followed by a well-attended wedding breakfast. One from which the newlyweds had soon slipped away, discarding their finery to tumble into the solid behemoth that was Nick's bed.

Later, the heart worm had slipped into Anna's vein, taking up residence, and within a day, her heart rate had increased from a worrisome forty beats per minute to over sixty. Her pale cheeks grew pink and her hands warm. Not a single seizure had transpired since. Cured. But the parasitologists of Lister Institute were left mystified, for soon after Anna's treatment, the roundworms extracted from the vial had indeed died.

Impressed, the Duke of Avesbury offered Colleen contract work, a chance to assist the Crown on a case by case basis. Her primary task? To restore her family's lands, ensuring the health and well-being of the cat sìth within its woods. Nick, content to relinquish his position with the laboratories, would accompany her, directing an attempt to locate a source of the nematodes that could be collected without endangering the wildcats while keeping a sharp eye out for cryptid hunters.

Isabella—a widow whose wealth depended upon the outcome of her child's delivery and the Crown's investigation into Lord Maynard's illicit activities—had waved away Colleen's invitation to accompany them. "Such nonsense. Go enjoy your honeymoon while I adjust to widowhood. I have much to do, even if it is under the watchful stare of that rat-faced cousin who hopes to lay claim to the title." Concerned, Colleen had agreed to travel to Scotland for the coming spring only after both Isabella herself and Lady Stafford promised to send regular reports. "I'll return in plenty of time for the delivery," she'd promised, not caring for the hint of purple tinging the skin beneath her aunt's eyes. "Or sooner, if you have any difficulties. Any at all."

For now, she stepped into the cobwebbed wonder that was the Craigieburn's entryway, then led her husband up the stairway and into the great hall. "Behold, the enormous fireplace I promised." A long-forgotten bed of wood lay, waiting. Drying for years upon the andirons and requiring no more than the touch of a match. "Shall we light the fire, or explore?"

Nick winked and held a burning match aloft. "I do believe the intent was to do both at the same time."

She laughed as he tossed it onto the tinder. The flames caught and in minutes, a fire crackled, chasing the chill from the hall. Without a soul to disturb them, they stretched out before the hearth upon a pile of tartan blankets and set about finding new ways to drive each other to distraction.

~~~~~
~~~~~

Made in the USA
Middletown, DE
29 June 2019